HAWKINS
OPTICS OF

"I think I have it. There's an opening some ten yards across and about five high right under that overhang."

For several seconds nothing happened at the aperture. Suddenly, an impossibly bright finger of bloodred light lanced out from the opening. Almost before the image could be registered it was gone.

"Jeez!" Hawkins said as he rubbed his eyes. "That was quick."

"It doesn't take long when a nuclear reactor is powering your giant laser," Manning replied. "All it takes is a single poof and you've blown the target out of the sky."

"One way or the other," Hawkins stated, "we've got to stop that thing. Our Navy pilots won't have a chance when the task force rolls in."

Other titles in this series:

STONY MAN II
STONY MAN III
STONY MAN IV
STONY MAN V
STONY MAN VI
STONY MAN VII
STONY MAN VIII
#9 STRIKEPOINT
#10 SECRET ARSENAL
#11 TARGET AMERICA
#12 BLIND EAGLE
#13 WARHEAD
#14 DEADLY AGENT
#15 BLOOD DEBT
#16 DEEP ALERT
#17 VORTEX
#18 STINGER
#19 NUCLEAR NIGHTMARE
#20 TERMS OF SURVIVAL
#21 SATAN'S THRUST
#22 SUNFLASH
#23 THE PERISHING GAME
#24 BIRD OF PREY
#25 SKYLANCE
#26 FLASHBACK
#27 ASIAN STORM
#28 BLOOD STAR

DON PENDLETON'S

MACK BOLAN®

STONY MAN™

EYE OF THE RUBY

A GOLD EAGLE BOOK FROM

WORLDWIDE®

TORONTO • NEW YORK • LONDON
AMSTERDAM • PARIS • SYDNEY • HAMBURG
STOCKHOLM • ATHENS • TOKYO • MILAN
MADRID • WARSAW • BUDAPEST • AUCKLAND

First edition July 1997

ISBN 0-373-61913-8

Special thanks and acknowledgment to Michael Kasner for his contribution to this work.

EYE OF THE RUBY

Printed in U.S.A.

EYE OF THE RUBY

CHAPTER ONE

Hong Kong

Mack Bolan looked completely out of place as he made his way toward the floating boat city in Aberdeen Harbour, at the south end of Hong Kong Island. There was no way he could hide his Western height and build among the throngs of Chinese that crowded the narrow street. To them, he was *quai loh,* a "foreign devil," and they gave him a wide berth. But since Westerners had been commonplace in the crown colony since its beginning, he didn't attract the attention he would have had he been across the border in China proper.

Even so, few of the Westerners ventured where he was going, among the Haklo, the boat people of Hong Kong who spent their entire lives on board the junks, sampans and other craft that made up this city on the water. Bolan wouldn't be going there himself had he not agreed to help his old friend Hal Brognola resolve a kidnapping involving the family of an American government official.

Normally a situation like that would have been handled by the efficient Hong Kong police. Kidnapping for ransom was an old Chinese tradition, and the Hong Kong Police Special Branch was good at handling that sort of crime. In this case, though, the kidnap victim was the young nephew of the Chinese American head of the U.S. trade mission to the crown colony. No ransom note had been received, but the indications were that the boy had been snatched by agents of the Red Chinese. And if that was the case, it was an attempt to put pressure on the U.S. government. Because of that, the kidnapping had to be kept quiet; word of it couldn't be allowed to leak out to the public.

The political situation in Hong Kong was extremely volatile, and the population was already on the verge of mass panic. In just a few short months, the ninety-nine-year treaty between Great Britain and China would expire and the Red Chinese would take over control of the island. The People's Republic of China had given their word that the democratic government would be allowed to continue and that the civil rights of the Hong Kongers would be ensured. Nonetheless, the realities of the Communist regime in Beijing were well-known in Hong Kong.

The already worried Hong Kongers didn't need to know that their government wasn't even able to protect the families of high-ranking foreign officials. That would destroy what little confidence they had that their government would be able to protect them when the takeover occurred. Thousands of Hong Kongers had already followed their fears and fled, and the thousands more who held British passports were ready to leave at the next hint of trouble.

Because of this need for complete secrecy, Brognola had asked Bolan to attempt a rescue, and the Executioner had been more than glad to do it for his old friend. He had zero tolerance for kidnappers of any kind, especially when a young innocent was involved.

It had been said on many occasions that Hong Kong was a city of a thousand secrets, but that no one who lived there could keep a secret for more than a day. It was also true that some secrets were easier to uncover than others. The trick was to go to the people who knew them all, the Triads.

The Chinese criminal gangs were older than the colony itself and had played a large role in its history and development. The fact that a hundred and fifty years of British rule hadn't been able to suppress them to any extent was only a sign of their great power. Little happened that they didn't know about, and that was why Bolan was on his way to talk to a Triad leader about the kidnapping.

The clock was running, and he needed information fast.

WHEN BOLAN'S WATER TAXI reached the landing at Aberdeen, he immediately spotted half a dozen young men in the crowd who were paying close attention to every Westerner who stepped off the boat. After noting their positions, he ignored them as he made his way through the crowd. He did notice, though, that they kept up with him all the way to the first of the boats that made up the floating city.

A maze of wooden walkways connected the boats, and he stepped out onto it. Following the directions he had been given, he soon arrived at a junk moored at the edge of the floating city. The ship was twice the size of any of the neighboring craft and looked like something out of a Chinese movie about the pirates of the previous century. The brightly painted decorations on the hull and deckhouse were fresh, the sails looked serviceable and a colorful family flag flew from the mast.

The man waiting to meet him at the head of the ladder was young and wore Western clothing, a white shirt with black pants. "Mr. Belasko," he said as Bolan climbed on board, "follow me, please."

Bolan was led down a ladder to a corridor below the main deck. The end of the passageway opened up onto a large cabin at the stern of the ship. The room was richly decorated with intricately carved wooden panels, delicate bamboo screens and colorful silk wall hangings. The artwork ranged from jade carvings to gold-inlaid statues of the ancient Chinese deities and would have made a first-rate museum collection anywhere in the States.

Four gunmen were positioned around the spacious cabin, and their eyes locked on him as he entered the room. Except for noting their positions, Bolan ignored them. He had been promised a safe meeting and, if Triads weren't good for their word, he wouldn't make it out of the room alive.

A man rose from behind a carved teak desk and walked forward to greet him. "Mr. Belasko," he said with a slight bow. "How nice to finally meet you face-to-face. I am Austin Chang."

Bolan bowed slightly in return but didn't extend his hand. Though Chang was dressed in an expensive Armani suit and spoke British-public-school English, he didn't follow the Western custom of shaking hands. Anyone who was worthy of his time was expected to know that small fact. Had Bolan tried to shake his hand, the meeting would have abruptly ended.

The Triad leader's expression didn't change when the big American passed the test. "How may I be of assistance to you?"

"Thank you for meeting me on such short notice, Mr. Chang. I'm sure you're aware that the young nephew of William Chun, the American trade representative to the crown colony, has been kidnapped by agents of the mainland government. He's just a boy, his father's only son, and I want to get him back to his family."

"That sad fact has made itself known to me," Chang admitted. Bolan wasn't surprised, since little that went on in Hong Kong would escape Chang's notice.

"And it is an unfortunate circumstance. A man's family should be sacrosanct."

Bolan let that little bit of hypocrisy pass without comment. He knew that the Triads often put pressure on a man's family to get what they wanted. They were also known to take out their anger and displeasure on family members. Nonetheless, the family was the most important thing to Chinese society, and kidnapping a man's only son was a serious matter.

"I agree," Bolan replied. "Family ties are important, and that is why I am here."

"But," Chang said, smiling thinly, "if you will excuse me, I did not know that you were related to the Chuns."

Bolan had to smile in return. "I'm only a friend of a friend," he said. "But I was happy to take up the obligation."

"And how is it that you think I might be able to assist you in fulfilling this obligation?"

Bolan was well aware that Chang was really asking what was in it for him and the organization he led. Chang was the chief dragon of the Golden Lotus Triad, one of Hong Kong's most active criminal enterprises. He didn't give favors lightly and would need a good reason to deal with a man like Bolan.

"First," the big American said, "I would like to offer you a small gift. It has come to my attention that your deceased brother's youngest son wants to go to the United States to study. I also learned that because of an unfortunate boyhood prank, he wasn't granted a student visa. That was unfortunate, because I'm told that he's an intelligent young man and is sure to bring honor to his family."

"He was a high-spirited youth," Chang agreed. "And he allowed his spirits to lead him astray when he was younger. Now, though, he is older and will be an asset to my brother's memory."

The would-be college student in question had been denied a student visa to the United States because he had a police record. It was nothing serious, just a school prank, but since he had been brought before a magistrate and was sentenced, it had been enough to keep him out.

"Were your brother's son to have a sponsor," Bolan elaborated, "his situation would be reconsidered. The man I represent will sponsor him, and the visa will be granted."

Chang bowed. "And in return for this gift, what can I do for the man you represent?"

"I need information to help me recover Mr. Chun's nephew."

"Just information?"

Bolan nodded. "The rest I'll handle myself so there won't be anyone for the kidnappers to vent their anger on."

The Triad leader studied him for a few moments. "You are much more than I was told to expect, Mr. Belasko, and I am pleased. It is rare that I meet a man who is so wise and so competent."

Bolan nodded to accept the compliment. He wasn't unknown to the major Triads, and their memories of him went back to the beginning of his career as the Executioner. Under more normal circumstances, it would have been worth his life to attempt to meet with a man like Chang. But these were not normal times in Hong Kong.

The most potent of all ancient Chinese curses was that a man live in interesting times, and the Beijing government had cursed the Hong Kongers big time. Their lives were about to become very interesting.

It wasn't only the capitalists and industrialists of Hong Kong who were looking over their shoulders as the Red Chinese takeover approached. The Communists were known to be harder on the Triads than they were on capitalists and bankers. In a Communist system, the government itself was a criminal gang, and it didn't put up with any competition on its turf. If the Communists cracked down on the Hong Kong Triads, there could be open warfare. But if it came to that, the Triads could only lose.

While Bolan was a known enemy of the drug-smuggling Triads, the Communists were an even more powerful enemy. In Asia as in the Middle East, the adage that the enemy of my enemy is my friend was no less true, and that's what Bolan was counting on to work for him this time.

He couldn't offer that the American authorities would look the other way while the Triads smuggled China White heroin into the country. Both he and

Chang knew that the war against the drug trade would go on. But offering to help Chang's family member put this on a personal level that allowed both of them to set aside their historic differences in the face of a common enemy.

"I will see what I can hear that may help you," Chang said. "But I cannot promise anything."

"I understand." Chang had risked criticism from the other Triad leaders by even agreeing to this meeting. Getting them to agree to help him was a long shot, but one that he had to take. They were his best chance to locate the boy without risking the consequences of making the crime public.

"I hope, though, that you hear something very soon. As you know, the longer something like this goes on, the more danger is involved for the victim."

Bolan knew that Chang would have argued strongly with the heads of the other Triads in favor of this unholy alliance between themselves and one of their oldest enemies. But Bolan was confident that they would take the long view this time instead of simply trying to kill him. Chang was a powerful man in the Hong Kong Triads, and the future of his brother's son was important to him. Plus, foiling the Communists at every opportunity was in both of their best interests.

"You will hear from me soon."

"Thank you."

BACK IN HIS HOTEL, Bolan made sure that he was ready to move out at a moment's notice. The clock had been running for almost two days now, and the longer a kidnapping lasted, the less chance the victim had of coming out of the experience alive.

As he worked, he took stock of the situation he was facing. The Bamboo Curtain that separated Hong Kong from the People's Republic of China wasn't much of a barrier for either side. Anyone who wanted through—refugees, agents or smugglers—didn't have to work too hard at it. He didn't think, however, that he would have to go into China proper to find John Chun, and he didn't think that the kidnappers had come from China, either.

Hong Kong had always been the eye of the political storm in China. When Mao's Communist forces finally defeated the Nationalists in 1949, hundreds of Communist agents joined the throngs of refugees who had crowded across the border seeking freedom. The Reds had more than enough agents in Hong Kong to kidnap anyone they wanted, and the rat warrens of the poorer parts of Hong Kong could hide an army.

But the Triads had a long reach, and if Austin Chang could point him in the right direction, Bolan should be able to effect the boy's release.

After preparing his gear, Bolan plugged his laptop computer into the phone jack and placed a modem call back to Stony Man Farm in Virginia. Hal Brognola needed an update so he could brief the President. The Chun kidnapping had spread the anxiety of Beijing's takeover of Hong Kong to Capitol Hill.

Even though his computer was fitted with Aaron Kurtzman's latest security precautions, he kept the call short. This was Hong Kong, and someone might be listening in.

CHAPTER TWO

The call Mack Bolan had been waiting for came right before noon the next day. "Belasko," he answered.

"Mr. Belasko," a man speaking accented English said, "you are to go to the restaurant right around the corner from your hotel, the one with the blue-and-white cloths on the tables. Go to the table in the back by the rear door and order your lunch. You will be met."

Though his caller hadn't mentioned Austin Chang, Bolan knew that his contact would be the Triad leader. Hopefully he had uncovered where the boy was being held. Though he didn't expect trouble, Bolan still slipped into the shoulder rig carrying the Beretta 93-R before leaving the room. He would have felt naked without it.

THE TABLE by the back door of the small restaurant was empty when Bolan walked in, and he headed straight for it. As soon as he sat down, the waiter came to take his order. Without bothering with the menu, he ordered a typical Hong Kong lunch: a bowl of noodles with ginger chicken and spring peas, and a Tiger beer.

As he sipped his iced beer, Bolan saw four hardcases enter the restaurant and position themselves to watch the doors. When they ignored him, he knew that they were the advance team for their boss, Austin Chang.

When the waiter brought his lunch, Bolan started to eat. Chang would come in his own good time, and he didn't want his food to get cold. He looked up from his bowl of noodles and spiced chicken when the back door opened and the Triad leader walked in. He was plainly dressed this time and slid into the chair across the table from Bolan without a word.

"The Pan Asia film-production company has a soundstage and production complex in the New Territories," he said as he slid a city map across the table. "The company is backed by the Communists, and my information is that the boy is being held there in an office in the back of building four, the costume shop. The night watchmen are in on the kidnapping, and they are armed. Will that be a problem for you?"

"Not really."

"I understand that he is still in good condition, but his kidnappers are not pleased at how the negotiations have been progressing, so I recommend that you get to him as soon as you can."

Bolan could understand that because there had been no negotiations so far. "Thank you for the information," he said.

"I hope you can make good use of it."

"I will, believe me," Bolan replied. "There is one more thing, though, that I need to know."

"What is that?"

Bolan's finger drew a circle on the map around the movie-company lot. "What is the best way to cut the electrical power to this area?"

"Power outages are common in Hong Kong," the Triad leader said. "I can see that is done for you. When do you need it to happen?"

"As soon as it is completely dark tonight."

"You move quickly, Mr. Belasko."

"There's a boy's life at stake. And as you pointed out, I can't afford to wait much longer. I have come too far to be too late to save him."

"It will be done at seven-thirty, then."

"I'll be waiting."

Chang got up and, as quickly as he had appeared, he was gone.

THE MOVIE-PRODUCTION complex Bolan looked down on wouldn't have seemed out of place in southern California. It was a state-of-the-art facility that turned out dozens of martial-arts films a year for a worldwide market. For the Chinese-speaking populations of Asia and the West, the movies were left in Chinese, but they were dubbed into a dozen other languages for the rest of the world's audiences.

Bruce Lee had introduced the wider world to the genre of the Chinese martial-arts movie, and his untimely death hadn't killed his audience. If anything, his death had made it only larger. Now Jackie Chan had taken up where Lee had left off and had led the genre to new bone-breaking heights.

For the purely domestic market, however, the prolific Hong Kong filmmakers also produced dozens upon dozens of Chinese opera movies, the classic "boy meets girl and overcomes evil to win her hand" plot. These films were rarely screened in the United States outside of America's larger Chinatowns, but they were runaway box-office smashes in Asia.

The sun was setting by the time the last of the film crews left the buildings. A fine, soft rain was falling, but that suited Bolan's purposes well. Rain always made guards less alert and it also muffled sound. From his vantage point, he could see the security guards take up their posts for the night watch. Several windows in the small building by the main entrance remained lit, and from the number of men walking in and out, it had to be the security force's operations office.

As soon as it was completely dark, Bolan carefully moved down to take a position close to the perimeter fence. Inside, batteries of lights placed around the compound had come on, and the lot was well lit. If Chang's people didn't kill the power, it was going to be difficult, if not impossible, to make the rescue.

BOLAN WAS COUNTING the seconds off when the entire neighborhood was plunged into darkness. Austin Chang's people were right on time, but he had expected nothing less. The Triad's honor was on the line, and they would do exactly what Chang had agreed to.

Bolan heard male voices shouting in the dark as he snapped the night-vision goggles down over his eyes. With the power out for the entire neighborhood, the lot was plunged into almost total darkness. The goggles, however, turned it into a glowing green landscape.

Hong Kong suffered from frequent power outages anyway, so no one in the film compound would panic and call the power company. But he had to get in there quickly and take out the backup generator so he could continue to enjoy the cover of the darkness.

The cyclone fence didn't appear to have sensors on it, but if it did, the power outage would have killed them, as well as the lights. It took only seconds with the pair of heavy-duty wire cutters for the Executioner to cut a hole big enough to squeeze through.

The diesel generator at the far end of the compound was under its own little roof to protect it from the rain. Seeing that he had beaten the guards to it, Bolan took the pliers from his side pocket and crimped the fuel line shut right under the fitting where it connected to the fuel tank. Cutting the line would have allowed diesel fuel to pour on the ground, and that would have been noticed. This way the generator simply wouldn't run, and it would require a close examination to isolate the problem.

After sabotaging the generator, Bolan melted back into the darkness and waited. A few minutes later, two guards carrying flashlights walked up to the control panel for the generator. The Executioner didn't understand what they were saying, but he recognized curses in any language. More angry curses sounded when the diesel wouldn't start. Finally, the two men walked away to report their failure.

With the cover of night ensured, Bolan drew the Beretta 93-R pistol from his shoulder rig and threaded the sound suppressor onto the muzzle. For him to have any chance of getting the boy out of there alive this night, he needed to make relatively silent kills. Even with the suppressor attached, the pistol would still emit a sound that resembled a discreet cough.

Beretta in hand, Bolan headed for his objective on the other side of the compound, the building that Chang had said was normally used to store costumes. If the Triad leader was as right about the building as he had been about everything else so far, it was now being used to store one frightened boy.

DURING THE TIME he had watched the compound, Bolan had counted more than a dozen guards, but he wasn't sure that he had spotted them all. He was hugging the walls when he heard footsteps approaching directly in front of him. With no place to hide until the guard passed, he crouched in the darkness and got ready to take him out.

Flicking the 93-R's selector switch to full-auto, he waited until the guard was almost on top of him before firing a triburst of 9 mm parabellum slugs into the sentry's chest. The man went down abruptly, the only sounds he made a sodden thud and a clink as the flashlight struck the concrete floor.

After rolling the corpse into the shadows against the wall, the Executioner moved on to his objective two buildings down. A guard packing an AK-47 stood by the door.

Rather than waste time working his way closer to the man, Bolan steadied his firing hand against the corner of the building and zeroed in on his temple. The Beretta chugged softly, and the guard's head snapped to one side.

Bolan was on him almost before he hit the ground, snatching up the AK-47. Trying the door, he found it open and dragged the body inside. After scanning the interior of the building and finding no more guards, he headed for the dim light that was showing under the door to an office on the opposite side of the room. Again, he hit paydirt the first time.

In the light of a single battery-powered lantern,

he saw a boy tied to a chair with a piece of surgical tape across his mouth.

"Are you okay, John?" Bolan asked the boy as soon as he removed the tape.

"Yes, sir," the wide-eyed boy replied. "Are you a policeman?"

"No, I'm just a friend of your father's. He sent me here to get you."

A single pass of the Cold Steel Tanto knife sliced through the ropes, and the boy was free.

"Now, listen carefully," Bolan said, leaning down to whisper to the boy. "This is important. Some of the men who kidnapped you are still here, and I have to sneak you past them. So I need you to stick real close behind me and don't say a word. If they spot us, we're going to be in trouble."

The boy nodded his understanding. It had been three days since he had been snatched, and he knew that the men who had grabbed him weren't to be taken lightly. Beyond tying his hands and feet tightly, they hadn't hurt him. But it had taken all the courage he had not to cry when they had told him that they would kill him if he didn't do exactly what they told him to.

Unzipping his waist pack, Bolan took out a rolled-up black kevlar vest. It was a Second Chance vest in a woman's size small, but it should fit the boy. "I want you to wear this until we get out of here."

"Is this a bulletproof vest, mister?"

"Yeah," Bolan said, stretching the point. It

would keep the child from being killed by a 9 mm or .45 pistol round, but wouldn't keep out a .357 or a Magnum bullet. And as it only covered his small torso, he needed to be kept out of the line of fire at all costs. "It'll protect you if anyone shoots at us."

"Awesome!"

"Are you ready?"

"Yeah."

"Stick close behind me. We have to go across the lot and get out through a hole I cut in the fence."

Bolan had reached the corner of the building when he heard several vehicles pull up into the compound. Shouts in Chinese told him that the kidnappers had gotten concerned about the sabotaged generator and had brought in reinforcements. It wouldn't be long before someone checked the building and found the boy gone.

When they reached the last building before the fence, Bolan saw two gunmen heading for the hole he had cut in the chain link. A shout in Chinese told him that they had spotted his bolt hole.

"They found the hole in the fence," he told the boy, "so we're going to have to go out through the front. When I tell you, run for the gate. When you reach the street, turn left and hide behind the building. I'll be right behind you."

The boy nodded and followed Bolan as they cut across the movie lot again. Edging along walls all the way, they took a long three minutes to reach the last building before the open main gate.

When Bolan saw that the way was clear, he turned to the boy. "Go now!"

The boy was off like a sprinter, fear driving his small legs. Bolan spotted a gunman coming out of the dark to intercept John, but the Executioner cut him down with a 3-round burst before he got a dozen feet.

This time, though, even with the silenced Beretta, his muzzle-flash was spotted. An automatic weapon opened up from the other side of the parking lot. Slugs ricocheted off the concrete above his head, and Bolan dropped to the pavement.

The gunman had to have thought that he had scored, because he stepped out into the open and yelled something in Chinese. From his prone position, Bolan lined up the man in his sights and snapped a 3-round burst at him.

The gunman soaked up two of the rounds, but still had enough strength left to trigger his AK-47 once more. Fortunately, though, he didn't have enough to aim the weapon, and the rounds went wide.

Bolan dropped the empty magazine from the butt of the Beretta and slammed home a fresh one before holstering the weapon under his arm. Drawing the .44 Magnum Desert Eagle, he flicked off the safety. Now when he put a round into a man, his target would go down as if he'd been hit by a speeding truck. The Magnum loads in the Desert Eagle would guarantee that.

The gunman's rifle fire had drawn more of the

enemy. Shouts and the sound of running feet converged on him. Picking out his targets with the night-vision goggles, Bolan fired the Desert Eagle three times in as many seconds, and three men went down. In the silence that followed, Bolan sprinted for the cover of the guard shack by the gate.

Crouched beside the shack, Bolan continued to pick his targets and fire. He had a commanding view of the lot, and not much return fire came his way.

When there were no more targets, he got to his feet and ran for the building where he had told the boy to wait.

JOHN CHUN STOOD by the wall of the building across the street, huddled against the rain, and Bolan saw that he was okay. As he sprinted across the street to join him, he caught movement out of the corner of his eye. He spun, the Desert Eagle in his hand tracking the figures, but he held his fire. He recognized the man walking toward him.

CHAPTER THREE

"Mr. Chang," Bolan said, lowering the Desert Eagle but not holstering it. "I didn't expect to see you here tonight."

The Triad leader smiled and made sure that both his hands were in plain sight. "I thought that you might need a little assistance. After all, these people are my enemies, as well. Political kidnapping is bad business. Someone might have associated this crime with a Triad, and that would have made us look bad."

He looked over to where John Chun stood huddled against the light rain. "Is the boy unharmed?"

"Yeah," Bolan replied. "Other than needing a shower, a soft bed and a couple of good meals, I think he's okay."

"I am glad to hear that." Chang sounded sincere. "This has been quite an ordeal for him."

"Speaking of young men," Bolan said, "my principal has been informed of your assistance in this matter and wants me to inform you that your nephew has been granted a renewable student visa.

He'll be able to study in the United States for as long as he wants."

Chang bowed deeply. "In the name of my brother, I thank you."

"It's nothing," Bolan replied. In the Orient, it was always good manners to depreciate any gift or favor that had been given, even when it had been given in trade for value received.

"If you are done here," Chang said, looking around, "I think we should leave. Your little fire-fight will not have escaped notice, and the police will be arriving soon."

"That would probably be wise."

"My car is waiting around the corner. May I offer you and the boy a lift back to your hotel?"

"Better than that, how about a ride to the American Consulate?"

When Chang raised an eyebrow, Bolan explained. "I need to get him back to his uncle without attracting too much attention."

"I understand completely."

"But," Bolan said as he shrugged out of his shoulder rig, "I need a place to park this for a while."

"I will have it delivered to your room."

"I appreciate it."

The Executioner had Chang drop him and the boy at the corner, and they walked to the consulate. At the door, Bolan flashed the Justice Department ID Brognola had provided and was let in immediately.

Moments later, the consul and the boy's uncle appeared, and there was a tearful reunion.

"If it's not too much trouble," Bolan said to the consul, "I'd like to use one of your secure lines to report back to Washington."

"Follow me."

Stony Man Farm

THE SUCCESS of Mack Bolan's Hong Kong mission brought a sigh of relief when he reported in to Stony Man Farm. Barbara Price took his call from the scrambled phone in the U.S. consulate as he recounted the rescue and the boy's reunion with his uncle.

"I'm going to take a few days off and get reacquainted with the city," Bolan said as he wrapped up his report. "I haven't been here in a while, and when the Beijing takeover goes down, we may need to know our way around this town. I have a feeling we'll be back."

"That's not a bad idea," she replied. "I'll let Hal know that you're staying on. Give me a call when you're ready to come home, and I'll arrange your transportation on one of the courier flights."

"If you don't mind, I think I'll book myself on a commercial flight this time. I'm getting a little tired of government-issue in-flight meals."

"You have a point there, but keep in touch and let me know where you're staying."

"I will."

As soon as Bolan hung up, Price got on the secure phone to Washington, D.C.

Washington, D.C.

HAL BROGNOLA GRINNED in satisfaction when Barbara Price gave him the word that the rescue mission had been a success. Once more, his old friend had come through for him and he could report another Stony Man success to the President.

In his role as the Justice Department's special liaison to the White House, Brognola was called upon to handle any number of sensitive tasks for the Man. Usually a sensitive operation requiring his attention involved neutralizing a potentially explosive situation for the greater good of the United States, or eliminating a global threat.

This time the task hadn't been that serious except to the boy and his family. Nonetheless, the mission had been considered sensitive because of the delicate condition of America's relationship with Beijing's hard-line leadership in the shadow of the imminent takeover of Hong Kong. The return of the crown colony to Chinese control for the first time in ninety-nine years was more than merely a matter of some expensive real estate changing hands. It was a power play that could have far-reaching consequences in the future—and not only for the nations of the Far East.

When the British crown signed the Hong Kong treaty with an impotent imperial China in 1898, no one had ever thought that the new crown colony would become one of the most important economic centers of the Far East. More importantly, not in their wildest imagination had people ever thought that by the time the treaty had run its course, Britain would once more be simply a small island nation, her far-flung empire stripped from her. Nor had anyone thought that China would be not only the most populous nation on earth, but also a major player in world politics.

Back in 1898, there had been no communism, no nuclear physics and Great Britain's coal-burning warships had ruled a vast empire through the strength of their guns. Today, in the dying days of the twentieth century, Britain's battle fleet was just a nostalgic memory, and the Chinese had weapons strong enough to destroy the world ten times over.

The future of the entire Pacific Rim depended in large part on what China did after they took over Hong Kong. If Beijing decided to adopt an expansionist agenda, only the military strength of the United States stood in the way of China's complete domination of the region—the U.S. and her longtime ally, the twenty-one-million-strong island nation of Taiwan.

Ever since the Nationalists fled to Taiwan to escape the conquering forces of Mao Tse-tung in 1949, the island had been a bone in the throat of the Communists, who wanted to incorporate it into their empire. Several times during the Korean War and the cold war that followed, China had put immense military pressure on Taiwan. Coastal artillery had pounded the small Nationalist-controlled islands between Taiwan and the mainland for months on end, and big air battles had been fought over the Formosa Strait.

In those forgotten wars, the United States had stood firmly by her old World War II ally. Since then, though, the relationship had been rocky. When Red China had been granted Taiwan's seat in the United Nations, the island lost its high status in American foreign-policy concerns.

Some of that status had been regained in 1996 when the Chinese threatened the island with missiles in a vain attempt to block the national democratic elections. And now the U.S. Intelligence community was picking up hints that the hard-line Beijing faction wanted to settle the Taiwanese question the same year that it took control of Hong Kong. With both of these areas under Communist domination, Japan and South Korea would be hard-pressed. It wouldn't be many more years before the Pacific Rim would be dominated by the Chinese, and the United States couldn't allow that to happen.

There was nothing the U.S. government could do to block the return of Hong Kong to China. They could, however, draw the line at Taiwan and make sure that the Chinese realized that the United States would counter any attempt to take over the island by military action. The question was how to do that without setting off World War III.

The rescue of John Chun had been a small but important part of that policy. It showed Beijing that America wouldn't be blackmailed or held for ransom. The fact that the situation had been resolved without the usual political posturing and media blathering also showed the hard-liners that the United States took them seriously.

Brognola idly wondered what the hard-liners would try next, because this sure as hell wasn't over yet. For now, though, he had another victory to announce. And in any war, every victory counted.

Taipei, Taiwan

THE NIGHT WAS QUIET in Taipei, the sprawling capital city of the island nation of Taiwan. But even so, Ken Cunningham felt his heart speed up when he ducked into an alley between the Red Lotus teahouse and the Joyful Song bird shop on the Street of the Snake. The American reporter stopped for a moment to steady himself before moving on. The alley was barely lit, but like most of Taiwan's capital city, it was clean for a city of its size. He would have never dared to walk down a back alley like this in his hometown of Philadelphia, as it would have been an act of suicide, an invitation to a certain, brutal death.

In Taipei, though, street crime wasn't the inescapable fact of urban life that it was in far too much of the United States. There were, of course, the inevitable petty crimes that were part and parcel of human existence. But a man didn't have to fear gangs of armed children or crack-crazed druggies who would kill you for your shoes or just for kicks. Taipei was a civilized city.

Nonetheless, the CNN reporter felt the adrenaline race through his veins like a runaway train, but he liked the feeling. He loved the way it sharpened all of his senses and made his movements quick and sure. Adding to the excitement was the fact that if he pulled off this coup, he would become one of the glitterati of TV journalism. Rather than living out of a suitcase in the armpits of the world, he would become one of the trench-coated idols reporting from the front lawn of 1600 Pennsylvania Avenue.

Halfway down the alley, he found the red-and-blue painted door. Taking a deep breath, he stepped up to it and knocked.

Cunningham was somewhat surprised by the middle-aged man in business clothes who greeted him. He had expected to see a younger man, a student. Taipei had always been a hotbed of dissent, and as in all of Asia, the dissenters were almost always the young.

"Mr. Cunningham?" the man said.

"Yes."

"I am Kwan Choi. I am so glad you could come. Please enter my humble home."

Cunningham followed the man into the house.

The American hadn't been in many Taiwanese homes, but he recognized good taste when he saw it. Kwan might not be rich, but he had educated tastes. Almost two dozen people had gathered in the large room, and they were talking quietly.

This wasn't quite the radical underground movement that Cunningham had anticipated. There were the students he had expected, but like his host, most of the people were older. And from what he had seen of the clothing worn by Taiwanese on the street, they came from a cross section of the island's society.

Unlike most TV journalists, Cunningham had done his homework on the politics of Taiwan. The majority political party was the Nationalists, the successors of the old Kuomintang Party of World War II. Since they had come to the island after the fall of the mainland to the Communists in 1949, they had ruled virtually alone. There were, however, dozens of minor parties from all over the political spectrum. But until quite recently, they had been vigorously suppressed.

Even with the open democratic elections of 1996, which had elected a new president and legislature, the Nationalist government of Taiwan was a little too structured for Cunningham's tastes. He couldn't argue with the results they had obtained since 1949, however; the island was one of the emerging economic powerhouses of Asia. For the most part, the standard of living was right up there with Korea and

Singapore. But there was always the unmistakable shape of the steel fist inside the silken glove.

As far as Cunningham was concerned, even though the island's government was democratic on the surface, it was little more than a military dictatorship. The people who had come here tonight only wanted what people all over the world wanted—a stake in guiding their own future. As he saw it, his job was to do whatever he could to see that they got that chance.

After Cunningham was introduced to the group, his host provided him with a young man who gave him a running translation of what was being said. Most of the meeting concerned finalizing the plans for the demonstration that would be held the following morning: where the groups were to meet the buses that would take them to the square; who was supplying the food and drink; other organizational details.

After that had been taken care of, Kwan announced that Cunningham's CNN crew would be filming the protest for a worldwide audience. The announcement was met with cheers that the reporter warmly acknowledged. It was moments like this that made his hectic life worthwhile.

"Thanks for inviting me to your meeting," Cunningham said as he shook hands with his host after the meeting broke up. "I learned a lot here tonight, and I can assure you that your people will get the TV coverage you want tomorrow. I have a full crew with three cameras, and we'll be on-site filming from the beginning to the end.''

"There may be trouble from the police,'' Kwan cautioned him.

Cunningham laughed. "We're CNN,'' he said proudly. "We're used to that. We've been thrown out of more countries than any two of the other networks combined. If your people show up, we'll film the demonstration, and it will be seen around the world.''

"We thank you.''

"No thanks are needed,'' Cunningham said with just the right amount of self-deprecation. "It's my job.''

"YOU DID WELL, Comrade,'' an older man said as he approached Kwan as soon as the dissidents left the house. "Mr. Cunningham will be very satisfactory for our purposes, almost perfect. The only way it would be better would be if he were a blond woman.''

"Thank you, Comrade.'' Kwan bowed to Houng Yen, the Beijing agent who was the leader of the Communist underground on the island.

"Remember, though,'' Houng said. "It is imperative that the American be shot in the head, and only when he is facing the police. It must been seen that he was killed by the puppet government.''

"It will be done. Our marksman is already in place tonight and he will be ready.''

"The rifle is the one that was stolen from the police armory?"

"Yes, Comrade, and the ammunition is from the police stocks, as well."

"Good."

CHAPTER FOUR

Early the next morning, Ken Cunningham checked himself in the mirror one last time as he waited on the sidewalk for the demonstration to begin. His California blond hair was just right, a little tousled, and the left breast pocket of his tailored safari jacket was unbuttoned. He had the casual but professional look that was so necessary to CNN stardom.

The demonstrators had gathered at the south end of the square, some two or three hundred of them. Most carried signs, many of them written in English for the benefit of the TV cameras. Men with arm bands marked with Chinese characters and holding bullhorns were exhorting their followers and leading chants. Cunningham's sound technician was recording the chants to use as background for the later broadcasts.

At the other end of the square, a thin line of Taiwanese riot police stood shoulder to shoulder blocking the street. They wore flak vests, helmets with full face shields and carried clear riot shields. There were no weapons that he could see beyond their long riot batons. But Cunningham had no doubt that armed troops were waiting in the riot vans parked behind the line of police.

Suddenly the chanting changed, Cunningham heard shouted orders and the demonstrators started forward in an orderly fashion. After making sure that the end of his pen showed above his jacket pocket, the reporter clipped the microphone to his lapel and stepped out onto the sidewalk.

He had the entire Taiwan CNN team with him today. Three cameras were covering the march, and the satellite feed was uplinked and running. Everything he did and said here today was being beamed directly to CNN's Atlanta headquarters and would be seen on the "Headline News" a half hour after he did it. Atlanta planned to use clips of his feed every half hour until the march ended, then they'd do a consolidated report for the rest of the day.

He faced the camera, took a deep breath and snapped his fingers out as he counted down for the cameramen. "Three, two, one. This is Ken Cunningham in downtown Taipei, the capital of the Republic of Taiwan. To my left, political dissidents from many of the nation's smaller parties are planning to march down this street this morning in a peaceful protest against what they see as a repressive government."

He turned away from the camera. "As you can see, the Taipei police have gathered at the end of the block to try to stop this peaceful expression of democracy in action. Much has been made of the recent so-called democratic election that saw the small parties on the ballot, but yet returned the long-ruling Nationalist Party to power. True democracy is something that the ruling party of Taiwan fears. Even though President Lee was elected in 1996 by a direct vote of the people, many of the people here today say that the long-entrenched power politics of the island prevent them from having any real say in the government."

Behind him, the chanting grew louder to drown out the orders to disperse being issued over the police bullhorns. That was Cunningham's signal to get out there and do his thing. For this to work the way he wanted it to, Cunningham had to be seen putting his butt on the line and he was prepared to do it. He wouldn't be dodging missiles, but from the look of things, he would be in line for a rubber bullet or two and maybe a face full of tear gas.

He didn't relish the prospect. But if that was what it took to become a star, he was ready for it.

With the cameras following him, Cunningham stepped into the mob as it surged toward the police. The demonstrators parted to let him through as they had been instructed to do. A few of them mugged for the cameras as he passed before going back to their chants. He moved out far enough to be in the crowd, but still stayed close enough to be picked up by the cameras.

Cunningham might have been a vain, overly ambitious media poster boy, but he had some small talent. For one, he had good powers of observation. When two men pushed past him with pistols in their hands, he instantly knew that he was in deep trouble. If those guys started firing, the police would have to shoot back to protect themselves.

He was prepared to face tear gas and rubber bullets, but he was damned if he was going to get shot at with real bullets. "Cut! Cut!" he shouted over his mike. "I'm coming out."

The cameraman was still taping when Cunningham started fighting his way clear of the crowd. Since he was taller by a head than any of the Chinese, it was easy to track him as he elbowed his way through the mob.

He was only three steps from the curb when someone in the crowd grabbed him and spun him. An instant later, the crack of a high-powered rifle sounded over the roar of the riot.

A 7.62 mm round took Cunningham high in the face, under his left eye. The full-metal-jacketed slug drilled through his head and blew a small piece of his skull off when it exited. The force of the blow spun him to face the cameras, and they caught the puzzled look on his face when he died.

As soon as the sniper saw that his primary target was down, he switched his sights to the rest of the crowd. Since it would look strange if only one person was shot, he sighted in on a man in the middle of the front rank and fired again. The man spun from the impact to his shoulder and went down.

The sniper then found a young woman on the other side of the crowd, a student from the looks of her. He zeroed in on her and put a bullet in her chest. She threw up her hands and fell back against the man standing behind her.

By now, someone had spotted his position and was shouting to the closest police officer. The cop looked up, and the sniper had to resist the urge to put a bullet in him, as well. But that wouldn't do. The deaths today had to look like an example of police brutality, which was why he was using a Taiwanese-made assault rifle, the primary weapon issued to the police and the army.

The cop was shouting into his radio when the sniper left his perch. Shoving his rifle into the middle of a rolled-up bamboo mat, he hurried down the hall of the apartment building for the back stairs. Once in the alley, he calmly walked down two doors, slipped into a building on the other side and disappeared.

BACK ON THE STREET, an enraged crowd surged past Ken Cunningham's body, trampling it in the rush. Several of the Communist agents in the crowds produced their pistols and started firing, as well. To their credit, the Taiwanese police didn't fire back indiscriminately with live ammunition. Crouching behind their riot shields, they lobbed tear-gas grenades and fired bean-bag rounds from their 12-gauge shotguns.

A successor to the old rubber bullets, the bean-bag rounds were the latest American contribution to riot control. Packed into a 12-gauge Magnum shotgun shell, they were lead-shot-filled nylon-mesh bags that unfurled when they came out of the barrel, forming a two-inch-diameter bludgeon. Theoretically a single hit from one of the rounds was enough to instantly incapacitate a man.

The first rank of rioters stopped dead in their tracks under the barrage of bean bags. One of the advantages of these rounds over the old rubber bullets was that they could be fired as quickly as standard ammunition from unmodified shotguns. That hadn't been the case with rubber bullets.

When the second rank tried to clamber over the bodies of the fallen demonstrators, it was also met with a barrage of bean bags. The roar of the shotguns and sight of the bodies hitting the pavement dampened the ardor of the demonstrators. Seeing that they weren't going to make any progress in the face of such firepower, the group leaders started shouting into their bullhorns for their followers to run.

The street was cleared in less than ten minutes, leaving only those who had been stunned by the bean bags behind. And the well-trampled body of CNN reporter Ken Cunningham.

REGARDLESS OF Cunningham's plan for self-aggrandizement, the CNN crew backing him up were true professionals. They hadn't ducked for cover when the first shots rang out. They had stayed at their posts filming Cunningham's death and the aftermath. Every charge of the crowd and every bean-bag round fired in return had been caught on tape, flashed up to the satellite in deep space and retransmitted to CNN headquarters. Within half an hour, the riot was being seen all over the world.

Cunningham earned undying fame that morning as he had wanted, but at the cost of his own life.

BACK IN THE HOUSE on the Street of the Snake, Kwan Choi debriefed the older man who had been at the meeting with Cunningham. The man, the senior Chinese agent in Taiwan, was pleased with the results of the demonstration. "How many of your people were captured?" he asked.

"Only two, Comrade."

"I will see that they are silenced," Houng Yen said simply.

"That would be best," Kwan agreed. Though one of the men in police hands had been a comrade of his for many years, the security of the movement always came first.

THE RESPONSE to Ken Cunningham's death in the Taipei riot was immediate and overblown, the way Beijing had known it would be. As had happened with the deaths of the American journalists who had been caught in the cross fire in the pre-Sandinista Nicaraguan fighting, the American media went ballistic.

Why the media didn't go into this routine when a reporter was offed by a leftist government was a question that only the opinion makers in the networks could answer. A journalist who was killed in Islamic nations or one of the socialist workers' paradises of Africa hardly merited mention on the six-o'clock news. But let one of the media brotherhood die in a Western-leaning nation, and all hell broke loose.

The scene of Cunningham's death played prominently on almost every CNN broadcast. At least a dozen times a day, the American TV-viewing public saw him hit in the head and go down. Even though the other networks had to pay through the nose to use the CNN tape, they got in on the action, as well. By the end of the week, it was calculated that every American had watched the scene at least two dozen times.

Along with that, the public was barraged with stories about the repressive, antidemocratic regime that held Taiwan in its steel grip. Along with the network heavyweights, even the Fox network got in on the act. No newscast was considered complete if it didn't include a rehash of the demonstration that day and why the people of Taiwan had been marching in the street.

Backing that up were interviews with self-proclaimed members of the political opposition, draft dodgers and anyone else who had a bone to pick with the elected Taiwanese government. Taiwan's military draft was also touted as proof that the island's rulers were bent on dominating the population. The fact that the Red Chinese had the largest land army in world history—with much of it poised to invade the island—was never mentioned.

Eager to get in on the prime-time coverage, a Fox camera crew tried to force its way into a Taiwanese military base and was politely denied entrance. Somehow a scuffle broke out, and Taiwanese MPs moved in to break up the melee. The entire affair was caught on tape by the other half of the crew, who had stayed back a safe distance. It was a classic forced confrontation so loved by "investigative reporters," but when the tape was edited and played on the evening news, the fire storm broke out anew.

THE NEXT DAY, a New York congressman best known for his attendance at photo ops with every socialist, Communist or Islamic fundamentalist leader in the world was recognized on the floor of Congress. As he played a tape of the demonstration, he launched into a tirade about the tragedy of Cunningham's death at the hands of a brutal police force that was trying to block a peaceful political protest.

Next he showed the edited tape of the confrontation at the Taiwanese military base and decried the

SS-like actions of the Taiwanese MPs. In conclusion, he proposed a resolution that the Congress condemn Taiwan for its "human-rights abuses" and immediately halt all American aid to the island republic until said abuses had ended.

Though the U.S and Taiwan had been allies since before the beginning of the cold war, the congressman's emotional resolution passed. It passed by only one vote, but the United States was now on record as condemning Taiwan simply for trying to maintain order on its streets and security at its military bases.

With that condemnation came the cancellation of a shipment of twenty American-made F-16C Fighting Falcon jet fighters that had been ordered and paid for by the Taiwanese government. Though ready for delivery, the planes were impounded at the manufacturer until the government of Taiwan improved its human-rights record.

However, not all of the United States went along with this media-sponsored farce. Corporate America had invested heavily in Taiwan and wanted to protect its investments. But the resolution blocked more than arms shipments to the island nation. High-tech equipment necessary to expand and modernize Taiwan's economy was also on the blacklist. More than one American CEO protested this government interference in free trade, but the protests went nowhere.

Another segment of the American public that was outraged by this decision was the large Chinese American community. With the exception of agents planted by the Beijing government, it was difficult to find a Chinese Communist in the United States. The older Chinese Americans knew firsthand what the Communists were like, and they made sure that the younger generations knew, as well.

Some of the Chinese American community might have had arguments with certain actions the Taiwanese government had taken over the years, but for the most part they saw the island nation as the only hope for their people now that Hong Kong was disappearing behind the Bamboo Curtain.

Like American CEOs, the Chinese American community didn't have a lot of pull on Capitol Hill. They did not, however, just let it slide. Prodemocracy activists held well-attended meetings and lectures to tell the people what Beijing was doing and to show solidarity with Taiwan.

THE PRESIDENT of the United States also wasn't pleased with the liberal knee-jerk reaction against Taiwan. The island nation was a bulwark against Red Chinese expansion, and it had to be defended at all costs. With the congressional resolution against him, though, his hands were tied, and there was little he could do to help the Taiwanese.

There was, however, the Sensitive Operations Group at Stony Man Farm, the only resource he had at his command that Congress didn't control. They couldn't mess with Stony Man, because they didn't know about it and that was why it had been set up. Sometimes a President needed an extra hand.

He reached for the phone on his desk and dialed a number in the Justice Department known only to him and the Stony Man team.

CHAPTER FIVE

San Francisco, California

For a human-rights activist, Jimmy Fong was a modest, sincere man. He took part in none of the self-serving grandstanding that was so much a part of the human-rights movement. He didn't have a fancy office, a PR firm booking his talks, nor did he head a nonprofit organization that paid his bills and expenses, as well as a handsome salary. Rather than being a high-profile activist who lived to see himself on the six-o'clock news, Fong was just an American citizen of Chinese birth who was concerned about the conditions of the people in his homeland.

That was only one of the reasons why there were no concerned white liberals at his lecture in the Chinese American Friendship Hall in the heart of San Francisco's Chinatown. The name of the building was an anachronism dating back to the dark, early days of World War II when the Asian giant had been America's staunchest ally in the fight against imperial Japan. When the building had been named, no one had thought that the day would ever come when America and China wouldn't be the best of friends.

Another reason that Fong's lecture on the latest outrages of the Beijing government hadn't attracted the usual civil rights crowd was that he wasn't enamored of communism as were so many American liberals. He had lost several of his relatives to the Maoist Cultural Revolution of the 1960s, and he had gone to prison himself in the aftermath of the 1989 Tiananmen Square demonstrations. He had no illusions about the realities of the Beijing government and even less about Chinese communism.

Some of his Chinese American audience were third- or fourth-generation Americans, and some of them were more recent immigrants who had fled Hong Kong before the impending takeover. Regardless of how long they had been in the United States, though, all of them were concerned about the future of their homeland, and they listened intently to the man who had put his life on the line so many times to promote democracy in China.

Fong's message was a simple one. He spoke of the danger China's takeover posed to the residents of Hong Kong and of the Beijing government's increasing pressure on the Taiwanese. He reminded them of the need for all Chinese, no matter where they lived, to support democratic reform in China. He talked of the particular need for the American Chinese community to extend their hands to their overseas brethren and help them in any way that they could, mostly financially.

Already the money that was sent by Chinese Americans to their relatives in mainland China was a sizable part of China's foreign-currency income. The money was badly needed to provide funding for small businesses and other capitalist ventures. Fong reminded his audience that the road to democracy was powered by the engine of small business, and it was a message that they understood. The American Chinese were among the best small businessmen in the world.

Fong had been speaking for a little less than half an hour when three men burst into the hall with weapons in their hands. Shouting in Chinese for everyone to keep their seats, they ran onto the stage and confronted him.

True to his character, the activist stood his ground and didn't try to escape as maybe a wiser man would have done. His courage had been proved many times before and, unfortunately, it didn't fail him this time.

While two of the intruders held Fong's arms, the third put a semiautomatic pistol to his head and pulled the trigger. The result was as if an explosive charge had been placed inside Fong's head. It literally exploded, blowing off the back of his skull.

Ignoring the blood and gore that soaked the front of his clothing, the gunman turned back to address the stunned audience.

"This man was a traitor to the Chinese people,"

he said in Cantonese, the most widely spoken Chinese dialect in the United States, "and the people called for his death. All traitors to the Chinese people will be dealt with this way."

As suddenly as they had appeared, the three gunmen disappeared out the back door of the lecture hall before anyone in the audience could react.

THE ASSASSINATION of Jimmy Fong hardly made a blip on the national news. Most of the stories that did mention it linked the killing to unspecified Asian-gang problems in San Francisco's Chinatown. Bare mention was made of Fong's activities on behalf of the prodemocracy movement in China, and even less was said about the topic of his speech that night.

Fong's assassination, however, didn't escape notice at Stony Man Farm. At the weekly staff meeting that covered world events that might be of interest to their SOG operations, his death was high on the agenda. After going over the debriefing regarding Bolan's resolution of the Hong Kong kidnapping, the San Francisco kill was next on the lengthy agenda.

"That's the third assassination of a Chinese anti-Communist leader in the past two weeks," Barbara Price said after Aaron Kurtzman recounted the event. "One in Singapore and two here in the States."

"And all of them were done in broad daylight,"

Yakov Katzenelenbogen commented. "Someone's trying to send someone a message."

"The explosive bullet to the head on this last one sounds like a pretty explicit message to me," Price said. "'Keep your mouth shut or we'll blow your head off.' The only question is, who's sending the message and why?"

"It sounds like the Beijing hard-liners to me," Katz replied. "The speech the assassin made after the hit about 'death to the traitors of the people' is pure Communist rhetoric and is right out of the Cultural Revolution's Little Red Book."

"But, isn't this a little out of their ballpark?" Price asked, turning to Kurtzman. "They're usually not too active here, are they?"

"As a general rule," Kurtzman answered, "I'd say that you're right."

"But...?" she prompted him, hearing the question in his voice.

"The 'but' is that we really don't have diddly on the Red Chinese agents in the States," the cybernetics wizard said. "Sure, we know that a few of the trade-mission people are dabbling in industrial espionage on the side, but we don't have much on suspected Chinese hit men or terrorists like we do with the Islamic factions. Chinese terrorism has never been a problem here before."

"It looks like it's just hit the top of the list now," Katzenelenbogen observed. "As Striker likes to say, once is happenstance, twice is coincidence, but three times is enemy action.''

''Do you think they could be using local tong people for these hits?'' Price asked.

''It's hard to tell,'' Katz replied. ''But since these have all been Chinese-on-Chinese hits, that's a distinct possibility and worth looking into. Most of what the tongs do, they do to their own people.''

''I'll access the national crime center and see what updates they have on the tongs.''

''And,'' Price said, ''if no one has any objections, I'm going to put Able Team to work on this and see what they can come up with before Hal comes storming in here and tells us to take care of it. Just for once, I'd like to be ahead of the power curve.''

''I agree,'' Katz said. ''With the Hong Kong kidnapping and the political rumblings in Taiwan, I'm convinced that Beijing's up to something and we should try to get a handle on it before it blows up in our faces.''

In his role as the Farm's tactical adviser, the gruff Israeli warrior liked to keep his potential enemies in plain sight so he could keep a sharp eye on them. Years of experience on the sharp end of the stick had made him really hate being blindsided.

''That suits me,'' Kurtzman agreed. ''And we're going to need someone on the ground this time because this is one area where I'm not going to be able to do much good from here. Even though China is modernizing as fast as they can, they're still years behind in computer use, and I can't get much on them in cyberspace simply because they're not there."

"I'll give Carl a call as soon as we're done here," Price said. "They should be able to move in and start working on it immediately."

"And," Kurtzman said, "I'll put my people to work just in case there is something we can find in cyberspace."

THE MEN OF ABLE TEAM had been cooling their heels in southern California, so Barbara Price's call to action was welcomed. The main problem with being in their line of work was that too much off-time tended to dull the reflexes, and that wasn't good.

It was a short trip to San Francisco, and using his Stony Man Justice Department cover, Carl Lyons set up a meeting with a Chinese-speaking SFPD cop the next day. But when they hit the bricks of San Francisco's Chinatown the next morning, it didn't take long for Able Team to come hard up against the problems of working in the city's Chinese community.

To start with, if you weren't Chinese, you couldn't blend in. And if you didn't speak Chinese, you were going to get very lonely. It was too easy for a man, or a woman, to pretend not to be able to speak English. Even though Able Team had a translator, they weren't breaking through the language barrier.

"For Christ's sake," Lyons said, his frustration bubbling to the surface after the fourth witness to the Fong killing said that he didn't have any information for them. "We're trying to protect these people. Why in the hell won't they talk to us?"

Roger Yee, the San Francisco cop who had been handling the language chores for the three men he thought were Justice Department special agents, smiled. "The people are frightened. The older ones have long memories, and they remember the bad old days under both the Communists and the Kuomintang. Besides, it's a close community and they have a distrust of strangers."

"Who are they?"

"They're the old Nationalists, the political party that runs Taiwan right now. During the civil war in China, they weren't much better than the Reds except that they were America's allies against the Japanese."

"But didn't the Communists fight the Japanese, as well?"

"Sometimes," Yee answered. "Other times, though, they helped them against the Nationalists. It's confusing, I know, but China has a long, confusing history and it isn't over yet."

"This is all very fascinating, I'm sure," Lyons interrupted. "But can we hold the history lesson for later? Right now, I have a hit team to find and I need more-current information."

"But we're getting information," Yee said. "The people are frightened, but that doesn't mean that they haven't seen the men we're after. It just means that they're a little reticent to say anything about them directly."

"So what have they said indirectly?"

"Well—" the Chinese American cop thought carefully for a moment "—reading between the lines, they've mentioned that the word is out on the street that it is unwise for anyone to speak out too loudly against the Beijing government. They've also said that many people are scared because of the killings of the activists and that they will be more careful about attending the meetings."

"That's all fine and good," Lyons said. "But that's all just background information. It's not the same as putting the finger on someone so we can put the hammer on him."

Yee had to agree with that, but this was the same wall his department had run into when they had investigated the killings. Beyond descriptions that matched almost every male of Chinese decent in California, they had nothing, either.

"So," Lyons continued, "now that we've canvassed all of the witnesses to the Jimmy Fong killing again, and still don't have squat, does your department have any Chinese snitches we can lean on?"

"Well..." Yee hesitated. "Chinese snitches

aren't exactly like the guys you're probably used to working with."

"How's that?"

"Well, for one thing they're Chinese, and 'leaning on them' doesn't really work very well here."

"It's always worked with me before," Lyons said.

"With Chinese?"

"Well, not exactly."

Blancanales recognized the look on Lyons's face and saw it as his cue to jump into the conversation. He needed to apply some of his people skills before the situation got completely out of hand.

"What have your snitches volunteered?" he asked.

"Well, most of it doesn't have anything to do directly with the Fong killing itself. Instead, they've been giving us tips about a new guy who's been moving a lot of China White recently."

Lyons and Blancanales locked eyes. As the name implied, most China White originated in the pharmaceutical labs of the Beijing government. They had a long-standing policy of using drugs to pay agents for information or to buy forbidden foreign technology. If there was a new player in the China White game, he could be their man. At least it was worth a look-see.

"Have they given up a name or anything specific?"

Yee shook his head.

Lyons wasn't too happy about their being teamed up with a local cop anyway and decided to cut Yee loose. If there was a drug connection to Fong's death, that would give them another avenue to explore. Plus, Yee's SFPD wasn't going to like the results of this investigation no matter how it went down, so he might as well go.

"Look," he told the Chinese cop, "thanks for your help, and we'll get in touch with you later if we need to talk to any more of the locals. We need to contact our home office and make a report."

Yee shrugged. "Sure."

CHAPTER SIX

As soon as Carl Lyons was cut free of Roger Yee, he set off on a new tack. First he called Stony Man to get Aaron Kurtzman to use his DEA contacts to try to access more information on the new China White operation. Then, since Lyons wasn't inclined to sit on his butt and wait for Stony Man to develop a lead, he came up with another idea.

They were on the ground, and since they had to do something, he decided that they should check in on a couple of Chinese American political meetings and troll for the bad guys. If they were in the audience when the hit team struck again, they could wrap this thing up quickly.

"Isn't that kind of a crap shoot?" Hermann Schwarz asked. "Kind of like closing your eyes before you take a swing at a guy? We don't have any way of knowing where they're going to hit next."

"You got a better idea?"

Schwarz shook his head. "Nope."

"Get your coat on, then. We're going."

"Aren't we going to look a little out of place in

there?'' Schwarz asked when the three of them walked into the Oakland Chinese American community center. The poster outside announced that a recent immigrant from Hong Kong would be giving a talk on the work of the martyred Jimmy Fong. ''I mean, we don't particularly look Chinese or like young white urban professionals who are seriously concerned about the evils of the world.''

''But we are seriously concerned about evil,'' Lyons reminded him. ''We're concerned about the evil bastards who've been shooting up these meetings.''

''But it's not the same thing,'' Schwarz insisted. ''We look like what we are, hardcases.''

''But we're hardcases on the side of righteousness, Gadgets,'' Lyons said seriously. ''Never forget that.''

''Right.''

This time there were quite a few Caucasians in the crowd. Though Fong's death hadn't made the top of the news, word had gotten out to the wider activist community that one of their own had been killed. The fact that Fong had kept a low profile and had been completely unknown prior to his death made no difference. He had given his life for his cause, and that was a good enough reason to attend this memorial for him and his work.

Lyons took a seat by the rear door of the meeting room so he could keep an eye on the entrance and exits. Blancanales took a front-row seat, and Schwarz loitered outside in the lobby to act as an early warning. As he had predicted, he got quite a few strange looks, but he was used to that.

AFTER SITTING THROUGH an uneventful lecture, the three Able Team commandos went back to their motel room to review their situation.

"I think we need to take a completely different approach," Blancanales said. "We're getting nowhere fast with what we're doing."

"What do you have in mind?" Lyons asked.

"Well, I'd like to keep pushing to develop something on the new China White importer. I know it's a long shot, but the guy's worth talking to. If nothing else, we'll be doing the nation a favor by getting him off of the street for drug dealing."

"What can we do that we aren't already doing?" Schwarz asked. "Remember, with all the other agencies looking into this thing, Barbara said that we're supposed to be keeping a low profile."

"Well, if someone new on the scene is moving a lot of China White around here, he's bound to have pissed off someone."

"Other than the cops and the DEA, you mean," Schwarz said.

Blancanales nodded. "I was thinking of the local Triads and tongs who have been the traditional dealers of that particular commodity."

"You're saying that we should get tight with them to try to find out who this new guy is?"

Blancanales shrugged. "Why not? We can screw

around here for days trying to work it out ourselves the old-fashioned way, pick up a couple of street dealers, bust a few heads, that old routine. Or we can go to the people who can probably give us our target's name, rank, social-security number and address right off the top of their heads."

Lyons smiled broadly. This appealed to his sense of irony, using the bad guys to catch the bad guys. "As it so happens," he said, "I know just the guy who might be able to help us, one of the old-time Chinese godfathers, Johnny Lin. If anyone would know who the new guy in town is, he would."

"Will he talk to you?"

"I don't know," Lyons said honestly. "But it's worth a try."

BARBARA PRICE HADN'T BEEN surprised when she'd received a call the night before from Hal Brognola saying that he would be coming to the Farm in the morning to brief them. He wasn't the only one who had seen the Asian storm clouds building, and she knew that Stony Man would be called to action before much longer. The Taiwan situation alone was worth looking into, and when the Hong Kong kidnapping and the assassinations were factored in, China's name kept coming up.

She noticed that Brognola didn't look too harassed when he stepped down from the unmarked Bell JetRanger helicopter that had transported him from his Washington office. His clothes didn't look as if he had slept in them for a week, and the unlit cigar in the corner of his mouth hadn't yet been chewed down to a sodden stub.

That was a good sign. Maybe his visit was merely to give them a "heads up" briefing rather than being a call to send the action teams to war again. But she knew that she couldn't pin her hopes on that being the case. More than likely, Brognola was just getting an early start on the carnage to come.

As always, the big Fed didn't say a word to her beyond a brief greeting as he followed her from the chopper pad to the farmhouse. Even though the Farm was one of the most secure installations in the country, Brognola didn't speak much in the open air. Old habits were hard to break.

The Stony Man team was waiting in the War Room when Brognola and Price walked in. The big Fed acknowledged them as he made his way to the head of the table and took his seat. "This is just a 'heads up' briefing," he said. "The President wants us to look into a couple of things and try to develop some information."

"The topic is China, right?" Price asked.

Brognola nodded. "Is Striker still in Hong Kong?"

She nodded. "He said that he wanted to reacquaint himself with the city and isn't due back until sometime around the end of the week."

"Good. I'd like him to take a look at the Taiwan situation for me as long as he's still in Asia. The

President is considering sending Phoenix Force to the island, and I can use his input if he wants to make a reconnaissance for us."

Strictly speaking, Mack Bolan wasn't a member of the Stony Man team. Nonetheless, he often took part in their operations when he wasn't on a mission of his own. Since he was on R & R at the moment, so to speak, Price didn't think that he would mind extending his vacation to include the island republic.

"As far as I know," she said, "he doesn't have anything else going on right now, so I don't think there'll be a problem. I'll talk to him tonight and set it up."

"Good." Brognola nodded. "The President isn't about to ignore the Communist threat there, not after the Taipei riot. But with the congressional resolution condemning Taiwan in effect, his hands are tied as far as doing anything official to help them. He would have to run it past Congress, and that's simply not going to fly right now."

"I understand."

Condemning an ally for protecting itself from a foreign-sponsored insurrection was stupid and short-sighted, but it was also typical of Congress. Sometimes, being a friend of the United States was a lot more trouble than it was worth. The Bosnians had paid that price a few years earlier, and now it was the Taiwanese's turn to be in the barrel.

"The second thing that the President wants you to get involved with is the recent assassinations of the Chinese prodemocracy activists here in the States. He needs to know if they are happenstance or if there is some kind of Beijing-sponsored campaign going on here, as well."

"We're ahead of you on that one," Price stated. "Able Team is already in San Francisco working on the activist assassination cases. The San Francisco PD has drawn a complete blank on them, and so far our guys haven't made much progress, either. But as you well know, the Ironman has his ways to make things happen."

Brognola was glad to hear that Price was one jump ahead of him on that one. He knew that the FBI, the ATF and every other federal and state agency was working the case, as well. But he had confidence in the abilities of Carl Lyons and his two partners to get the goods before the rest of the agencies even got their desks organized, their pencils sharpened and their coffeepot plugged in.

For one thing, Able Team wasn't hampered by the legal niceties that bound the hands of the police and federal agencies. Swift, certain justice had long been known to be the most effective way of dealing with those who preyed on society. The problem was that the law too often didn't allow that to take place, so it fell to the Stony Man action teams to make it happen.

"Good," he said. "I'll let him know. Beyond that, I want everyone focused in on the Asian theater right now. The feeling in the intelligence communities of everyone involved is that the hard-liners are back in power and that we can expect more problems, particularly over Hong Kong and Taiwan.''

''Is there anything specific?'' Kurtzman asked.

''Nothing and everything.''

WHEN CARL LYONS WALKED into the Golden Pavilion restaurant on the outskirts of Oakland, he paused inside the door to let his eyes adjust to the darkness. Most of the lights were turned off, and only a single table in the back by the kitchen was lit. The table was set with a pot of tea and two cups, a sign that this was a social meeting. The Chinese man seated at the table looked to be in his sixties, but the big ex-cop knew that Johnny Lin had to be seventy-five if he was a day.

Lin's reputation wasn't unknown to Lyons. The man had been a gangster for a long time and had his hand in a number of things in the Bay Area. Off-track betting, opium dens, ''businessmen's insurance,'' girls—you name it and, if it happened in the Chinese community, Johnny Lin was rumored to be involved. It was true, however, that he had never been connected with the narcotics trade except maybe for a little opium, and that all went to users in the Chinese community.

Lin also ran a very disciplined group of hoods. They didn't rob the poor, didn't prey on the innocent and they didn't kill for sport. He ran his organization like an old-time warlord, but he took care of his people. He supported Chinese charities and even sent deserving sons and daughters of his employees and clients to college.

What all this meant to Lyons was that, as far as crooks went, Lin wasn't very high on his list of priorities. Although the former LAPD detective wasn't one to give a bad guy a break, he also knew that all bad guys weren't alike. The world would be a better place if men like Lin didn't exist, but compared to the real criminals of the Bay Area, Lin hardly rated the label. More than anything, he was simply a businessman who catered to the all too human vices of his own people.

Nonetheless, Lyons was still a little apprehensive about meeting the gangster. Lin had never been in formal trouble with the law, but he wasn't known to particularly like policemen. Even though Lyons hadn't been with LAPD for years, he knew that to the Chinese underground he was still a cop.

He didn't even want to think of what Lin would do if he really knew what Lyons did for a living now.

"I'm glad that you could meet me on such short notice," Lyons said as he came to a stop beside the table.

"It is my pleasure," Lin answered. "Please have a seat. Can I offer you tea?"

"Thank you."

Lyons waited until a cup had been placed in front

of him before breaking the silence, but Lin beat him to it.

"I understand," Lin said, "that you and your associates are looking for the Beijing killers."

Lyons had come to ask Lin about the China White trade, but the old man was one step ahead of him, so he had nothing to gain from being coy. "That's true."

"What will happen to them when you find them?"

Lyons met Lin's eyes squarely. "They will be dealt with."

"That is good. They are giving us Chinese a bad name, and I don't like that."

"If you're so worried about your cultural image," Lyons said, "why don't you take them out yourself?"

"I can't do that," Lin answered. "It wouldn't look good."

"To who?"

"To the rulers in Beijing. Though they are an ocean away, as you are finding out, they have a long reach. But if you deal with them, it will not reflect badly on me."

Lyons knew that he had just hit the jackpot, but he still wanted to be cautious. "Why are you offering this information to me?"

Lin took a sip of tea while he formulated his answer. "This country has been good to me," he said. "And I feel that I should give something back to it for the chance it has given me to become a wealthy man."

"You could try giving up a life of crime," Lyons suggested. "That would be a good gift."

Lin smiled. "If I did that, my people would just fall prey to the barbarians on the streets. As long as I am strong, the black and Mexican gangs leave my people alone to live their humble lives in peace."

Lyons knew that there was a lot of truth in that. For the most part, the Chinese communities in California suffered a lot less crime than did the other Asian enclaves. Part of that was the fact that the tongs and Triads policed their own communities and made sure that brutal young men like the vicious Vietnamese gang bangers who preyed on their own people, didn't become a problem.

"I will be in contact with you soon," Lin said. "And Sergeant Lyons..."

"Yes?"

"When this is finished, you will not say anything about me to anyone, will you?"

"No way," Lyons replied, shaking his head. "It would be bad for my image if it got out that I had been consorting with known criminals."

Lin smiled. "We understand each other, then."

"I'm afraid that we do."

CHAPTER SEVEN

Taipei, Taiwan

Mack Bolan stepped off of the China Airlines Boeing 757 and entered the passenger concourse of Chiang Kai-shek International Airport. The hour-and-a-half flight from Hong Kong had been pleasant, though not uneventful. Immediately after the jetliner had taken off from the colony's Kai Tak Airport, a Red Chinese J-8 Fantail jet fighter had appeared off its wing and escorted the airliner to international airspace.

The fighter hadn't acted in a threatening manner, but it had been a not too subtle reminder that China ruled the skies over the South China Sea. It was also a reminder to anyone who visited Taiwan that he or she was entering territory that was contested by the world's largest nation.

Security at the airport was heavy, but Bolan had no trouble going through passport control or customs. He was completely clean, having left his hardware in Hong Kong to be sent to him later by diplomatic courier. Congress might have cut off almost all contact with the Taiwanese government, but Barbara Price had still been able to use Brognola's Justice Department influence to take care of that chore for him.

Outside the terminal, Bolan hailed a Toyota cab for the twenty-mile ride to downtown Taipei and his hotel. Taipei had grown since the last time he had been there. The city now held some six million people and was starting to look a lot like Singapore, the current Jewel of the Orient. The core of the city was all modern construction with tall buildings, wide thoroughfares and parks. It was neat, clean and looked prosperous.

After checking into his hotel, Bolan took another cab to the American Consulate to retrieve his bag, which had arrived from Hong Kong in the diplomatic pouch. The seal he had affixed to it was still intact, so he knew that the tools of his trade had arrived unmolested.

After having a quick meal in the hotel, Bolan went out to reacquaint himself with the city. Also he had to make a phone call and didn't want to do it from the hotel. The big American's contact with the Hong Kong Triad leader Austin Chang had paid off with more than just helping him rescue young John Chun from his kidnappers. Before leaving the crown colony, he had contacted Chang again and had been given an introduction to a Triad contact in Taipei, a man named Tung Wu.

Many of the Taiwanese Triads had gone legitimate, at least on the surface. In the economic boom of the past two decades, there had been more money to be made in business than in the more traditional Triad ventures, smuggling and extortion. Not surprisingly, the contact Bolan had been given was the president of a small but prospering electronics firm.

Tung was surprised to receive Bolan's call that evening. But after hearing the code word the American had been told to give him, he immediately agreed to a meeting the following morning.

TUNG'S ASIA-TRONIC wasn't one of the electronics giants of Taiwan that had fueled the island's recent economic boom, but it was big enough to be profitable. Tung had carved out a sizable niche market producing microprocessors that went into videogames and other small consumer applications.

"I am pleased to meet you, Mr. Belasko," Tung said when the American was shown into his plush office on the top floor of his manufacturing complex. "Certain colleagues of mine have asked me to give you every assistance that I can, and I will do everything possible to help you."

After receiving Bolan's call the night before, Tung had made some calls of his own and had been briefed on the reason for the American's visit.

"I appreciate that," Bolan replied.

"We have, as you would say, common enemies and it makes sense for us to join forces on this. The sooner that the men who are behind the unfortunate death of Mr. Cunningham are exposed, the sooner relations between our two nations can get back to what they had been before that regrettable and tragic incident.

"And," Tung said with a shrug, "this current situation is also—how do you say it?—bad for business."

Bolan didn't ask which business it was, the traditional or the modern, that Tung was concerned about. But whichever, if the Triad leader's economic concerns could be turned into information he could use, it really didn't matter.

"So, what do you know about those who were behind Cunningham's death?"

"It all goes back to last year when we had the first free and open election of a president," Tung said.

"How had your presidents been elected before?"

"Previously the people voted for the party, and the party's head man then became the president. Rather like the British do with their prime minister."

"Anyway, as you will remember, Beijing threatened us then by conducting missile tests close to our shores until your government intervened. The hardliners were frustrated when Beijing backed down from the threat of your American fleet. They had been ready to go to war and take their chances, but they did not feel that they were strong enough to take on the American Navy and risk war with Washington as well. Now, though, the situation has changed."

"What's different this time?"

"They think they are strong enough now," Tung said simply. "In the past year, several more-liberal members of the Central Committee of the People's Republic have had accidents or have died in mysterious ways. They have been replaced with men who are dedicated to returning Taiwan, as they say, to their control, and their plan has been implemented.

"There has always been a large number of Beijing's agents in Taiwan. Most of them have been in what I think you call deep cover. Now, though, they have been activated and will carry out their orders to undermine our security. Part of that plan has been successful in that the Cunningham incident has driven a wedge between our two governments."

"Unfortunately that is true."

Tung looked Bolan straight in the eye. "What are your intentions when you find the people who are behind Cunningham's death?"

Bolan locked his cold blue eyes on the dark ones of the Triad leader. "They'll be eliminated."

This solution to a problem wasn't foreign to Tung's way of thinking. In fact, it was very Triadesque. Nonetheless, even with what he had been told about Belasko's actions in Hong Kong, he was surprised to hear him say it so bluntly.

"You are not concerned about the Taiwanese authorities, then?"

"Concerned, yes," Bolan replied. "But not to the point of letting that concern come in the way of getting the job done. I can assure you that I won't get in the way of the Taiwanese police or other local authorities. And when I am finished here, I'll leave the evidence behind to prove that these men were the ones they have been looking for themselves. I wouldn't want them to lose face."

Tung laughed. "You are a wise man for a foreigner. You are blunt like most of your countrymen, but you are also subtle and that is a good thing. We Chinese are a subtle people."

"There was nothing subtle about Cunningham's death," Bolan argued."

"But," Tung replied, "he was killed that way to have an impact on you Americans, not on us. And I must say that it had the desired effect. We Taiwanese are now all on our own at a time when we are facing a great danger and need our friends at our side."

"But just as the American Congress suddenly turned its back on you, it'll as quickly reverse itself. If I can prove a Red Chinese connection to Cunningham's death, America will stand by Taiwan again."

"Then I'll pray that you have great success and have it soon," Tung said. "As a businessman, I want only to see a speedy return to normalcy."

"So do I."

"I will be in contact with you soon," the Triad leader said.

"I'll be waiting."

WHEN HAL BROGNOLA FLEW to the Farm again, he met with just Barbara Price and Yakov Katzenelenbogen to get a quick update on the ongoing missions to take back to the President. Now that both Bolan and Able Team were in the field, the Man was expecting fast results.

"The President isn't going to be happy to hear about this," Brognola said, shaking his head when Price told him about Carl Lyons's meeting with Johnny Lin.

"In fact, he's going to go ballistic when I tell him that Able Team has joined forces with a Chinese gang. It was bad enough when Striker had to use that Triad in Hong Kong to find the Chun boy, but I could explain that one away because of it being an overseas operation. I don't know how I'm going to explain this to him."

She shrugged. "Just don't tell him about it. All he really needs to know are the results we get, not how we arrive at them. You've been running the show around here long enough to know that."

There was a certain amount of truth to that. No President really needed to know exactly how Stony Man worked in the field. "But I know he's going to ask me," Brognola said.

"Lie to him. You've stretched the truth before."

Brognola sighed. "I know I have. Someday I'm going to get caught at it, and he's going to have my ass thrown in jail."

"No chance." She grinned. "You know far too much to be allowed to live. If you ever get caught, they're just going to kill you and dump your body in a ditch somewhere."

"That makes me feel so much better, Barb."

As radical as it sounded, there was an element of truth in what she had said. Stony Man Farm was the guardian of far too many secrets for it ever to be exposed to the light of day. And those secrets weren't only American. There was hardly a Western government that could afford to have the knowledge of Stony Man activities made public.

"How's Striker's mission going in Taipei?" Brognola asked, changing the topic.

"He's in place," Price said, trying to figure out a way to tell him that Bolan had hooked up with another Triad to give him the inside line he needed. But, as had been the case in Hong Kong, it was necessary.

"Do you have Phoenix Force standing by?"

"They're on call," Katzenelenbogen replied, "and the mission pack has been put together. All we need are the results of Mack's recon and we're ready to go."

"What's the cover story?"

"With the congressional sanctions in place against Taiwan," Katz said, "we can't send them there with a traceable U.S. connection, so we're falling back on a Canadian cover. They're using the geological-survey-team legend again. There's enough interest in oil and mineral exploration of the islands around Taiwan that it will pass inspection. The mission equipment will go packed as their survey gear."

"Good," Brognola said, nodding. The mission

set-up this time was a little trickier than usual because of the congressional sanctions. But political obstacles were a fact of life in his line of work.

"When do you have Phoenix Force scheduled to move out?"

"They'll be here tonight," Katz said. "The briefing's in the morning, and they'll fly out to California right after that. Their plane's loaded and waiting for them."

Brognola glanced at his watch. "I've got to run. There's a reception for the new drug czar that I have to attend. But if you get anything new from either Lyons or Striker, break in and tell me."

"Will do."

AFTER KATZENELENBOGEN and Price saw Brognola off for his flight back to Washington, the pair returned to the communications room. "I noticed that you didn't come clean with Hal on Bolan's Taipei Triad connection," Katz said with a grin.

Price smiled back. "I didn't want to strain him too much. He gets himself in trouble if he has too much that he has to lie to the President about."

"It is a hell of a thing, though," he said, "when you really stop and think about it. Here we are, supposedly the nation's last bastion against evil, getting into bed with some of the oldest criminal gangs in existence so we can save the world from the Communists."

"Well," she said, "the way I see it, when you're going up against the government of the largest nation on earth, you need all the help you can get. If we're still around when this is all over, then we can worry about having been contaminated by working with the Triads. But if this thing turns into World War III, it won't really matter, will it?"

"You're becoming cynical, and that's supposed to be my specialty."

"I can't help it. It goes with the job."

The old Israeli warrior smiled. How true that was.

"JOHNNY LIN SENDS his regards," the man said as Schwarz quickly patted him down for hardware.

"He's clean." Schwarz stepped back.

"Have a seat." Lyons nodded toward the couch in the living room of their suite.

Being careful to keep his hands in sight, the messenger walked over and sat on the couch. "I am Jim Lin," he said, "Johnny's grandson. He sent me to tell you that he has a line on the men you are looking for."

"Great," Lyons replied. "Where are they?"

"We don't know exactly where they are yet," the younger Lin said. "But we have a line on a guy who has been dealing with the Beijing government big time."

"What do you mean 'dealing'?"

"I mean trading high-tech information and equipment for China White."

Lyons was glad to see that his hunch was once more paying off. Having it confirmed this way was better than working it on his own.

"Industrial espionage and drug dealing, that's a nice combination."

"You got it."

"Who is this scum-ball?"

"His name is Kevin Wong," Lin said. "And he runs a yuppie antique boutique in the city. He's been importing heroin and antiques from the mainland in exchange for blacklisted high-tech equipment and industrial information."

"He's a spy, as well as a drug dealer."

Lin nodded. "That's what it looks like, and my grandfather would consider it a great favor if Mr. Wong went out of business, if you know what I mean. He says that people like him give the Chinese people a bad name. Heroin is bad business."

"Opium is good?" Schwarz asked.

Lin shrugged. "The poppy is an old Chinese vice, and we know how to handle it. Heroin is destructive, and no one can keep it in check."

"One way or the other," Lyons promised, "Wong's history, believe me. The best he'll get is a life sentence in a federal slammer. But that's only if he cooperates and gives it up easily. But if he wants to go down hard, I can do it that way, too. It's going to be up to him how he wants it."

"Granddad told me that you'd say something like that."

"Your grandfather's a smart man."

CHAPTER EIGHT

Kevin Wong felt as if he had stepped between a rock and a hard place, and he didn't like the sensation of being slowly crushed. Watching the evening news report about yet another assassination of a prodemocracy Chinese American activist, this one in Vancouver, B.C., brought it all crashing down on him. Not for the first time he sincerely wished that he hadn't gotten involved in this mess.

At the same time, he really didn't understand what the fuss was all about between the Communist Beijing government and the old farts who kept trying to keep the dead Nationalist cause alive. The Nationalists had Taiwan wrapped up for themselves, and they should be smart enough to know better than to keep harassing the mainland government. As far as he was concerned, the Communists weren't all that bad. In fact, they were damned good to do business with—at least for someone in his line of work.

Wong didn't like to call himself a drug dealer. The term had bad connotations, and he didn't see himself as a bad man. He liked to style himself as being in the import-export business. And he was. He imported China White from the mainland and exported information and technology that the Beijing government needed to expand their economy.

It was a painless arrangement, and it had given him an almost exclusive dealership for a superior product. It was true that he had some competition from the local branches of the Triads, especially from the Hong Kong–sponsored groups. But his Beijing contact had told him that as soon as the Red Chinese took over Hong Kong, the Triad operations would cease to exist. This was good news, as the demand for his product was on the rise and not only within the Chinese community.

Cocaine had gotten a bad name over the past few years, and the trendy, upscale party drug in California now was the ultrarefined form of heroin known on the street as China White. There was a ton of money to be made on the stuff, and he wanted to get as much of it as he could. That was why he had made his original contact with the Communists to set up his profitable arrangement.

He'd had no problem supplying the technological information and equipment that Beijing wanted in exchange for their heroin. He thought that it was completely absurd for the American government to try to keep mainland China in the Dark Ages by restricting her access to the latest technology. It was obvious to him that the quicker the Chinese were able to modernize, the quicker they would become a major U.S. market—to the benefit of both nations.

His business with the Chinese had been going smoothly, and the money had been rolling in. Then this political bullshit started up again, and he had been forced to get involved with more than the import-export trade. In the beginning, no one had said anything about his having to get involved with something as dangerous as political assassination. When his contact had come to him, though, the Beijing agent made it quite clear that he had no choice but to do what he was told if he wanted to continue living. And since life was good for Kevin Wong, he did what they wanted. So far it hadn't been all that much. He just feared what else they might want.

A two-bedroom apartment in Oakland had been leased in his name, and he was paying the bills. His contact had told him that he would be reimbursed for his expenses, so he wasn't worried about that. He was concerned, however, about the fact that his name was on the lease. If this didn't turn out the way his contact promised that it would, he'd be sucked into the aftermath and he didn't want to get tagged as an accessory to murder, particularly not to a political assassination. That was a federal rap.

Beyond initially securing the apartment and making sure that it was furnished the way the tenants wanted, Wong hadn't had much contact with the six Chinese who were staying there. On the occasions that he did, he spoke enough Cantonese to get by, and the six men spoke basic English along with Cantonese. They also spoke another Chinese dialect he didn't understand at all, which they used to talk among themselves.

So far his contact with the Beijing agents had been minimal. Not all of them stayed in the apartment at the same time. Usually only three of them were there at any one time, and he had no idea where the other three stayed. Because of that, he could truly say that he had no idea what these men were doing in the States and he was almost comfortable with the situation.

Then, just a few days earlier, his contact had asked him to start going to the political meetings of the Chinese American organizations that supported Taiwan, and he didn't know how to get out of it. He wasn't a spy, and he didn't know how to be one. On top of that, he wasn't really well connected to the Chinese community. His grandparents were all dead, his own parents lived in the mostly white suburbs and he didn't even have many Chinese customers in his shop. His only real connection with San Francisco's Chinatown was the accident of his birth.

He was a third-generation American, and he didn't think of himself as Chinese, not even as Chinese American. He saw himself simply as an American, and it would be difficult for him to fake being really concerned about what happened to Taiwan. As far as he knew, he didn't have any relatives living there. In fact, the only real contact he had with any of the overseas Chinese was with his Communist trading partners in the People's Republic. Because of that, he didn't think that he would be too welcome at a meeting of old-fashioned, hard-core Nationalists.

There was also the simple fact that he didn't want to get any more involved with this mess than he already was. As it stood now, if something went wrong, he might be able to talk his way out of the fact that he had leased the apartment. He could say that he had been asked to do it for one of his mainland trading partners. But if he started spying on people to set them up them for assassination, he would never be able to explain that away. The problem was that he didn't know how to get out of it.

KEVIN WONG'S STORE, the Ming Treasure House, was a trendy import boutique that catered to yuppies with a flair for Oriental decor. Unlike the often flimsy and poorly made Chinese goods found in many places, Ming's offerings were first-rate. Wong's Beijing connections also allowed him to import a limited amount of genuine Chinese antiques in addition to well-made modern reproductions.

When Able Team went looking for proof that Wong was involved with the assassinations, the first place they went was to his store. The fact that it was after-hours and his security system had been activated wasn't a problem. Lin's information packet on him had included the keypad code to turn off the shop's burglar alarm. Schwarz didn't even have to break a sweat getting them inside.

"Man, he's got some nice stuff in this place," Schwarz said as he admired a porcelain temple dog from the Tang dynasty.

"Put that damned thing down," Lyons called out from Wong's office, "and get your butt in here. We've got a lot of stuff to go through."

"Okay, okay."

While Lyons and Blancanales started to sift through Wong's paperwork, Schwarz booted the computer on his desk, hacked his way through the simple password security system and started tripping through the files. Most people in the drug business who ran a business to launder their drug money left traces of their transactions behind. The three of them were old hands at spotting the signs of money laundering.

Two hours later, though, they hadn't found the smoking gun.

"We're wasting our time here," Schwarz said as he backed out of Wong's system. "I haven't found diddly."

"Me, either," Blancanales added.

"I want to hit his warehouse next," Lyons suggested.

"Let's do it."

The three let themselves out the way they had come. Schwarz paused at the security system's keypad and activated the alarm again. There was no point in advertising that they had been there.

WONG'S WAREHOUSE was located in a light industrial area rather than in the warehouse district, which was both good and bad news for Able Team. It was good in that it meant that there would be few, if any, people working in the area at that time of night. By the same token, it also meant that if they were spotted, they probably would be reported.

Schwarz parked the van behind the building next to the warehouse and set the silent alarm. That way, if anyone messed with the truck, they would hear it over their comm links.

Interestingly enough, the windows of Wong's warehouse were both painted over and barred. He wasn't taking any chances that anyone would get a glimpse of what was going on inside. Since Lin had reported that the importer was dealing in China White, as well as antiques, that wasn't surprising. Lin hadn't been able to provide a keypad code for the security system here, so Gadgets finally got to make himself useful.

Figuring that Wong wouldn't have wired his burglar alarm to a police response center, he didn't have to worry about tipping off the cops. But a quick look at the wiring revealed that it apparently was connected to someone's phone, and the chances were good that person was Kevin Wong. He would certainly want to know if someone was breaking into his warehouse.

It took Schwarz only a few seconds to remove the face of the control box and expose the wires behind the keypad. Taking an electronic random-number generator—a cracker, as it was known to computer hackers—out of his waist pack, he clipped it to the exposed input wire.

For a keypad security system to be any good, it needed to incorporate a wrong-number counter. That device would sound the alarm if someone tried to simply punch in random numbers in hopes of stumbling onto the correct six-number sequence as Schwarz was now doing electronically. Wong hadn't bothered to spring for the more expensive system, so it took less than two minutes for the cracker to work out the keypad's numerical sequence and switch off the security system.

"We're in," Schwarz said.

"Hurry up with the door," Lyons whispered. "We're exposed out here."

Schwarz stopped inside the door and looked to both sides to see if there was any kind of security backup. Most drug warehouses had security systems on top of security systems, and he didn't want to get cocky and tip Wong off that someone was breaking in.

"We're clear."

"Where are the lights?" Blancanales said.

Schwarz hit the switch and whistled. "Payday."

The warehouse was filled with shelving units, which were stacked with boxes and crates bearing the logos of America's top electronics and cybernetics companies.

"What do you want to bet that most of those goodies are on the restricted-technology export list?" Blancanales offered.

"That's a sucker bet," Lyons replied. "Of course it is—just look at the stuff. It's all top brand-name electronics."

"There's a lot of defense-industry material here, as well," Schwarz added as he walked past the racks. "This gear is all military avionic and positioning-system stuff used in a number of weapons systems."

"Do we call the Feds in on this?" Blancanales asked.

"Not yet," Lyons stated. "I want to get my hands on this Wong guy before they do. If they get him, he'll just lawyer up and they'll have to cut a deal before they get anything out of him."

"You want to talk to him tonight?" Blancanales asked as he glanced at his watch.

"Why not?" Lyons said. "We're not getting any younger."

"Suits me," Schwarz added. "The night's shot anyway."

KEVIN WONG'S HOUSE was in an upscale neighborhood. It wasn't the most expensive house on the block, but it wasn't a fixer-upper, either. Obviously Wong's enterprises were paying off handsomely.

The security system covering the house was little more than a basic unit, but it did have a phone link that was probably connected to an emergency response center. The system presented little challenge, and Schwarz disabled it in record time.

"It's clear," he reported.

"Okay," Lyons said, pulling the .357 Colt Python from shoulder leather. "It's show time."

Leaving Schwarz outside in case he had missed an alarm, Lyons and Blancanales moved in to make the snatch. Since they didn't have a layout of the place, the two men swept the ground floor first. Usually in a house of this style the bedrooms would be on the second level. But reconning the ground level first ensured that they didn't miss signs of the presence of anyone in the house other than their target. The younger Lin hadn't known of Wong's living arrangements, so they needed to check. A bedroom guest could complicate things.

When the ground floor showed no signs of overnight visitors, no twin glasses on the coffee table by an empty bottle, they headed for the stairs. Usually human nature decided that if only one bedroom was going to be occupied, it would be the one closest to the bathroom. And it would usually be the one to the immediate right of the bath, as it was in this case.

Lyons's and Blancanales's rubber-soled boots

made no noise on the thick carpet as they approached Wong's bed. "Kevin Wong?" Lyons asked as he shone his flashlight in the man's face.

Wong opened his eyes.

"You Kevin Wong?"

"Yeah. What are you—?"

"Get your clothes on," Lyons said, jerking him out of bed. "You're coming with us."

"But..." Wong fell silent when he saw the pistol in Lyons's hand.

"Get dressed and keep your mouth shut."

Stunned, Wong sat on the edge of his bed and reached for the clothes he had taken off before he went to bed.

As soon as the man had on his shirt, pants and shoes, Blancanales slipped a plastic riot restraint over his wrists and a strip of duct tape over his mouth.

"You can walk or we'll carry you."

Resigned to his fate, Wong walked out of his house and was led to the van parked around the corner.

CHAPTER NINE

Kevin Wong looked as if he was about to pass out in fear when Schwarz and Blancanales hauled him out of the van and he saw that he wasn't being taken to a police station. But with the tape across his mouth, all he could do was try to voice his concern. Once inside the interrogation room, they slammed him into a chair and bound his wrists to its arms and his ankles to the legs with plastic riot restraints.

"Who are you people?" Wong asked as soon as the tape was removed from his mouth. "Why did you bring me here?"

"We're looking for some Chinese," Schwarz said, "and we've been told that you can tell us where they are."

"I don't know anything about any men," Wong answered automatically.

"But," Schwarz said with a grin, "I haven't even told you who we're looking for yet."

Wong's eyes shot around the room, but he didn't see a way out of his predicament. "I think I would like to talk to my lawyer."

"You want a lawyer?" Schwarz asked. "What do you think this is, a goddamned police station?"

"Wait a minute." Blancanales stepped between them as if on cue. "Obviously Mr. Wong's a bit confused, so we'd better explain it to him."

He leaned over their prisoner. "If I understand you correctly, Mr. Wong, you think that we are some kind of police officers and that we want to talk to you about some Red Chinese assassins who have been killing Chinese American activists. Well, you're right about part of that."

Wong's blood ran cold. How in the hell did they know that he was connected with the Beijing hit team? "I can explain," he said hurriedly. "But I think I need to talk to a lawyer first. If you get me a lawyer, I'll tell you everything I know about them."

Blancanales backed off. "Unfortunately for you, Mr. Wong, I think that you still don't understand your situation here. You see, we aren't the local police. We're not even federal agents."

The Politician grinned broadly to Wong's all too apparent confusion. "We're what you would call a private party, and we don't have much contact with lawyers."

Now Wong really got scared. If these guys really weren't cops, he didn't have anything to bargain with. Suddenly he thought about the China White he had been unloading. Had he unknowingly crossed the line into another drug lord's heroin turf? But if that was the case, why were these guys asking him about the Beijing agents?

"Whoever you are," he said hurriedly, "I can explain everything."

"What's this 'everything' that you're going to try to explain to us?" Blancanales asked.

"Well..."

So far Lyons had been sitting back and letting his two partners play a Mutt-and-Jeff interrogation routine with this guy. It was working as well as it usually did, but now he wanted to get into the game. The only thing more effective than the good cop–bad cop routine was the variation on the theme known as bad cop–completely whacko cop.

It was a role Lyons really enjoyed playing.

Storming across the room, he shoved Blancanales out of the way and pulled the .357 Colt Python from his shoulder holster. Wong went into a blind panic when Lyons jammed the muzzle of the pistol against his forehead. But cuffed to the chair as he was, there was no place for him to go.

"Please," he sobbed, "don't shoot me."

"Give me one good reason why not, asshole," Lyons snapped. "You're wasting my valuable time, and I don't like that. I've got work to do, and if you can't help me—" he paused and thumbed back the hammer on the Colt "—I guess I'll just have to talk to somebody else."

"Please," Wong wailed. "I'll tell you everything you want to know about them. I know who they work for because he forced me to help them. I really didn't want to get involved, but I didn't have any choice. He said that he'd kill me if I didn't help him."

"So you helped them kill someone else," Lyons said, sneering. "That's real cute, and it's called being an accessory to a political assassination. That's a big-time federal beef. The very least you're looking at is doing life in a federal slammer if you don't help us put an end to their operation fast."

"There are six of them," Wong said. "I don't know how they got into the country, but I know where they live."

"Do you have their names?"

"Only their last names," he said as he rattled off six Chinese names.

"Slowly," Schwarz said, "and spell those names."

"THAT DIDN'T TAKE very long," Schwarz said after he put a pair of stereo earphones over Wong's ears to make sure that he couldn't overhear what they were saying.

"He was a pushover," Lyons stated. "He's just a nickel-and-dime punk, and he's in way over his head on this. I'm surprised that Beijing trusted a guy like him for an operation this important."

"Maybe they didn't have anyone else in place to use as a support man."

"What're we going to do with him now?" Blancanales asked Lyons. "Dump him on the DEA for the heroin or the FBI for the restricted electronics?"

Lyons shook his head. "We're going to hang on to him for a while. I want to use him to get us into that safehouse of his. Those guys aren't going to be the kind of pushovers that Wong is, but his smiling face at the door might get us inside."

"We need to keep at least one of those bastards in one piece," Blancanales reminded him when he recognized the glitter in Lyons's eyes. "We're going to want someone to talk to when it's all over."

"That's why you're going to be carrying the SPAS loaded with those new bean-bag rounds."

Blancanales closed his eyes for a moment and shook his head. "Man, I was afraid that you were going to say something like that. I'm going to go for head shots with them, though. And I don't care if he has a headache for a week. I'm not going to get wasted, because we need to talk to one of those guys."

"Go for crotch shots for all I care," Lyons said. "Just make sure you take one of them out."

"But only one, Ironman," Blancanales insisted.

"That should be enough." Lyons shrugged. "We don't have enough chairs in here to talk to the rest of them anyway."

"Do you want to check in with Barb and let her know what we've learned so far?" Schwarz asked.

"Just send her a quick E-mail, then break communications. I don't want Hal coming back on-line and telling us that we have to share the goodies with the FBI. We developed this one and we're going to run with it."

Schwarz grinned. "You got it."

BARBARA PRICE SMILED as she read Gadget Schwarz's E-mailed report on their capture of Kevin Wong and the results of his interrogation.

It was good to get a break every so often.

Once more, Lyons and his teammates had come through. And it was just in time. The most recent assassination of another Chinese prodemocracy activist in Vancouver, B.C., had shown that the U.S.-based hit team was moving farther afield. They needed to get this thing wrapped up as soon as humanly possible.

When she tried to get back to Able Team and found that they were off-line, she knew instantly what Lyons was doing. Once he was rolling, he hated to have anything get in his road, particularly things like go-slow messages from Hal Brognola. Wanting Lyons to have a free rein she decided that she wouldn't pass on this information to Brognola just yet.

After all, she was the Stony Man mission controller, and that meant that the details of mission coordination were her call. There would be time enough to brief the Justice man when this particular action was all over.

THE NEXT MORNING, Schwarz untied Kevin Wong and helped him work out the kinks from a night spent in a sitting position. As soon as the prisoner could walk again, Schwarz escorted him to the bathroom.

"What are you going to do with me?" Wong asked after he came out.

"Well," Schwarz said, "we're going to pay a visit to your tenants and have a little chat with them, too. We thought you'd like to come along and make the introductions."

"Please, don't make me do that. They'll kill me if they see you with me. I know they will."

"No, they won't," Schwarz said jovially. "We'll keep you alive so we can slap your ass in jail."

"I'll go to jail, but I can't go over there."

"Oh, yes, you can. We'll take real good care of you. Now, how about a little breakfast first? You don't want to do something like this on an empty stomach."

When Wong poured himself a cup of coffee, Schwarz walked over to Lyons. "You want me to give this guy a Kevlar T-shirt? If it gets nasty, we may need him in one piece so we can talk to him again later."

"Sure, if we have a spare."

"I've got him covered."

KEVIN WONG WAS REALLY scared now. The terror of the night before was completely gone, and sheer panic had replaced it. But with the short guy pressing the silenced semiautomatic pistol against his side, he had no choice but to climb the stairs to the hit team's apartment. On the drive over, he would have probably risked jumping from the van had it not been for the small electronic device that had been clipped to the back of his belt.

This device, the short guy had explained, was a remote-control bomb that was triggered by a control box in his pocket. "If you try to make a break," he had said, "I'll just press the button and they'll have to bury you in two coffins. And I recommend that you stick real close to me no matter where we're at. If you get more than forty or fifty feet away, it'll automatically detonate and cut your spine in two."

Wong still had no idea who these guys were, but they had him more scared than he had ever been. There was absolutely no doubt in his mind that they would kill him if he didn't do exactly what they said, particularly the cold-eyed blond guy who appeared to be the leader.

At the top of the stairs, the blond man had his silenced submachine gun ready as he checked out the hallway before motioning for the other two to join him.

"Remember," the short guy whispered in Wong's ear when they reached the door. "I've got my finger on the button, so don't screw up."

Wong knocked, and the door was immediately

opened by the man who called himself Pang. "I need to talk to—" Wong began.

Suddenly Schwarz thrust him aside and triggered his silenced Beretta pistol. Two 9 mm rounds took the Chinese in the face and knocked him backward.

Blancanales and Lyons burst past Wong with their weapons lowered. The man on the other side of the room dived for a weapon on the coffee table, and Blancanales triggered his SPAS-12 shotgun, sending one of the bean-bag rounds screaming across the room.

The deployed bag hit the Chinese in the shoulder and spun him. A second shot hit him in the middle of the back and dropped him to the floor like a sack of cement.

Lyons raced past him, heading for the bedrooms in the back. A brief shout was cut off, and all was silent.

"Clear," Lyons called out from the back room.

"We're clear in here," Schwarz announced as he dragged the body of the first man inside to clear the door.

Wong stood inside the apartment, pressed back against the wall and trying hard not to look at the dead man at his feet. Now he was certain that these guys were Mob hit men of some kind. Cops, even Feds, wouldn't have gone in shooting the way they had. They hadn't given the Beijing agents any chance at all to surrender. He felt lucky to be alive himself and realized that he'd better not try to pull anything on these guys. They'd kill him in a heartbeat.

"My guy's still alive," Blancanales said as he bent over the man he had taken out with the beanbag rounds. "He's going to have major bruises, but we'll be able to talk to him."

"Good," Lyons said. "You and Gadgets get him and Wong down to the van while I take a quick look around here."

"We going to leave the bodies behind?"

Lyons thought for a moment. "Yeah. When the other three come back and find them, they might think that the one we grabbed did in his buddies and split. It may help confuse them."

On the ride back to the motel, Wong rode with his hands cuffed behind his back, as did the Red Chinese agent. He was relieved that the Beijing man's eyes were blindfolded. He didn't think that he'd be able to keep it together if the man was staring at him.

CHAPTER TEN

The Beijing hit man was conscious by the time Able Team got him back to their motel room. He was smart enough, though, not to try to struggle. He was in enemy hands, but as a trained agent, he knew better than to give his captors an excuse to hammer on him.

"But I don't speak good Chinese," Wong protested when Lyons told him to talk to their prisoner. "And I don't think that this guy speaks much English."

"How the hell did you communicate with these people, then," Lyons asked, "sign language?"

"The guy who answered the door speaks—" Wong shuddered "—or at least he did speak pretty good English. And their leader sounds almost like an American. But I've never talked to this guy before in either English or Chinese."

Lyons didn't press the linguistic point. If they didn't have a good translator, they might as well not even go through the exercise.

The problem was that he knew better than to try

to get their Chinese American SFPD liaison man to help them with this. Officer Yee would go ballistic if he learned about their raid on the apartment and the bodies they had left behind. Even with the air conditioner left running at full blast, someone was going to find them in a couple of days anyway. But since nothing had been left there to connect the corpses to Able Team, SFPD wouldn't have a clue.

"Why don't you call your Chinese godfather?" Schwarz suggested. "I'm sure he can loan us someone who can talk to this guy."

"Good idea, Gadgets."

Lyons quickly placed a call to Johnny Lin and, without explaining what was behind his request, asked if he knew of a confidential interpreter Lyons could borrow for a couple of hours. Without asking why such a man was needed, Lin said he would send someone immediately.

THE MAN JOHNNY LIN SENT to assist Able Team was the same grandson who had tipped them off about Kevin Wong's activities. As Lyons quickly briefed him on the raid, Jim Lin looked the gunman up and down. There was nothing special about him that he could see. The man could pass completely unnoticed in any Chinese population, but that was the mark of any good agent. How good he was at keeping his mouth shut was yet to be seen.

"I need to find out where those other three Beijing agents are," Lyons concluded, "And I need to find out fast. Do you think you can get it out of him?''

''It's worth a try.'' Lin shrugged. ''I speak enough of the Chinese dialects that we ought to have at least one them in common.''

''Get him on his feet,'' Lin told Schwarz and Blancanales. ''When you question a Chinese, you want him standing up so he'll know who's in charge. If he can't stand, prop his ass against the wall.''

Taking the prisoner by the arms, the two stood him on his feet and removed the tape from his mouth.

Lin locked eyes with the prisoner and stared at him for a long moment. ''Two of your comrades are dead,'' he said in Mandarin, ''and the other three are being captured as we speak. It will go easier on you if you cooperate with the authorities. You can start by giving me your name and your military unit.''

''I don't have to answer a Yankee half-breed like you,'' the man replied in Cantonese, a sneer curling his lip. Among the mainland Chinese, it was considered a disgrace to have European blood in your family. And it was widely believed that most Chinese Americans were so contaminated.

Without saying a word or changing the expression on his face, Lin kicked the prisoner in the testicles. The gunman dropped to the floor like a rock, his hands covering his crotch as he fought to catch his breath.

"Dog excrement," the younger Lin grated in Cantonese. "You are a complete disgrace to our people. If you want to keep your sacred jewels intact, you will watch your filthy tongue. I am of the honorable Lin family, and we are pure Han back to a time when your ancestors were still mountain barbarians living in caves and eating dog meat."

"Get him back on his feet," he told Schwarz. "This might go a little better now that I have his attention."

"You sure as hell got mine."

A fairly long conversation commenced, with Lin getting in the gunman's face and shouting and the prisoner giving short answers in reply. With a final shout, Lin turned to Lyons. "He says that he doesn't know when the other three are due to come back."

"Do you believe him?"

"I'm not sure," the gangster admitted. "I don't know if he realizes the seriousness of his situation yet. These guys can get pretty arrogant when they want. He's still giving me the agent-of-the-people bullshit."

"What's it going to take to get anything more out of him? Beat him to death?"

Lin grinned. "I can always threaten to send him back to China alive so that he'll have to explain why he failed to carry out his assignment. He probably won't want to have to go though that. Beijing isn't big on rewarding failure."

"Do whatever you have to do," Lyons said. "But I need that information."

"I'll get it." Lin smiled confidently. "It just may take a little while."

"WHAT ARE WE GOING to do with those two?" Blancanales asked the next time Lin took a break. "We're starting to get quite a collection of thugs around here. We can't really afford to spare the manpower keeping an eye on them while we're looking for those other three."

"Can your grandfather help us lock these two guys up for a couple of days?" Lyons asked Lin.

"I think so. Let me give him a call. And—" he hooked a thumb back towards the gunman "—we're making a little progress. He said that they flew in from British Columbia on phony Canadian passports."

"That's nice to know," Lyons said, "but it doesn't help us much."

Schwarz thought for a moment. "I can try INS and see who else this guy came in with. Maybe I can get some names, at least the passport names."

An hour later, four of Lin's associates showed up at the motel room and took control of Able Team's prisoners. "I'll keep working on him," Lin told Lyons.

"Good. We'll be in touch."

LYONS'S PLAN to stake out the apartment of the Beijing hit men wasn't working out. After watching the place for a day and a half, they had nothing to show for it. The other three Red Chinese agents hadn't shown up. But they had had no other option. Lin's best efforts hadn't produced any more useful information out of their captive.

"I think we need to talk to our hit man again." Schwarz said. "There's something about this I don't like."

"What do you mean?"

"Well, Wong said that all six of the Beijing boys didn't stay here at the same time, and we assumed that meant that they were on the road looking for someone to kill when they weren't here."

"And?" Lyons prompted.

"Maybe this apartment isn't the only place where they've been staying. Maybe they didn't completely trust our friend and found themselves a second safe-house on their own. After all, six guys staying in a small two-bedroom apartment can get a little crowded."

"That's a thought," Lyons said. "But the question is, are we going to be able to shake that second address out of our prisoner? Lin said that he feels he's gotten everything out of him that he can short of beating him to death."

"Let's chat with Wong again. At least we can talk to him ourselves and, after a couple of days with Lin, he might have remembered something we can use."

"It's worth a try," Blancanales said. "We sure as hell aren't getting anywhere here. And I think we need to talk to him about his drug supplier, as well. I keep thinking that we're missing a connection somewhere."

WONG WASN'T HAVING a good week. He'd thought that things would get better when the three white guys turned him over to the Chinese gangsters they were working with. But that hadn't proved to be the case. These Chinese were treating him like crud on their shoes. They refused to speak English to him and wouldn't speak his name. At least they were feeding him.

He had no idea what had happened to the Beijing agent who had survived the raid on the apartment. The last he had seen of him, the Chinese gangsters were taking him away, too. Maybe the assassin was being held captive in another room of this house, but there was no way for him to know. He hadn't been out of his small, windowless room since he'd been locked up.

He had completely lost track of the days he had been held captive. For that matter, he didn't even know if it was day or night. He was dead tired, as he hadn't been able to sleep for more than an hour or two at a time. He was still wearing the same clothes he had put on in his bedroom the night he had been captured, and he would have paid through the nose for a long hot shower.

Hearing footsteps outside his door, Wong automatically stood. It hadn't taken him long to learn the rules of the house. He wasn't allowed to sit in the presence of anyone. The first time he tried it, he'd been slammed facefirst into the wall. The gangster who walked in now was Lin, the chief interrogator, and Wong stiffened to attention. His incarceration had taught him good manners.

"Dog excrement," the gangster said in Cantonese, "the honorable long noses are here to talk to you again. Even though they are foreign devils, you will be polite to them and you will answer their questions or you will answer to me."

"Yes, Honorable Uncle."

"Do not call me that honorable name," Lin said. "My family has never had dog excrement like you in it."

Wong closed his eyes. Every time he tried to be a good Chinese and speak politely to these assholes, they threw it back in his face. If he ever got out of here, he was going to change his name and claim that he was Polynesian, anything to keep as far away from anything Chinese that he could.

When the door opened again, Wong saw the blond leader of the three white men walk in, followed by the other two. The blonde was almost the last guy in the world he wanted to talk to right now. The only thing that could be worse would be to have to face Zhang Liu, the leader of the Beijing team.

He had seen him only once, but that had been enough.

"Your other three tenants still haven't returned to their apartment," Lyons said, opening the conversation. "You wouldn't happen to have any idea where they might be staying, would you?"

"No sir," Wong said very respectfully. "As I said before, the only place I ever knew them to be when they were in town was at that apartment."

"And they never discussed any of their plans with you?" Schwarz asked. "Like where they were going or what they were going to do?"

"No, sir." He had gone over all of this several times before, but if they wanted to keep asking him the same questions, he'd be glad to answer them. Anything to make the time pass.

"The only thing they ever talked to me about was directly related to their living at the apartment. Things that they needed, supplies, food, that sort of thing."

"Did they ever ask you to get maps or phone numbers for them?" Blancanales asked.

"No," Wong said. "They never asked me for anything like that."

"Okay." Blancanales changed tactics. "Let's talk about your drug supplier. How does he fit into this program?"

This wasn't a subject Wong wanted to get into. So far he had managed to keep his American contact out of the conversation by giving up the apartment and the Beijing team, and he wanted it to stay that way. He was still hoping that he could somehow extricate himself from this mess and go back into business, maybe in L.A. or farther south.

"I don't know what you mean," he answered. "I—"

Lyons's hand snaked out, grabbed Wong by the front of his dirty shirt and jerked him forward. "You're wasting my time, asshole," he thundered, "and I don't have a lot of time to waste. I want to know who you were trading the technology to for the China White, and I want to know right now!"

Wong cowered under the verbal assault. But he had taken much worse in the past couple of days and was getting hardened to it. At least this guy yelled at him in English, and he could completely understand what he was saying. His Cantonese had dramatically improved over the past several days, but he could not recommend the gangsters' method of language study.

Nonetheless, maybe it was time for him to come clean on his business contacts, too. Anything to keep the blond guy from eating his face.

"Well," Wong said, "his name is Bill Hu, and he works for the trade mission downtown."

"The Red Chinese trade mission?" Blancanales asked.

"Of course."

Lyons smiled. Now he had it. "I need only one more thing out of you," he said. "And if you do what I want, you may get out of this thing alive after all.''

Wong felt his heart leap. ''You mean that you're going to turn me loose?''

''No,'' Lyons said bluntly. ''I mean that you'll still be alive when I turn you over to the DEA to face trafficking charges.''

Wong's heart fell. At least, though, he would be alive. ''What do you need?''

''I need to use you as bait to suck in the rest of the Beijing hit men.''

''Oh, no!'' Wong said. ''I can't do that. They'll kill me if they see me. They'll blame me for what happened at the apartment.''

''The government will kill you if you don't,'' Lyons argued ''Under the new antiterrorist laws, being convicted of a terrorist act where someone was killed is worth the death sentence. And being an accessory to such an act is as good as actually pulling the trigger. The only hope you have of staying alive is to help me get this guy. If it works, I'll see that you get off on the terrorist charges and only do time for the drugs.''

''How do I know I can trust you?'' Wong asked. ''I don't even know your name or who you work for.''

''You don't need to know my name to know that you're in deep shit, son. And as far as trusting me, you really don't have a choice. You either help me and have some kind of chance, or I'll see that you face terrorist charges and a certain death sentence. It's just that simple."

Something about the matter-of-fact way that the blond man recited the facts convinced Wong that he was being told the plain, unvarnished truth. And as frightened as he was of the Beijing hit men, he was even more afraid of being strapped to a gurney and plugged into a lethal injection machine. At least with Zhang Liu, he would have a chance of surviving. No one survived the injection machine.

"Okay," Wong said softly, "what do you want me to do?"

CHAPTER ELEVEN

Taipei, Taiwan

Mack Bolan met Phoenix Force's C-130 Hercules turboprop transport when it taxied to its parking spot on the tarmac at Taipei's Sungshan Airport. In recent years, the city had grown up around it, and the airport was now in the middle of Taipei. With the international flights now being serviced by Chiang Kai-shek Airport, Sungshan mostly handled domestic and cargo flights.

David McCarter was the first of the team to step out of the plane. Since he was posing as the geological survey team's leader, he had to clear the men and their gear through customs before they could leave the plane. He was met by two Taiwanese customs officers, and he escorted them on board the aircraft. One of them flipped through the thick cargo manifest while the other one poked around inside. Five minutes later, they stamped their passports and signed off on the manifest.

"That didn't take long," McCarter observed

when the two customs officers walked off, leaving them to their own devices. "They hardly looked at a thing. Just a peek and a tickle, and they were gone."

"It helps to have friends in low places," Bolan replied. "It only cost Hal five thousand dollars for that speedy customs clearance."

"It was bloody well worth it, too," McCarter said. "We have a full mission load tucked away in there."

"We're probably going to need every bit of it before this is over. I've got a line on half a dozen Red agents, and I just got started."

"When do *we* get started?"

"Let's get everything sorted out first. We're in no hurry. They're not going anywhere and right now they're not causing any more trouble."

"That's just the way I like it."

THE HOTEL where Bolan had booked rooms for himself and Phoenix Force was a midrange businessmen's establishment in the middle of town. It wasn't fancy, but it was clean and was in keeping with their cover story. A contract survey team didn't stay in the Taipei Hilton. Once the commandos had checked into their rooms, they met in Bolan's suite for the mission briefing.

"Here's the drill," Bolan stated. "As you all know, because of the recent congressional sanctions, we're here without the knowledge of the Taiwanese government."

"What's new?" Calvin James asked. "I wouldn't know how to act if someone actually invited us in for a change."

"But since we're after the same people that they're after, it's not as bad as it could be. Taiwan has a large police force, an active internal-security service and a large army that we're going to have to be very careful not to bump up against."

"What happens if we do attract the attention of the authorities?" Rafael Encizo asked. "Do we have a 'get out of jail free' contact?"

"Not up front," Bolan replied. "Stony Man will be able to get us out, but it'll take some time, so we'd better not get caught."

James shook his head.

"We're going to kick off the operation tonight," Bolan continued. "Our first customer is a petty thief who's been bragging to one of the working girls in a local cathouse. He's saying that he was a big shot in the riot where the CNN reporter was killed. We're going to drop in on this guy when he visits his girlfriend tonight and take him away for a little chat."

Bolan looked over to Encizo. "Rafe, I want you and Gary as backup on this. We'll have a local with us to finger our man and to help us with the language."

Encizo nodded.

"Who's the local we're working with?" McCarter asked.

"He's a Triad informant who's been assigned to work with us."

"Isn't that leaving us exposed?" McCarter asked, raising an eyebrow. "I don't like working with those Triads."

"Normally I'd agree with you on that. But this time it's different. The Triads want to work with us, and we really need their help. Anything we can do to get Beijing to back off and leave the island alone is to their advantage, too."

McCarter shook his head. "It's a hell of a thing when we have to get in bed with the bloody Triads, Mack. I can remember that not too long ago we were killing the bastards, and I'm sure that they remember, too."

"I haven't forgotten, either," Bolan said. "But since we don't have any government resources on the island this time, this was the only way I could put this thing together. I used Triad contacts in Hong Kong to get that kidnapped boy back, and they were very reliable. I'm expecting the same thing to be the case here."

"I still don't bloody well like it."

"Well, until someone around here starts speaking Formosan and Cantonese, we don't have much of a choice, do we?"

"More's the pity."

"While Gary, Rafael and I are making the

snatch," Bolan said, getting back on the topic, "the rest of you will be setting up our operations base and making noises like we're a geological survey team."

"What are we supposed to be looking for this time?" James asked.

"Oil, gold, whatever."

CHO'S HOUSE of Great Joy was a big name for such a ratty little establishment, and it was no different than any number of other Asian whorehouses Bolan had seen over the years. The smell of stale beer, sweat, incense and cigarette smoke was thick enough to cut with a knife. The scantily clad girls all wore the same artificial smiles that masked boredom and greed when they saw the two Americans walk in. Their third-rate cathouse wasn't a usual stop for the tourist trade, but maybe the gods had smiled on them this night and their luck had changed.

They quickly dropped the smiles, though, when they saw Shan Wei walk in behind them. They knew him well, and if the long-nose tourists were with the Triad informer, they were here on business, not pleasure. The girls knew that their amah always paid the insurance faithfully, so they knew it wasn't a raid. Beyond that, a smart girl didn't want to know what their business was.

The Triad man asked the woman behind the desk a question, and she answered immediately. Motioning for Encizo to stay at the front door, Shan led Bolan and Gary Manning through a beaded curtain to a hallway with the girls' rooms on both sides. Each room had a door with a lock on the inside that was mostly for show. When he located the right door, Shan simply kicked it open and walked in.

Their target had had more than a couple of beers this evening, and his exertions had left him drowsy. He started when the door flew open, but before he could focus his eyes, Manning jerked his arms behind him and slipped a plastic riot restraint down over his wrists.

"Who are you?" the man asked in both Chinese and Formosan. "What are you doing to me?"

Shan pulled a thin-bladed knife from the back of his belt and pressed the point into the hollow of the man's neck under his ear. "Shut your mouth or you die right here."

"You can't do this to—" The man abruptly stopped talking when the point of the knife pierced his skin.

"Move!" Shan grated in Chinese as he jerked the man to his feet.

"You stay here!" he told the scantily clad girl. "And keep your mouth shut."

This wasn't the first time that the girl had seen someone snatched from a whorehouse. She knew that she wasn't in any danger, but kept silent anyway. Even for a Triad member, Shan was crazy and she didn't want to press her luck.

It was only a few feet to the back door, and this time Shan undid the lock instead of kicking it open. If he angered the amah who ran the place, he would lose his discount.

Manning opened the rear door of the Toyota sedan that had been parked in the back alley, stuffed the prisoner into the back seat and slid in beside him. Shan got behind the wheel, and Bolan took the front passenger seat. A single honk of the horn brought Encizo on the run, and he got in the back on the other side of the prisoner.

THE TRIAD SAFEHOUSE was down a side street in an older section of town, the kind of place where no one would notice a few screams in the night. After parking the car on the street, Shan led the Phoenix Force commandos and their prisoner inside. By now, the man was fully alert. There was something about being kidnapped that sobered a man quickly.

"Listen to me carefully," the Triad gangster said as he slammed the man back against the first available wall. "I am the Honorable Shan Wei of the Glorious Lotus Triad, and you will tell me everything I want to know or I will give you to these foreign devils. They will slowly skin you alive."

"But what do I know that would interest an honorable man of position such as yourself?" the prisoner asked.

"That remains to be seen. It is these honorable foreigners who want to talk to you, and you will answer their questions or you will incur their wrath, as well as mine. Do you understand?''

The prisoner glanced over at Bolan and nodded.

''I think he's ready to talk now,'' Shan said, smiling.

''What did you tell him?'' Bolan asked.

''Just that you would skin him alive if he didn't.''

''Crude,'' McCarter stated, ''but effective. Shall we begin?''

Shan turned back to the prisoner. ''They want to know how to find the men who ordered the killing of the TV reporter Cunningham. But before you open your mouth, be sure that you do not lie to me. I know what you told that diseased whore at the House of Great Joy. You bragged to her that you are a big man in the People's Party and that you played a big part in the famous riot.''

''Honorable Uncle,'' the prisoner said, not remembering Shan's name, ''I told the whore that so she would think that I was a big man. You know how that is.''

''No, I do not. I do not have to lie to whores to improve my manhood. I am not a piece of Communist dog excrement like you. And since I am not a woman, you had better tell me the truth.''

''I was at the riot, yes,'' the prisoner admitted. ''But I had nothing to do with the death of the reporter.''

''Who did?''

"It was not me, Honorable Uncle," the man said. "All I did was carry a sign."

"And who told you to do that?"

The prisoner mumbled a name.

"Who is he?"

"My team leader in the People's Party."

"WHAT DO YOU WANT ME to do with him?" Shan nodded toward their prisoner.

"I don't want him talking to anyone until this is all over," Bolan said. "What do you suggest?"

"Do you want me to kill him?"

"It might be best if he just disappeared for a while. We might need to talk to him again later."

The Triad representative shrugged. He didn't really care what happened to the man one way or the other. People like him were found dead every morning, but if the foreign devils wanted him held, he would be held. He could always be killed later.

"How about the man he mentioned, his team leader?"

"I do not know of him, but I can make a phone call and see if I can locate him for you."

"If you can, I'd like to talk to him tonight, as well."

Shan didn't care if the long noses wanted to talk to half the island's population. His orders were to help them do anything they wanted.

"WE MAY HAVE a problem, Comrade," Kwan Choi said when he walked into the crowded office in the back of the small restaurant in the dock area of Taipei.

Houng Yen, the secretary of the Taiwanese Communist underground, better known as the People's Party, looked up from the papers on his desk. A problem at this point in time wasn't something that he wanted to have to deal with. Not when they were apparently so close to the end of the long struggle.

Even as the top Communist operative in Taiwan, he didn't have a need to know exactly what was being planned. But it was difficult not to know that there were great plans being put into action. He had been instructed to stockpile thirty days' worth of supplies for all of his operatives and to stand by for further instructions. Change was in the wind, and he didn't need anything else on his mind right now.

"What is the problem, Comrade?"

"Two of our lower-ranking men seem to have disappeared last night."

Houng frowned. "What do you mean, seem to have disappeared?"

"What I mean is that the police do not have them, and neither does the army."

"Are you certain?"

"There is no doubt," Kwan assured him. "All of our comrades in both the police and the army report that they have not been arrested."

The PRC had always had their agents in Taiwan, men and women, who were dedicated to the cause of Chairman Mao and his successors. However, Communist fervor went only so far, and there were only so many who would put their lives on the line for a political belief. Fortunately, though, the fact that the Taiwanese economy was booming made the recruitment of spies and agents an easy matter for the PRC.

In a booming economy, there were always those who weren't enjoying the good times and were resentful of others who were. Now that the PRC had a surplus of foreign exchange, much of it had been put to good use paying a small army of agents on the island republic. For every politically motivated agent, there were a half dozen who were loyal to Beijing because the Communists paid well.

These men and women could never hope to rise very high in the Communist structure, but they were useful pawns in Beijing's campaign to overthrow the island's government. In fact, had it not been for these agents, the riot that had so stunned the American people couldn't have taken place. Though it would be no great loss if these two ended up dead, it was still something that had to be looked into, particularly now that the final days were upon them.

"Look into this immediately," Houng said, "and take extra security precautions. I received a report about one of our operations in Hong Kong that worries me."

"What was that, Comrade?"

"One of our best units there had kidnapped the

nephew of the Yankee trade commissioner to the British. They were going to hold him and force the Yankees into the embarrassing position of having to negotiate with Beijing for his release, but something went wrong. A small commando team learned of the boy's hiding place and raided it. He was released, several of our men were killed and not even a word about the affair was mentioned in the press."

"How did that happen?"

"No one seems to know, and what makes it even stranger is that apparently even the American government is not sure what happened."

"How can that be? Surely they sent one of their special-operations units to rescue the boy and they just want to keep it secret."

"That is not the information Beijing has. They are certain that it was not a sanctioned operation. And if someone is working against us like they did against our cell in Hong Kong, I will need to report it to Beijing as soon as possible."

"I will look into it immediately."

CHAPTER TWELVE

It didn't take long for the Phoenix Force warriors to learn that the Beijing-sponsored People's Party underground in Taiwan was organized in the classical cell structure the Communists had always used. When the last Communist was long dead and buried, the legacy of Lenin would live on in the highly successful cell organization that he had invented to hide his revolutionaries from the czar's police.

The two men Phoenix Force had captured and interrogated so far were both low-ranking members of their lower-level cells and knew only the other people within their own cells. Had they been the cell leaders, they would have known a contact person in the cell above them. As it was, they knew no one above their own level.

"This is getting us nowhere fast," McCarter commented the next morning. "We really don't have bugger all to show for our efforts so far."

Bolan nodded his agreement. "It's been a long time since I've seen a cell structure, and I'd forgotten just how efficient its security can be."

"We need to snatch someone from the next level up if we're going to get anywhere."

"At the rate we're going," T. J. Hawkins said, "we're going to be here all year doing it that way."

"Unless," Encizo said, entering the conversation, "we luck out and stumble onto a high-ranking man, hopefully someone on the second level down who can give us the top guy."

"Is there anything we can do to help our chances?"

"Not really," Encizo stated. "That's why it's set up this way. It's a bitch to work your way to the top of the pile. Just ask Czar Nicholas's secret police. Those bumbling fools never did catch up with Lenin, and he was right under their nose."

"Actually there is something we can do," Bolan broke in. "I think that we can dangle some bait and draw in a top-level man. The problem with a cell structure is that it's all top-down leadership. The men on the lower levels can't even scratch their asses without permission from the top, and the request has to go up the chain of command. So if we present what looks like an opportunity for them, they'll have to bring in a high-level man to make an on-the-spot decision for them."

"What are you going to use for the bait?" McCarter asked.

"Me," Bolan told him.

McCarter shook his head. "That's a no-go, Mack.

If you're going to do something like that, you're going to use one of us."

"It won't work that way, because they don't know who you guys are. But remember, they know me. And even if they've forgotten, I can always remind them that I'm the guy who whipped them in Hong Kong. That's got to be enough to get a reaction out of them."

"Barbara and Hal aren't going to like this," Encizo said emphatically.

"What's not to like? I've got the five of you to back me up."

"They're still not going to like it."

"That's why we're not going to tell them what we're doing until after we're done."

Encizo shook his head, but he knew better than to try to change the Executioner's mind.

THAT EVENING, Shan Wei drove the Stony Man warriors to a small apartment building where a People's Party man was known to room with another man, his cousin, who was also known to be an active party member.

"Don't take any chances up there," McCarter cautioned as the commandos took up positions around the building.

"I won't," Bolan said.

"I still wish you'd take Rafe or Calvin along with you for backup."

"I can't risk anyone seeing a second long nose.

For this to work, the word has to get back that I'm working by myself like I did in Hong Kong.''

When everyone was in position, Bolan and his Triad contact went up to the second floor to make the snatch. In the dimly lit hallway, the Executioner paused outside the door, drew his silenced Beretta 93-R and flicked the selector switch to semiauto. He didn't think he'd need the hardware in a country where the citizens weren't allowed to own firearms, but he hadn't lived as long as he had by taking chances.

When Bolan's gloved fingers flicked out the third time, Shan slammed his foot against the cheap door lock, and the door flew open. The big American stormed in, the Beretta leveled, and shouted ''Stop'' in Cantonese.

Two men, wearing only shorts and undershirts and seated at a small table under a naked light bulb, froze, their chopsticks halfway to their mouths. When Shan told them to put down their eating utensils and to stand, they instantly obeyed.

''Which one of you is Lee Chou?'' Shan asked.

When one of the men looked at the other, Bolan grabbed him and slammed him up against the wall. Shan told the other guy to sit against the other wall and keep his mouth shut. The man meekly obeyed as he always obeyed men with guns.

This time, though, Bolan and Shan didn't hurry their prisoner to the car waiting below. Instead, while the roommate cowered on the floor, they openly interrogated their man about his affiliation with the outlawed Communist underground. They also questioned him about his participation in the now infamous riot that had killed Cunningham and asked him who his leaders were.

After almost an hour, Shan and Bolan took their man away. After making sure that the two gunmen were gone, the cousin quickly put on his clothes, hurried out of the building and down to the street.

THE FOLLOWING MORNING, Kwan was back at the small restaurant office of the People's Party. "Another one of our men was captured last night," he reported to Houng. "But this time he was with another comrade who was able to get away, and he made a report on the attackers."

"What did he say?"

"There were two of them, and he thinks the leader was an American. He was accompanied by a Taiwanese who he thinks is a petty Triad gangster."

"That is interesting," Houng commented. "I did not know that the Americans would dirty their hands by working with the Triads."

"The most interesting thing," Kwan said, "is that while our informant does not speak English, he knows a few words of the barbarian language and he heard the two men talk about Hong Kong several times among themselves. He also heard the Triad man question his cousin about his involvement in the riot when Cunningham was killed."

"What did this Yankee look like?"

Kwan repeated what he had been told.

Houng thought for a moment. "That sounds like the man the Yankees sent to Hong Kong to deal with our kidnapping operation there. Beijing reported that only one man was used on that raid."

"But," Kwan replied, frowning, "you told me that several of our men were killed and that the complete cell was destroyed. How could one man have done all that? He would have had to be a super-warrior, and I didn't know that the Yankees had men like that."

"Never underestimate the Americans," Houng cautioned. "I got to know some of them very well during the Vietnam War. The Yankees are a young people, and there is no doubt that they are brash barbarians, but they aren't weak."

Houng paused when he realized that he had just contradicted the Beijing party line about the decadence of American society.

"At least not all of them are weak," he explained, "They produce some of the strongest men I have even seen. I interrogated captured American pilots in Hanoi when we were still allied with the southern barbarian dogs. The Vietnamese would torture them beyond human endurance, and still many of them would defy their captors.

"Some of them broke, of course. There is only so much a man, any man, can take. But some held out even unto death. I, on the other hand, usually did better with them than the Vietnamese because I treated them like men. I could reason with them and gain their confidence. From them, I gathered much information without laying a finger on them.

"But, yes," Houng said, returning to the problem at hand, "the Americans have some skilled warriors, never doubt that. And it may be that one of them has come to Taipei to seek revenge."

"But I don't understand," Kwan said. "The Yankee Congress has imposed sanctions on the puppet government here. Why are they sending a commando to track us down? That is not logical."

"The Yankees are usually not subtle, and emotion rules them more than logic. They are an excitable people and, when they are wounded, they want immediate revenge. They have foolishly broken their agreements with their old ally by sending an assassin to attack our cells. Someone in the Yankee government wants revenge for the death of that reporter, and that is why he is here."

"But to go to these lengths because of the death of only one man? That doesn't make any sense to me. None at all."

"I agree," Houng said. "But as I learned in Vietnam, that is also a characteristic of the Yankees. When one of their pilots was shot down, they would risk even more planes and men trying to rescue him. Often we would purposefully not capture a downed pilot, but let him run free just so we could draw even more planes into a trap. It worked almost every time."

Kwan shook his head in amazement. The only Americans he had ever seen had been tourists and businessmen, and they had all been contemptible barbarians. They would have never shown courage like that.

"And it appears that it is working that way for us again. They have apparently sent one of their top operatives to Taiwan to extract vengeance for the reporter's death. But he is one man alone, and we are many. If we can neutralize this man and then expose him as a Yankee assassin, it will create even more local animosity against the Americans and widen the gap between the two governments even further."

The communist leader smiled. "This can be of great benefit to us, as well as being a great embarrassment to the Americans. Good work, Comrade Kwan. I will forward this information to Beijing immediately and see how they want to deal with this man."

TUNG WU HAD his Triad soldiers scouring the city, trying to pick up on anything they could about the Beijing underground, but it was slow going. Not all of the Taiwanese who voted for the People's Party were Communists, and not all of the Taiwanese Communists were involved in the People's Party.

By now, Shan Wei was a common visitor to the

small warehouse the team had leased by the airport. He would drop by in the morning to make his report and then once again in the late afternoon. Two days after the snatch, he brought Bolan a message from his boss, Tung Wu.

"This may be it," Bolan said when he told McCarter that the Triad leader had information for them.

"Let's hope so," the Briton replied, who had been busy with Phoenix Force flying a few aerial geological-survey missions to keep their cover intact. "The lads are getting bored."

"THE PLACE YOU ARE looking for," Tung told Bolan, "is called the Tsang Liu Monastery."

"A monastery?"

"Yes. And there is also a shrine to a saint there, a famous priest who lived several centuries ago. People from all over Taiwan come to visit it and to pay their respects."

"Where is this shrine?"

Tung unfolded a topological map of the island and tapped an area. "Here in the mountains of the Taroko National Park just south of here."

Taiwan was some 245 miles long and eighty-nine wide, but those simple measurements didn't tell the whole story of the nation's topography. Like many islands, Taiwan was actually the top of a mountain that stuck up above the surface of the ocean. The top formed an extended ridgeline that ran from north to south, effectively cutting off the east and west coasts from each other.

Within that chain of mountains was some of the most beautiful terrain in all of Southeast Asia. From the majestic thirteen-thousand-foot peak of Yu Shan to the serene Sun Moon Lake and the three big national parks, the center of the island was a good place to hide out if you didn't want to be found.

"You're sure that this is the place?"

"Oh, yes. The information comes from the highest authority, the second-in-command of the foreign-operations section of Beijing's Intelligence service. It seems that he likes to talk to his mistress about what he does during the week because she pays so much attention to him when he does."

Bolan smiled. That was the oldest trick in the intelligence game, the honey-pot gambit, and it worked almost every time. "Your organization is well placed if you can gather information like that."

"We have our sources," Tung said cryptically. "What will you do with this information?"

"My orders are to deal justice to those who were responsible for Cunningham's death," Bolan said.

"That is a dangerous mission. You will run the risk of widening the rift between our two governments if you are discovered."

"That's true," Bolan replied. "But it's even more dangerous for us to let Beijing think that they can do things like that to us with impunity. Plus we'll make sure not to be discovered—and we'll make sure that your police know who these men really were. They just won't know who killed them."

"You have a point there, Mr. Belasko. And if there is any way that I can assist you in this venture, you have only to ask."

"I can't think of anything right now," he said. "But I'll let you know if anything comes up."

CHAPTER THIRTEEN

Kevin Wong's drug contact and spymaster worked at the PRC's trade delegation in San Francisco. It was almost a mandatory tradition in governmental affairs that trade representatives and cultural attachés were expected to be spies. In this case, however, the man known as William Hu wasn't one of the registered Beijing delegates. Instead, he was listed as an American citizen who had been hired as the office manager for the mission.

This was the perfect job for a spymaster who was doubling as a drug distributor. In the conduct of his job, he had to be in contact with dozens of American companies to secure goods and services for the mission. It was routine work and not the sort of thing that anyone would pay much attention to. Until now, that was.

The orders he had been given to assist the Beijing hit team were compromising his cover, but there was little he could do about it. Beijing had made it clear that the leader of the assassins, Zhang Liu, was calling the shots. Zhang was a powerful man in the hard-line faction, and he was accustomed to having his commands instantly obeyed. His order for Hu to meet him at a restaurant by the famous Fisherman's Wharf was a good case in point. The tourist attraction was no place for a private meeting, but Hu had no choice.

"Your man Wong betrayed us," Zhang said, coming right to the point. "His disappearance proves it. Whoever attacked the apartment had to have known that it had been leased in Wong's name, and the only way they could have known that was for Wong to tell them."

"A thousand pardons, Comrade Zhang," the spymaster said. "I knew, of course, that Wong was a weak vessel, but he was all I had available to work with. And until now, he has been very useful to my technology-export operation. Beijing has been very pleased with what I have been able to procure for them."

"That is not important now," Zhang snapped. "Your only concern is to find Wong so he can be eliminated."

Zhang hadn't become Beijing's top overseas fix-it man by allowing a setback like the apartment raid to keep him from completing his mission. That didn't mean, though, that he ever allowed an enemy to strike at him without taking him down in return. Wong and whoever had killed his team members had to be punished.

Hu wasn't used to being talked to that way. He,

too, was a valuable agent and had been in place for almost a decade now. To become involved in Zhang's mission any more than he already was would only risk his being exposed. But he also knew that Zhang was in command of this operation and that it had the highest priority.

"Even if he is in the hands of the police, Comrade?"

"No matter where he is," Zhang stated flatly. "And no matter the cost, he must be killed."

"Because of what he knows?"

The assassin's face hardened. "Because he betrayed me and caused the death of three of my men," he snapped. "You are to spare no effort in finding out Wong's fate. If he is still alive, I want to know where he is being held. At the same time, I want to know the names of those who were responsible for the attack on my men. After I deal with Wong, I will deal with them, as well."

"Isn't that outside of your mission objectives, Comrade?" Hu asked. "My information was that you were tasked with eliminating those who are speaking out against the Party."

"The mission has been expanded so I can deal with these men."

"Has this change in your plan been approved by Beijing, Comrade?" Hu risked asking. If he was going to put his ass on the line, he wanted to know why he was doing it.

"I would worry about my own affairs," Zhang

warned, "and leave me to mine. I cannot fulfill my mission if I do not know where my enemies are. Until they are dead at my feet, I cannot continue."

Hu wanted to mention that almost the entire population of the United States could be numbered among Zhang's enemies, but he refrained. The assassin wasn't known to have a sense of humor. Plus, from the evasive answer Zhang had given him, Hu knew that he hadn't cleared his personal vendetta through Beijing.

In the long run, it was of no concern to Hu if Wong was eliminated or not. In fact it probably would be better if he was killed because he knew too much. As far as Zhang's going after whoever had raided his safehouse went, that also was of little concern to him. It was dangerous, to be sure, and it was outside of Beijing's instructions. But from the beginning, he had felt that attacks on the prodemocracy activists were a mistake anyway. All it did was draw attention to their so-called cause and made martyrs of them.

As he had proved so well, the best way to operate in a decadent capitalist society was to do as he had always done, keep a low profile and not draw attention to himself. If Zhang failed, as Hu felt sure that he would, he would have no one to blame but himself. But for Hu to keep the blame from falling on him, he would have to cooperate fully with Zhang—and, of course, file his own independent reports.

Hu had played the role of an American citizen for

so long that he thought more like a Yankee than a Han. The concept of "cover your ass" was second nature to him now, and he would sure as hell do it this time. If Zhang went down, he had no intention of going down with him.

"I will do everything I can to assist you," he told the assassin. "I will set all of my resources to work finding Wong."

"And the men who attacked the apartment."

"Them, as well."

ZHANG LIU WAS GOOD at what he did. His belief that he was the People's Republic of China's top operative wasn't too far off. He was smart, he was fearless and he had good instincts, all of which were essential to being a good secret agent and assassin. However, Zhang had been born in China and he was a racist to the core.

Being a Chinese racist was different than being an American racist, because his racism wasn't based on skin color. Instead, it was based on birth. If a man wasn't one hundred percent Han Chinese, the major ethnic group in China, as far as Zhang was concerned that man rated lower than a dog. And to Zhang, the overseas Chinese were all polluted by interracial mixing with the locals. The Taiwanese, the Hong Kongers, the Singaporeans and mostly the American Chinese were all semibarbarian scum.

To Zhang, the true barbarians—all whites, blacks, Oriental and everyone else in between regardless of national origin—were uncivilized animals and barely human.

Because of this extreme cultural arrogance, Zhang tended to ignore the Chinese Americans he came in contact with. He used them as camouflage because the Yankee barbarians couldn't tell a true Han from a half-breed, but he paid little attention to the very people he moved among and that was a mistake.

Johnny Lin's soldiers had been keeping a close eye on him for more than a day now after having stumbled onto him while they were watching William Hu in the same way.

Hu was very cautious. His years of successfully hiding completely in the open had made caution his second nature. But since Zhang didn't trust Hu, either, the deep-cover agent had been forced to meet Zhang at a place of Zhang's choosing instead of his. Two of Lin's men had simply followed Hu to the meeting and fingered Zhang.

Now that Lyons knew who he was and where he was, it was time to bring this operation to a quick conclusion.

KEVIN WONG DIDN'T HAVE to pretend to be scared when he placed the call to the man he knew as Bill Hu. He was deeply afraid, and it showed in his voice.

"I thought I told you never to call me here," Hu said automatically before he remembered that Wong had been missing for several days. "Where are you calling from?"

Wong glanced over to Schwarz, who was taping the conversation. "I'm calling from a motel in Oakland."

"Where have you been for the past couple of days, Kevin?" Hu asked. "I've been trying to contact you."

"I was kidnapped and held prisoner."

"What happened?" Hu asked tensely.

"All I know is that I was sleeping in my own house and woke up to some guy waving a gun in my face and telling me to get dressed."

"When was that?"

When Wong gave him the date, Hu felt his blood run cold. That was the night before the attack on the apartment, so maybe Zhang was right when he said that Wong had betrayed the Beijing team. If that was the case, this might be the day that he implemented his long-established escape-and-evasion plan. If Wong had been turned, he was in danger, too.

"Who were the men who captured you?"

"Three were white guys. Later they were joined by some kind of Chinese gangsters, I think."

"What did they do with you?"

"They took me to a house and locked me in a room. Then they started asking me questions about where I was getting the China White and who I was selling it to. I tried to play dumb, but they knew I was dealing."

Hu paused to think. If Wong had been picked up by one of the Triads or tongs because of a drug-turf dispute, that put Zhang's problem in a completely new perspective. If whoever had raided the apartment hadn't been tipped off by Wong, that meant that there was a completely unknown enemy out there, maybe a federal agency.

"Did you tell them about me?"

"No, I swear. I didn't tell them a thing about you."

Hu wasn't so sure about that, but he wanted the rest of the story first. "How did you get away from them?"

"There was something big going on," Wong replied. "I didn't hear much because they always spoke so fast. But there had been a big fight somewhere, and some of the gang had been shot. Anyway, they weren't paying much attention to me, and I was able to sneak out."

"I want you to come in," Hu said. "Zhang wants to talk to you about something that happened to his men."

"What are you talking about?"

"Someone raided the apartment you leased and killed some of his men. He wants to talk to you about it."

"But why does he want to talk to me?" Wong didn't have to fake sounding concerned: it was all too real. "You can tell him that I didn't have anything to do with that."

"He wants to talk to you himself."

"But I have to leave town fast. Those gangsters are going to be looking for me."

"Listen, Kevin," Hu insisted, "you have to talk to Zhang. You sure as hell don't want him looking for you. You know what he's like."

"Okay, I'll talk to him, but I want you to be there, too, and I want to talk in a public place. And when that's over, I'm clearing out. I'm going to the East Coast and I'm not ever coming back."

"I can help you relocate, Kevin," Hu offered. "I have contacts back East. When we get together, we can make plans so you'll have someplace to go to. You don't want to have to go to some strange city where you don't know anyone. So, when can we talk?"

"I've got to do some things first," Wong said. "Then we'll talk."

"Where can I reach you?"

"I'll call you," Wong said, and abruptly hung up.

He turned to Lyons and was relieved to see that he had a smile on his face for a change.

"That was good, Kevin. You almost had me convinced. Let's hope that you convinced him, as well."

"What happens now?"

"You'll wait awhile and then you'll call back later and arrange to talk to Zhang like you promised."

Wong shuddered. "Do I have to?"

"You do if you ever want to get clear of this." Lyons lost his friendly tone of voice. "You screwed up big time, and you're in shit up to your belt buckle. Like I said, though, if you play ball with me, I'll do what I can for you on the terrorist charges."

"I appreciate that."

"No sweat," Lyons said. "I'd do the same for any slime-ball."

BILL HU SAT and stared at the wall of his office for several minutes after Kevin Wong hung up on him. This wasn't quite the same as having located Wong, but at least he knew that he was still alive. Now he had to sit and wait for the next phone call. Suddenly he had a thought. There was an AT&T phone store across the street, and they could help him locate the elusive Kevin Wong. Putting the Back In Thirty Minutes card in the window, he locked his office door and headed across the street with a smile on his face.

ZHANG RADIO CHECKED all of his guard posts at the abandoned cannery on the outskirts of Oakland one more time. His two remaining men and the six Vietnamese Red Cobra gang members were in position. Like all mainland Chinese, he didn't have any great love for the southern barbarians, as the Vietnamese were commonly called, but he had to admit that sometimes they could be useful. Particularly in this case, when he had no other experienced Han operatives to use.

It had been clever of Hu to have discovered the phone number the traitor Wong had called from and even more clever to have found out that the motel room he had called from was supposed to be rented to three long noses. The meeting was an obvious trap, but a trap could be turned around. Hu's contacts with the Vietnamese Red Cobra gang had provided him with enough firepower to turn the tables. Wong and the three long noses he was working with would die tonight.

He had no idea who the Yankees were, but they had to be the men who had hit the apartment. He didn't believe Wong's story that he hadn't talked to them about it. Of course he had. How else could anyone have found out about the safehouse? And he would learn who the long noses were when he searched their bodies in a little while.

Once Zhang had eliminated these Yankees, he was considering recruiting a few of the Red Cobras to replace the three men who had been killed at the safehouse. There were still more Han traitors Beijing wanted him to eliminate, and he was known for carrying out his assignments.

First, though, he had a battle to fight. When it was over, he would plan his next assassination. There were still a dozen or so names on the list who would pay for their treachery to the People's Republic.

AT HIS POST inside the abandoned building, Nguyen Cao's hands almost caressed the smooth, oiled stock of the AK-47 assault rifle the Chinese guy had given him. It was a beautiful weapon, and there was no way that he could have afforded to buy one of the full-auto AKs on his own. The semiauto AK look-alikes that were for sale everywhere were affordable, but they were just not the same as the real thing he had in his hands. It could pump out 600 7.62 mm rounds a minute from the 30-round magazine.

He hoped that the enemy gang did show up tonight. He wanted a chance to try out his new piece. And it would be great to actually fight alongside his gang brothers for the first time. Nguyen was new to the Red Cobras, and he hadn't had a chance to prove himself a man yet. This was a rare chance to actually fight someone instead of just holding up a liquor store or mugging a Mexican, and he was ready.

All of the Cobras were packing the new full-auto AKs this night and were wearing the chest-pack-style magazine carriers that had come with the rifles. Nguyen thought that they all looked like NVA soldiers in a Vietnam War movie. All they needed were the green sun helmets with the red stars on the front. And like the NVA, they would bring death to these Yankees.

CHAPTER FOURTEEN

Even though Carl Lyons had arranged this setup himself, now that he was on the ground he didn't like the looks of it. He'd been in the business long enough to know trouble when he saw it, and this was definitely it. Regardless, he was committed and he wasn't about to back out now. It had been difficult to get Zhang to agree to meet Wong at this remote location, and he didn't think that he would be able to do it a second time.

Calling it off would sour the deal, and he wanted to get this wrapped up as soon as he could.

He was, however, glad that Johnny Lin had made him an offer of half a dozen of his most experienced gunmen. Normally he didn't like to get outsiders involved in his business, but he was glad to have them on hand tonight. If Lin's information that the Beijing agents had made a connection with the Red Cobra gang was true, Lyons might need the extra guns before this was over. The Red Cobras were one of the most troublesome of all of California's Vietnamese gangs, and they were known to be heavily armed. Going up against a dozen of them, along with the rest of the Red Chinese, wasn't going to be a cakewalk.

Even though they were walking into something that had trap written all over it, it looked as if they still had the element of surprise with them. They hadn't run into any guards on the approach, and now they were in place. He read this as an indication that the Beijing hit man was a little too confident, and he liked his opponents confident; it made them do stupid things.

He didn't know why it was almost a tradition for criminals to want to pull their ambushes in built-up areas. If the Beijing assassins wanted to get the drop on Able Team, they should have tried doing it in the open somewhere. It would be much simpler. But once again, he had been invited to walk into a firefight in a deserted industrial area.

This time, though, the building was an old one-story cannery. It was built of wood, not brick or concrete, which meant that there would be little cover inside capable of stopping a slug. But it should be mostly open inside instead of being partitioned into rooms, and that suited his purposes. It would be more like fighting in the open, even inside the structure.

He glanced at his watch and saw that he had another five minutes. To pass the time, Lyons checked the loads in his weapons again. Waiting was always a bitch.

JIM LIN HAD ALWAYS tried hard to live up to his grandfather's expectations, but he'd never had to go into a firefight before. In fact he had never even shot at a man before. The Lin organization managed to conduct its business without having to contribute to the violence that was so common in southern California. They were always prepared to defend themselves, of course, but had rarely needed to do so.

As his grandfather had put it, helping Lyons this night was the same as defending themselves. The Beijing assassins were giving all of the Han a bad name. His grandfather was right, but the younger Lin was still apprehensive. No one ever knew how he would react to being shot at until it happened for the first time.

Carl Lyons hadn't minced words when he had briefed Lin and the half-dozen other gunmen. Although he hadn't come right out and said it, he had indicated that no matter what happened here, no matter who was killed, the police wouldn't become involved except to carry off the bodies of the enemy dead. That didn't bother Lin in the least. In fact, he was glad to hear it. It did make him wonder, though, and not for the first time, exactly who Lyons and his two partners really were. He knew Lyons had been a cop at one time, but that didn't explain what he was doing now.

The only thing that made any sense to him was that the three mystery men had to be some kind of clandestine CIA hit team. He had always thought people like that were just the fictional stuff of movies and paperback thrillers. But here Lin was putting his life on the line for three guys who acted as if they gave lessons to James Bond.

He had to admit, though, teaming up with them was more interesting than most of the things he usually did for his grandfather. He hated to say it, but his life had so far been like that of any other mid-level businessman. It wasn't very exciting.

WHEN HIS WATCH clicked down, Gadgets Schwarz tapped his throat mike and spoke softly. "Anytime you're ready, Ironman."

"Copy," came Lyons's curt reply.

"I'm go," Blancanales radioed back.

"Lin?" Lyons asked.

"I'm in place," the gangster replied, "and my men are ready."

"Okay," Lyons growled. "Let's do it. One minute from now!"

Schwarz counted down from sixty to zero before triggering the M-203 grenade launcher under the barrel of his M-16. The 40 mm projectile arched out and flew through the open door at the end of the long low building, detonating a second later with a blinding blue-white flash.

Five seconds later, Blancanales fired another 40 mm round into the other end of the building. Again the blinding flash erupted with the power of an arc light. Jacking open the breech of his grenade launcher, he loaded an HE frag round. The next time he fired, he would be putting out more than just a bright light.

"Let's do it!" Lyons shouted over the comm link. Snapping down his night-vision goggles, he raced for the open end of the building in front of him.

NGUYEN CAO WAS completely blinded. He had been looking right at the area where the first grenade had landed. His eyes felt as if they had been seared out of their sockets, and the pain threatened to split his head. He staggered to his feet, still clutching the AK-47.

When he heard a weapon firing in front of him, he spun in that direction and triggered his assault rifle. The weapon in his hands bucked on full-automatic, spraying 7.62 mm slugs in a wide arc. He only stopped firing when the bolt locked back on an empty magazine.

"Nice shot, asshole," a voice said behind him, "but you missed."

As he turned to face the voice, Nguyen heard two quick shots and felt hammer blows to his back. He fell facefirst, dead before he hit the floor.

Lyons stepped around the body and took cover behind a section of plywood partition. The half-inch ply wouldn't stop bullets, but there was a distinct lack of cover inside the cavernous cannery. The long lines of the conveyer belts in the middle of the floor were serious cover, but from the muzzle-flashes, most of the area was occupied by the opposition.

From his right, he heard the characteristic thump of a 40 mm grenade launcher and the detonation of the grenade almost instantly. Screams followed immediately, and he stuck his head out to see two figures running for the open doors that led to the loading docks.

Steadying his Heckler & Koch MP-5, he triggered a short burst at the lead man and saw the slugs stitch him across the back. The guy following him dived for cover on the open floor, but that didn't save him. Lyons walked a second burst across him from hip to shoulder.

The gunman twitched and was still.

SCHWARZ DIDN'T KNOW IT, but he had drawn the ace. He was up against Red Cobras, and they were making every mistake in the night-fighting manual. For one, most of their shots were going high. A man naturally fired high at night, but that was fine with the electronics expert. Lying prone, he carefully chose his targets and put bullets in them.

One gunman stood so he could see better as he blazed away on full-auto. Waiting until the AK's magazine cycled dry, Schwarz put a bullet in the man's chest, knocking him off of his feet.

Suddenly he heard shouts in Vietnamese as the Red Cobras decided that they'd had enough. He did, however, get one more hardman on his way out the door.

BLANCANALES SLIPPED through the open side of the loading dock and took cover behind one of the massive wooden pillars holding up the rafters. He was tracking a target when a short burst of AK fire slammed into the pillar, sending splinters into his face.

Ducking back, he tried to find his opponent, but the gunman knew how to fight. He was snapping out short, controlled bursts, and the rounds were on target.

"Ironman," he said over the comm link, "someone's got me pinned down by the opening to the loading dock."

"I got him," Lyons sent back. "Keep your head down."

Using his night-vision goggles, the big ex-cop picked up the muzzle-flash of the guy who had Blancanales pinned, but all he could see was the weapon. The gunman had good cover behind what looked like a wooden partition. Slinging his MP-5, Lyons unholstered his Colt Python. The 9 mm rounds might not make it through the wall, but the .357s would. He drew a bead on where the gunman's head should be and tripped the hammer. The big Colt roared.

Lyons paused to observe the results and realized

that there was no more firing. "I got him, Pol," he radioed to Blancanales.

ZHANG LIU COULDN'T believe what was happening. His carefully planned ambush was falling apart. The vaunted Red Cobras had started to run at almost the first shot. He bitterly regretted having trusted the Vietnamese to do the job. If his own team had still been intact, this wouldn't have happened. At least his men would have stood and fought. As it was, his two remaining men were hard-pressed. Peng was down and Chin was trapped. Nonetheless, they were expendable and he wasn't.

Leaving his last man to his fate, the Beijing hit man carefully headed away from the firing. Once outside the building, he ditched his AK-47 and ran for the car parked out of sight behind what had been the main office building. He didn't bother to look back.

JIM LIN LOOKED a little green around the gills as he helped Lyons identify the last of the bodies. Not only had he not shot anyone before, but he also hadn't been around many freshly killed bodies. But since Lyons couldn't tell a Chinese from a Korean, someone had to sort out the casualties so they could figure out who, as well as what, had gone down in the brief firefight. Fortunately none of Lin's gunners lay among the dead. Two of them had been hit, but their wounds weren't serious and they were already bragging about them.

"This man's Vietnamese, too," Lin stated.

"So that only gives us two Chinese bodies, right?" Lyons asked.

"Right. The rest were Red Cobras."

"Damn, that means that one of them, probably Zhang, got away."

"Now that we know what he looks like," Lin reminded him, "we'll be able to catch up with him no sweat."

Lyons wasn't so sure of that, but Lin had come through for him tonight and he didn't want to burst his bubble. The young gangster was proud of having come through his baptism of fire, and as Lyons knew so well, that was more important to a young man than anything else that had happened to him so far in his life.

"Get your people together," Lyons told him, "and get on the road now. We'll meet up with you at the safehouse."

"Yes, sir," Lin answered automatically.

All the way back, the young Chinese wondered why he, a criminal, had called some kind of Fed, "sir."

ALL KEVIN WONG COULD SEE in the cold blue eyes of the big blond man was bad news. His nemesis was dressed in a night black combat suit. The black greasepaint on his face was streaked with sweat, and his hands were filthy. Obviously he had just come from killing somebody, and Wong hoped that he wasn't next on the butcher's list.

"I'm out of it now, aren't I?" Wong asked hopefully.

Lyons smiled grimly. "Don't you wish."

"But you said that as soon as I gave up Zhang and Hu that you'd turn me over to the Feds."

Lyons had never seen anyone who was so anxious to sit in a federal lockup for twenty years. But considering his options, Wong probably had the right idea.

"I lied," he said. "I still need you to make a positive ID on Zhang for us. Then you'll be done, I promise you."

"But you've had men tracking him for a couple of days now," Wong said. "You know what he looks like."

"They might have made a mistake. You wouldn't want me to kill the wrong man, would you?"

Once more, Wong realized that he'd been suckered. He also knew that he had no choice but to do whatever the blond man wanted him to. Anyone who talked so calmly about killing someone like Zhang would kill him just as easily. The security of a federal prison cell was looking better and better to him with every passing moment.

BARBARA PRICE SAT and reviewed the notes she had taken during her conversation with Carl Lyons. She particularly noted where she was going to have to send a Justice Department cleanup team in the morning. Not really a cleanup team, though. The local authorities would have already policed up the bodies. She needed to send in the spin doctors to muddy the waters so Able Team's bloody footprints wouldn't be noticed in the carnage.

The incident would go down as having been a shoot-out between rival Asian gangs, and that would be the end of it. The federal government's only interest would be in the automatic weapons that had been found on the scene. That was completely plausible and wouldn't be connected to the activist killings in any way. Even though only one of the Beijing hit men was still alive, he was believed to be the leader of the group, and Brognola wanted him in the bag, as well.

She still hadn't told Brognola the extent of Lyons's unholy alliance with the Lin organization. The big Fed had a lot on his plate right now, and Lyons was making good progress. Telling the Justice man *how* he was making such good progress would just raise his blood pressure, and it was high enough already because of the Phoenix Force operation in Taiwan.

Sending one of the SOG teams into action inside a friendly nation was always tricky. It was even more difficult this time because of the riff between the two governments. Brognola hadn't been able to pull his usual strings and set up a local clandestine contact, and Phoenix didn't even have an embassy contact to fall back on. Nonetheless, Bolan reported that the mission was moving well.

Once more, his Triad contacts were proving to be the key element in that operation. From what she had seen from the overseas Triads on this gig, anytime they wanted to go legitimate, they could farm themselves out to intelligence services. They sure knew more about what was happening in Asia than all the Western spy agencies put together.

Hitting the Buddhist monastery was going to be tricky, but she had to trust Bolan's judgment on that one. He would be sure to leave enough evidence behind so the Taiwanese would understand what had gone down. They wouldn't know who had taken out their enemies, but they would know that it had been a righteous hit. Later, a discreet hint would be passed along that the United States had given their longtime ally a hand.

CHAPTER FIFTEEN

"We have our target," Bolan announced to Phoenix Force as he unfolded the map the Triad businessman had given him. "There's a Buddhist monastery in the mountains that's been used by the Red Chinese as an espionage operations center for several years now. My information is that a senior officer of the Communist secret service will be holding a conference with the local Communist cell leaders the day after tomorrow to try to solve the problems we've been causing them lately."

"It's nice to have the opposition confirm that we've been doing our jobs," Encizo stated. So far, they had rounded up seven Communist cell members and were working on two more.

"Let's have a look." McCarter bent over the map of the island.

After spending several minutes trying to read the closely spaced elevation lines on the map, he looked up. "I think we need to do a little more surveying," he said. "If we're going up there, we need a good recon of those mountains."

"I hope you're not planning to do it on foot," James remarked. "According to the map, that sucker looks like it's nothing but straight up and down."

"As a matter of fact, I was thinking of an aerial recon," McCarter reassured him. "I'm not walking up there as long as we have the Hercules available. I want to fly up and down that ridgeline and take a few close-up pictures. If we have to go up there after those bastards, believe me, I want to take the easy route."

"That's music to my ears," said Jack Grimaldi, the Stony Man pilot. "I've been sitting on my ass so long that it's beginning to feel like I've had my wings clipped."

"What I don't understand," Encizo said, "is that with all the troops on this island, how in the hell have the Reds been able to hide a terrorist base up there?"

"The Taiwanese authorities know that the shrine's up there, all right," Bolan replied. "They just don't know what it really is."

"Say again?"

"The Chinese don't have an official religion, but a lot of them are Buddhists. If the monastery's been used as a base of operations as I was told, the military might not have looked too closely at it because it's in plain sight."

"Speaking of respect and all that," Hawkins commented, "how is it going to go down with the locals if we get caught busting a Buddhist shrine? I don't think they're going to like that very much.''

McCarter smiled. ''We'll just have to make sure that we don't get caught, then, won't we?''

EARLY THE NEXT MORNING, Jack Grimaldi filed a flight plan—under the name of their cover organization—that would take him over the central portion of the island to conduct another aerial geological survey. Bolan went as his copilot, and McCarter went as the cameraman.

When the plane landed an hour and a half later, the photos were quickly developed and faxed to Stony Man Farm along with Bolan's report and his proposal to launch an assault on the monastery.

While they were waiting for approval from the Farm, McCarter started putting the mission together.

''After looking carefully at all of the ground approaches,'' he said, ''I think our best way to get up there is to drop down on them from above. The mountain is too hard of a climb, and the trail is too easily interdicted. I don't want us to have to fight our way up.''

''Jump in?'' Hawkins asked. ''You've got to be joking, man. There's no place around there flat enough to use as a drop zone. You try to jump in there, and you're going to end up with a mountain peak up your ass or at the bottom of one of those valleys, and you'll still have to walk up.''

''There is one drop zone site close to the top,''

McCarter corrected him. "Granted, it's not very large, only a hundred yards or so across, but clever lads like us should be able to hit it spot on."

"Oh, boy," Hawkins said. "And you're talking about a night jump, aren't you?"

McCarter smiled. "But of course."

"You would be."

"And I want you to be our jump master."

"Great! That means that I'll be the last guy out of the plane, and I'll end up landing in the pucker brush or falling off a cliff because I'm at the end of the stock and can't catch up with you."

"Not a problem with parawings," the ex-SAS commando stated. "We'll be jumping with those new Bat Wing steerables. You can land them in a three-yard circle from over twenty thousand feet."

The mention of jumping from twenty thousand rang an alarm bell in the ex-Ranger. "You're not talking a HALO jump on top of it, are you?"

"Why not? I don't want them to hear us coming."

Hawkins was almost reduced to talking to himself as McCarter walked over to the map. "I figure that I'll have Grimaldi drop us off at twenty thou or so, ten miles offshore. We'll pop the canopies at ten thou, then we'll glide in to the DZ."

"What are we going to do about navigation?" Hawkins asked, trying to find a way to talk him out of this. "We won't have Pathfinders to mark the DZ for us."

"We're going to do that for ourselves tomorrow. More accurately, you and Manning are going to play tourist and visit the shrine. On the way up, you'll plant a remote-controlled marker to guide us in that night."

"On foot?"

"That's the way the rest of the pilgrims do it. There's a major highway that passes right by the trail up to the shrine. From there, it's just a few miles up the trail."

"How much is a few?"

McCarter leaned over the map. "Ten or twelve."

"Wonderful."

HAWKINS STOPPED when Manning halted on the mountain trail and tried to catch his breath. The two of them had been humping the mountain track to the monastery for two hours, and the going was rigorous. They were now high enough that the air was thin, as well.

On the way up, they had passed three way stations where the monks provided water and rest stops for the pilgrims making the trek. These stations were small but substantial rock buildings and could easily double as bunkers to delay intruders until reinforcements could arrive. McCarter had been right in planning a parachute insertion.

"There it is," the Canadian said, pointing with his chin to the small clearing on the left.

McCarter had said that the planned DZ was small,

and Hawkins saw that he wasn't kidding. Rather than being the hundred yards across that the Phoenix Force commander had said, it looked to be more on the order of sixty. It would be tight, but it was doable if the first jumpers who touched down cleared the drop zone on the double.

"Let's go have our lunch over there." Manning pointed to a tree line on the north edge of the clearing.

"Suits me."

Aside from the way stations, the two men hadn't seen any sign of surveillance along the trail, but they had to act as if they were under observation at all times. Since it was midday, there was nothing unusual about stopping for lunch. Even tourists had to eat sometime.

After finishing their prepared lunches, Hawkins reached into his rucksack and took out the small remote-controlled beacon that would guide them into the small clearing. Using his sheath knife, he cut out a square piece of turf the size of the olive-drab-painted box and dug two inches of dirt out of the bare ground and scattered it all around. After putting the box in place, he trimmed the turf block, made a hole for the antenna and replaced the turf on top of the device.

"If someone stumbles onto this thing before we jump, we're going to be in deep shit," Hawkins commented as he readied the device.

"If it doesn't activate on command," Manning

said with a shrug, "we'll just abort and glide our parawings down to the alternate DZ in the valley."

"And then walk up here?" Hawkins raised his eyebrows.

"You better hope it works."

"You got that right."

Manning checked the tourist map he had bought at the first way station. The shrine was just around the bend, and they followed the trail, then spent an hour looking around like real tourists before starting back down.

When Hawkins and Manning got back to their leased office building in Taipei, they found the rest of the team putting the finishing touches on the mission prep.

"I take it you planted it?" McCarter asked.

"That clearing's more like sixty yards across," Hawkins reported, "but it's doable. I put the marker centered on the north edge, so we'll have to touch down to the south of it."

"Good. Get your personal gear ready, grab a bite and then rack out until 2300. The Farm gave us the go-ahead, and we're launching at 2330."

"Just enough time to put a spit-shine on the old jump boots," Hawkins said. "I never jump with dirty boots."

STONY MAN PILOT Jack Grimaldi was on oxygen as the C-130 Hercules turboprop cruised at twenty-one thousand feet over the South China Sea ten miles off the east coast of Taiwan. After leaving Sungshan Airport an hour before, he had climbed to altitude and had taken up a course that sent him down the west side of the island and now, after making a one-eighty turn at the southern end of the island, he was cruising back up the other side.

"Green light's coming up in three minutes," the pilot called back over the intercom to the Stony Man team. "I'm dropping the ramp now."

"Roger," came David McCarter's clipped voice.

Grimaldi pulled the lever that lowered the rear ramp of the cargo plane to provide a platform for the men to jump from. They could have exited out the side door, but for this kind of a night HALO jump, it helped if they went off a platform in pairs.

"Ramp's down," the pilot radioed. "Red light's on."

"Roger red light, we're taking our positions."

In the back of the plane, the six Stony Man warriors checked each other's HALO gear one last time before lining up in pairs on the open ramp. A HALO—high-altitude, low-opening parachute jump—was a hard way to go to work.

Along with the weapons and ammunition loads they would need when they hit the objective, they were burdened with the larger than usual parawing chutes, a twenty-eight-foot reserve and the oxygen tanks and masks they would need for the first ten thousand feet of their jump. In addition to all this, as the team's jump master, Hawkins had a satellite navigation link and the remote control for the DZ beacon.

In the cockpit, Grimaldi watched his navsat screen and counted off the seconds. For this to work, the team had to jump at exactly the right spot, and he couldn't reduce speed because it would draw attention to the flight.

When the count reached zero, Grimaldi's gloved hand reached out and hit a switch. "Green light," he radioed. "Good hunting."

"See you on the ground," McCarter said as he dived off the rear ramp.

One by one, the three pairs of jumpers stepped off into the clear night sky and immediately assumed a spread-eagle skydiving position as they plunged toward the dark sea below.

As soon as the last of the jumpers had cleared the plane, Grimaldi pulled the ramp back up, engaged the autopilot and sat back. The flight plan called for him to continue on his planned course for another half hour before turning back to Taipei and landing at Sungshan Airport. At this time of night, no one would notice when he exited the plane by himself.

HAWKINS FELL through the cold night sky at terminal velocity, a little over 120 miles per hour. The other five jumpers were ahead of him, and he could track them by the small diode lights on the backs of the jump helmets. Checking the position of the lead jumper with his GPS navsat readout, he saw they were right on course.

When Hawkins's wrist altimeter indicated that he had dropped below ten thousand feet, he took off his oxygen mask and breathed in the night air. At that altitude, it was still chilly, but he could smell the water below and caught warmer smells from the island.

"Coming up on eight thousand," he radioed to remind the team of their deployment altitude.

When he passed the eight-thousand-foot mark, he tripped the release for the parawing strapped on his back. The opening shock sent the crotch straps of his parachute harness slamming into his groin, but that was just one of the small joys of being a jumping junkie.

When he looked up and saw that the triangular black canopy had properly deployed above him, he keyed his throat mike. "Five, deployed," he radioed.

Now he was riding a manned kite that was capable of being flown almost like an airplane. With a glide ratio of better than nine to one, he could almost make the coast of mainland China from where he was if he wanted to give it a try. As it was, his navsat readout showed him that he was only some eight miles from the drop zone.

Hell, he could damned near make that in an old-fashioned round chute. With the parawing, it was a piece of cake, as McCarter would say.

He looked around and saw the other five chutes below him. Since he had jumped last, they had all deployed before him. This way he could keep an eye on them as they silently flew through the night sky.

"Feet dry," McCarter radioed to tell the rest of the team that they had crossed the east coast of the island and were now over land. Their mountaintop drop zone was now only some six miles away.

Two miles out, Hawkins pushed the button on his control pad to activate the DZ beacon. Instantly he saw the invisible infrared pulses in his night-vision goggles as brightly as if they were white light strobes. The pulses didn't light up the boundaries of the DZ the way a strobe would have done, but they gave the team its aiming point for the final approach.

Pulling on his right-hand control toggle, Hawkins gently banked the parawing to line up with the small DZ. Already he saw a parawing glide into the clearing and touch down. That would be McCarter, followed closely by Bolan.

Hawkins was the last one down, and as soon as his feet touched the dirt, Manning and James were on hand to collapse his parawing. Punching his harness release, he shrugged out of it and took off his helmet.

As soon as all six of the parawings and jump gear were in a pile, James took a remote-control thermite device from his pack and placed it under the pile. When they triggered it on their way back out, it would incinerate the evidence of their arrival, leaving only melted nylon and plastic buckles.

"The DZ is clear," he whispered over his comm link.

"Let's get it done, then," McCarter ordered. "Five, move out. Three, cover him."

"Roger," Hawkins and Manning replied.

CHAPTER SIXTEEN

Since Hawkins and Manning had been up the trail just the previous afternoon, the ex-Ranger took the point with the Canadian walking his slack. With his night-vision goggles in place, the moonless night took on the ghostly green glow of night combat. Hawkins was well accustomed to looking at the world though green-colored glasses, though; his years as a Ranger had seen to that.

The day before, it had taken him and Manning less than ten minutes to make the walk from the DZ to the shrine, but this time they moved slowly. Bolan's Triad informer had reported that there were between twenty and thirty "monks" at the shrine. With odds like that against them, the only way they could make this night's action work was if they kept the element of surprise, and that meant moving cautiously.

At the end of the trail, the ridgeline flattened out into the narrow plateau the monastery and shrine had been built upon. A stone wall had been erected to enclose the compound and to allow the ground to be leveled. Outside the enclosure walls were simply the sloping sides of the ridgeline, cliffs and jagged rocks.

That meant that as soon as the Stony Man warriors got into the enclosure and secured it, there would be no place for the monks to escape to. It also meant that there was no easy way for the commandos to get off the mountain, either, if things went against them.

At the entrance to the shrine's grounds, Hawkins halted inside the ornate gate and scanned the open area in front of him. He and Manning hadn't seen any obvious signs of perimeter security on their earlier visit, but that didn't mean that there wasn't anything in place to guard against nocturnal intruders. It would be easy enough for the Communist monks to have heat or motion sensors hidden around the perimeter.

He was about to signal the others to move up when he heard the thunder of paws racing across the gravel toward him. Snapping around, he brought up his silenced H&K MP-5 just in time to fire a burst of 9 mm slugs into the dog's chest. The animal collapsed and died, teeth bared, not six feet in front of him.

He had just been confronted with the oldest silent security system in the world—a dog with its vocal cords cut. It was a foolproof, low-maintenance system that relied on the dying screams of the intruders to sound the alert. There was now no doubt at all that they were at the right place. Peaceful Buddhist monks would have no need to guard their monastery with attack dogs. And if these "monks" had one dog on patrol, they probably had human sentries to back them up, as well.

"One," Hawkins whispered over the team comm link, "this is Five. Be advised that I just took out a silenced guard dog, and he was a big bastard. We'd better keep an eye out for more of them and their handlers."

"One, roger," McCarter answered. "Wait there. I'm coming up."

When the Phoenix Force leader slid in beside him, Hawkins pointed out the corpse of the dog.

"Rottweiler," the Briton whispered. "Nasty brutes."

After waiting a few minutes to see if there were any more four-legged sentries, McCarter called the rest of the team forward.

James headed out around the left side of the shrine to look for the communications room. In the photos, a small outbuilding at the rear of the shrine appeared to have some kind of disguised antenna array, and it was a likely candidate for a radio shack. Since they didn't know what kind of manpower the Reds could call upon for reinforcements, it was essential to take out their radios before they went any further.

Hawkins backed up James while Bolan and McCarter secured the front of the enclosure. On the other side of the building, Encizo and Manning slipped along the inside of the wall, their night black combat suits rendering them almost invisible against the backdrop of dark stone.

Encizo was making his way from one stone monument to the next on his side of the enclosure when he spotted a man leaning back against one of the monuments that littered the grounds. The guard wasn't wearing the saffron robes of a Buddhist monk. Instead, he was wearing some kind of dark fatigue uniform and cloth cap. The AK-47 slung over his back and the canvas magazine carrier on his chest were pure Red Chinese.

Motioning for Manning to stay where he was, the little Cuban slung his subgun and pulled a Ka-bar fighting knife from his boot sheath. The Canadian drew his silenced Beretta 92 as a backup.

Drifting forward like a shadow, Encizo quickly closed the gap on the sentry. He was almost on him when something spooked the man just as Encizo made his thrust. The Chinese violently twisted to one side, tearing the knife out of Encizo's grasp and tried to bring his AK-47 to bear on his assailant.

The Cuban stepped back and was going for his pistol when he saw a dot of red light appear on the guard's forehead. An instant later, a 9 mm slug erased the red dot, and the Chinese went to his knees.

Encizo caught the man's AK before it could clatter to the gravel and laid it at the base of the wall.

"Gracias, amigo," Encizo said when Manning rushed up to him.

Manning smiled in the dark. *"De nada."*

"This is Two," Encizo radioed to McCarter. "The south side is secured. One guard taken out."

"One, roger," McCarter acknowledged. If one guard and one dog were all the Communists had guarding the grounds this night, this was going to be a piece of cake.

IN THE GUEST ROOM of the monastery, Sun Yu stirred suddenly and sat up on his narrow cot. He didn't know what had awakened him. He couldn't hear anything more than the normal sounds of the sleeping monastery around him. But he had learned a long time ago to trust his instincts, particularly when he was in enemy territory, and his gut told him that something was wrong.

He'd had a long trip from the Chinese mainland to reach this mountaintop base, and an even longer meeting with Kwan Choi and the other leaders of the Taipei People's Party cells, and he was exhausted. But as Sun Tzu had written, a man or an army was always in the greatest danger when tired.

He knew that the guard dog was loose and the sentries were posted, but whatever had awakened him still had to be investigated.

The Beijing agent always slept clothed when he was in the field. So, sliding his feet into his sandals and shrugging into his PRA-issue quilted jacket, he was dressed. Taking the 9 mm Makarov pistol from the table next to his cot, he walked into the silent corridor. Glancing out the window at the end of the hall, he saw that the moon wasn't up. It was the perfect time for an attack.

There were no indications that the Yankee action team that had been operating in Taipei knew about the monastery, but he couldn't take that chance. They had proved to be resourceful, far more resourceful, in fact, than Beijing had expected. That was why he was on the island, to put an end to their activities. Whoever these mysterious Yankees were, they had to be neutralized.

He was reaching for the handle of the door that led out of the main building to the separate radio shack when he heard the click of something metallic.

Pressing back against the wall, he held the Makarov ready and peered through the crack of the ancient door frame.

A shadow moved past his field of vision, and the shadow wasn't wearing the uniforms of the guards.

"To your posts!" Sun shouted to rouse the sleeping troops. "We are under attack!"

"AW, SHIT!" Hawkins muttered when he heard the shout from inside the building. He knew this had been going too well. Reaching down to his ammo pouch, he pulled an M-26 fragmentation grenade and released the safety pin. He held the explosive egg in reserve, however, until he found out if the shout meant business.

Ahead of him, James shifted into high gear. Sprinting the last few yards to the radio shack, he kicked the door open with his combat boot and stormed in. The man speaking into a handheld microphone spun to face him, a semiautomatic pistol in his other hand. James triggered his MP-5 subgun, sending a silenced 3-round burst into his chest.

The gunman pitched over, both the pistol and microphone falling from his suddenly nerveless hands.

Catching movement from a bunk in the dimly lit end of the room, James saw a man sitting up. Not waiting to see if the guy was armed, he triggered another short burst to put him back to sleep forever.

After making sure that there were no more nasty surprises in the shack, he triggered two more bursts into the radio equipment, stitching the transmitters. He had been too late to keep the radioman from making that one call, but they wouldn't be making any more calls for help this night.

After changing magazines in his subgun, he backed out of the shack and clicked on his throat mike. "This is Four," he called to McCarter. "I didn't get to the radio operator in time. He was talking to someone when I zeroed him. I secured the equipment, though, and they can't call out now."

"One, roger," McCarter's clipped voice came over his earphone. "You and Five keep working the back of the compound. We have the front and the flanks covered."

"Four, roger."

Just then, the clatter of an AK-47 on full-auto came from one of the windows in the main building. James dived for cover behind a nearby stone monument to escape the firestorm.

Zeroing in on the window beside the rear door, Hawkins threw the grenade and heard the glass break.

The bomb detonated with a thump, but there were no cries of pain. Seconds later, though, assault rifles blazed from almost every window of the main building. He had obviously chosen the wrong window to egg.

He, too, dived for cover and began snapping short bursts at the muzzle-flashes.

THE INSTANT the first shot rang out, Bolan and McCarter sprinted for the ornate portico at the front of the shrine's main building. The huge wooden doors were closed for the night, but there were no barriers that confounded C-4 plastiques.

The explosive blocks the Stony Man team carried had an adhesive strip on the back and were already fused with variable timers. Ripping off the covering tape, the two men slapped the preshaped charges against the middle of the door join where the crossbar would be on the other side. Since the default setting on the timers was sixty seconds, they simply tripped them and took cover against the walls.

A minute later, the detonation of the demo charges shattered the crossbar, and the massive doors were thrown open by the blast.

Bolan and McCarter tossed flash-bang grenades inside, followed by a barrage of fire as both men emptied their magazines. Ducking back, the two men changed magazines and readied fragmentation grenades.

On a three count, they tossed the bombs into the darkened corridor. This time the twin detonations brought screams of pain.

Going through the door low, the two commandos led with their silenced MP-5s spitting flame. Even after the fragging, the besieged Chinese were ready for them and returned their fire round for round, forcing the two to seek cover.

"This isn't cutting it, Mack," McCarter radioed from behind a statue right inside the door. "We'd better get our butts out of here."

"I'll pop a flash-bang," Bolan replied.

When the grenade detonated with an eye-searing flash, the two men stepped out from cover, emptied their magazines down the corridor and raced for the front door. Reaching the safety of the outside again, they changed magazines and got ready to try something different.

SUN YU REALIZED that all of the sounds of firing were coming from inside the monastery. And to his experienced ear, the weapons all sounded like AKs or Makarovs. He had heard no return fire, but he knew that his men were taking serious casualties. That indicated that the enemy was using silenced weapons, which meant that the attackers weren't Taiwanese. The island's police or army would have used their normal, nonsilenced weaponry.

The use of silencers was the mark of professionals, maybe the Yankee CIA or their Special Forces.

No matter who they were, it was obvious that Beijing's plan to isolate Taiwan from all American support hadn't been successful. In the American newspapers and television, the Nationalists were on their own; Congress had said so. But if the Yankees were sending in professional hit squads to ferret out the People's Party cell leaders, the widely publicized political moves were just carefully crafted disinformation. Beijing needed to be warned about this so they could adjust their plans accordingly.

But since the radio room had been one of the first things that had been attacked, he had to escape so he could carry the message back himself.

"I think your mysterious Yankees are paying us a visit," Sun told Kwan.

The Taiwanese Communist was stunned. "But that is not possible, Comrade Sun! How could they have known that you were going to be here?"

"That does not matter," Sun snapped. "All that matters is that I must get out of here so I can make my report. Beijing must be informed of this situation."

"But what about the comrades here?" Kwan asked. Almost all of the upper-level leadership of the People's Party cells were attending the meeting. If they were killed, it would take years to rebuild the organization.

"They can fight or die. And if they die, they can be replaced. I am going to escape up the mountain, and you can come with me if you want. We can hide up there until the raiders are gone."

"I will get some men to come with us," Kwan offered.

"Make it quick. And tell the others to give us cover when we leave."

Kwan grabbed the first two men he found and ordered them to pull back and go with him. After Sun ordered covering fire, the four hurried out the back door of the main building. Crouching to keep low, they dashed across the open ground to the rear wall of the shrine's enclosure.

Vaulting over the low wall, they hugged the ground until they saw that they weren't being pursued. When Sun was sure that they had gotten away clean, he ordered the two men to guard his back as he led the way up the overgrown trail for the mountain.

CHAPTER SEVENTEEN

The Tsang Liu Monastery had been built on a small plateau along the ridgeline of the mountain with only a single access route. The pilgrim's trail coming in from the highway through the valley ended at the shrine. But Sun Yu knew from his earlier visits that there was a smaller, unmarked path behind the monastery that continued north to the mountain's peak two miles away. If he could reach that trail unseen, he could wait out the attack on the mountain.

"Keep close to me," he ordered Kwan.

"And you two," he added, turning to the other two men, "guard our backtrail and make sure that I am not followed."

"Yes, Comrade."

"I'VE GOT FOUR GUYS escaping over the back wall," Encizo reported over the comm link. "And from the way they're moving out, I'd guess that there's a way up the mountain from there."

"Can you block them?" McCarter asked.

"They've got Gary and me pretty well pinned down," Encizo replied. "We're under cover now, but if we try to follow those guys, we're going to get whacked."

"I'm on the way, Rafe," Bolan answered. "You two keep your heads down and give me covering fire."

"No sweat."

Taking the other side of the enclosure, Bolan radioed to let James and Hawkins know that he was coming through. They stepped up their fire to keep the enemy gunners' heads down as the Executioner raced down the side of the building. By the time he reached the end of the walled enclosure, the four Chinese were already climbing the unmarked trail heading for higher ground. Though the trail was overgrown, he could see enough of it to follow them.

Ever careful of running into an ambush, he headed up the trail, his MP-5 at the ready. Even though the moon wasn't out, Bolan had no trouble picking out all four men in the ghostly green vision of his night-vision goggles every time they exposed themselves.

Two of the Chinese were holding back behind the front two, acting as rear guards. The man closest to him had disappeared into a clump of brush, but Bolan was picking up his heat signature through his goggles. To flush out the gunman, Bolan snapped a short burst of 9 mm rounds at him.

Panicked, the Chinese stood to get a clear shot and blazed away with his AK-47, but Bolan had moved out of the line of fire. From his new position, he stitched the gunman across the chest with a long burst from the MP-5.

The gunman dropped his AK and collapsed to the ground.

Slinging the subgun over his back, the Executioner drew the .44-caliber Desert Eagle from his belt holster. Now that there was no more need to hide the sound of the gunfire, he wanted to get back to using his favorite tool.

The second man also tried to make a stand in the open. He stepped out and started firing blindly down the trail. Bolan took cover behind a rock and waited.

The Chinese sprayed half a magazine of 7.62 mm slugs before the bolt of his AK-47 locked back on an empty magazine. He rather foolishly kept standing in the open as he fumbled at his chest-pack magazine carrier. Bolan stepped out from cover, the Desert Eagle held in a two-handed grip.

It was a long shot, even for a hand cannon like the .44, but in the hands of a master shootist, it wasn't impossible. When the weapon was lined up with the target's center body mass, Bolan stroked the trigger. The boom of the Desert Eagle echoed from the jagged rocks, followed by a death scream.

KWAN WAS IN A STATE of barely controlled panic. Every time a shot sounded, he jumped. His night vision had never been any good, and with no moonlight he was literally stumbling around in the dark. He couldn't even see how many men were after them.

"They are going to kill us if we do not surrender," Kwan said.

"You fool," the Beijing agent replied. "We cannot surrender to them. I have to get back to Beijing and tell them about this."

"Maybe I could surrender," Kwan offered, "and then have the comrades of the People's Party in the police release me from the jail. I could tell them that I was the last one, and they wouldn't look for you."

Sun stepped closer to Kwan, his right hand held low. When the muzzle of the Makarov jammed against Kwan's side, he triggered the pistol twice.

The man stiffened and slumped against him, dead.

Sun let the body fall to the ground. Looking around, he spotted a good place to climb up into the rock cliff. From there, he would be able to ambush whoever was following them when they stopped to check Kwan's body.

BOLAN HEARD the muffled pistol shots and knew that it had not been fired at him. When he saw only one man now on the trail, he knew what had happened. Someone had been judged a liability and had been eliminated.

A few more yards up the trail, he spotted a warm, man-size mass on the ground through the goggles, which had to be the man who had been sacrificed. Seeing this was a setup, Bolan took cover and scanned the area for the fourth man, who would be waiting in ambush. When he couldn't find him in the brush, he started to scan the rocks above the trail and picked him up climbing the rock face.

As he drew a bead on him, Bolan saw him lose his grip and plunge through the air. He fell only twenty feet or so, but he hit hard and was lying still when the Executioner approached him.

"Keep your hands where I can see them," Bolan warned, the Desert Eagle centered on the fallen man's chest.

"I think my left arm is broken," the man said in accented English. "I cannot move it."

When Bolan made no comment, Sun tried again. "I am an officer of the People's Liberation Army," he said.

"I figured that," Bolan said, keeping the Desert Eagle trained on the Chinese. "You're a long way from home."

"Who are you?" Sun asked as he painfully pulled himself to a sitting position. "And why did you attack us?"

"Let's just say that I work for the American people, and I'm here to deliver a message. Your people in Beijing have got to understand that killing American citizens carries a penalty. You should never have killed a man on live television."

Suddenly Sun's left hand snaked out from behind

his back, the spikelike Chinese throwing knife appearing like magic as it shot from his hand.

Pivoting on his right leg, Bolan twisted out of the path of the flashing blade as he triggered the Desert Eagle. The heavy .44 Magnum slug took Sun directly over the heart, blowing a fist-sized exit hole in his back. The hammer blow flattened him against the rock, killing him instantly.

The Executioner smiled grimly as he holstered the big-bore Israeli pistol. He had seen the left-handed throw many times before; it was in every Oriental martial-arts expert's little bag of tricks. Since most Orientals were right-handed, they rarely expected an offensive move from the left hand. Being an American, however, Bolan never trusted a man's left hand any more than the right unless it was empty and in the open where he could see it.

Not bothering to search the bodies, Bolan headed back down the mountain. From the sounds of things, McCarter was mopping up down there and would be finished by the time he got back. He took off toward his teammates at a dogtrot.

BOLAN WASN'T even breathing hard when he arrived back at the monastery's grounds. The firefight had ended, and only the Phoenix Force warriors were left on their feet. James and Manning were throwing buckets of water on a small fire that had started, while the other three commandos were checking the bodies to make sure no one was feigning death.

"We counted nineteen bodies," McCarter reported, "and several of them were in PLA uniforms."

"You can add four more up on the mountain," Bolan said, "and I think that two of them were high-ranking officers. At least they were packing pistols instead of AKs."

The American military was unique in that it required that its officers be proficient with rifles, as well as pistols, the customary officer's side arm. In Asian armies, that wasn't the case. The guy with a pistol was almost always an officer or a high-ranking NCO.

"Do you want to do a document search before we go?" McCarter asked.

Bolan glanced at his watch. "No, we need to get going. Plus I want to leave everything here for the Taiwanese to find. We want them to know why we hit this place, and they'll need to go over that material themselves to figure it out. With luck, they'll find enough here that they'll be able to shut down most of the cells on the island."

"That would be a nice bonus."

This time McCarter took the point as the team started down the mountain trail. It had taken more time than he had planned to clean out the monastery, and with the clock ticking, they had to get off the mountain before dawn. The pilgrims usually started their treks to the shrine as the sun came up over the mountain's peak, and the last thing the Stony Man team needed was to get spotted running away from the scene of a massacre.

The Taiwanese police shouldn't have too much trouble figuring out that this hadn't been a hit on harmless Buddhist monks. The Chinese People's Liberation Army–issue radios, uniforms and weapons would tell the story well enough. But the mystery of exactly who had taken out this nest of Communist agents should keep them busy long after the Stony Man team was gone.

When the team passed the clearing they had used for their drop zone, James keyed the remote control for the thermite device they had left with their discarded parawings and jump gear. The incendiary charge ignited with a blinding white flash. In seconds, the nylon chutes were burning brightly. By the time the fire burned itself out, little would be left behind and nothing that could identify them.

Bolan felt satisfied as he followed McCarter down the trail. It had been a perfect mission. They had gone in, done their job and were now getting out and no one would be the wiser. This made Stony Man three for three against the hard-liners, and while he wanted to think that Beijing might think twice before trying again, he knew better. China was on the move, probing for the free world's weak points, and he knew that Stony Man had not seen the last of Beijing. But they hadn't seen the end of Stony Man, either.

DAWN WAS BREAKING when the six Stony Man warriors reached the bottom of the mountain path where it intersected the highway running through the Taroko Gorge. Keeping well hidden in the tree line, Bolan took the small radio from his assault pack and switched it on.

"We're ready," he said.

"We come now," the voice on the other end answered. Shan, their Triad driver, was supposed to be behind the wheel of the truck, and apparently he had brought another Triad along to keep him company on the trip.

The truck that pulled into the parking turnout bore the colorful markings of the Three Seas Fish Market. The name was rendered in both English and Chinese characters over a painting of a large tuna fish. A strong aroma of fish backed up the bright logo.

"Here's our ride, lads," McCarter said.

"I like my fish as much as the next man," Hawkins grumbled when he saw the company logo, "but hitching a ride in the back of a fish truck is a bit much."

"You can always thumb it," Manning suggested.

"No, thanks. My dogs are barking. I've had about all the exercise I can stand for one twenty-four-hour period. I'm ready to ride for a change."

The truck pulled to the side of the road, and Shan got out of the cab. "Hurry," he said as he opened the doors in the back of the vehicle. There was an aisle between the stacked crates of seafood.

As soon as the six men had taken their places on the bench that had been bolted to the front bulkhead of the cab, Shan and his passenger stacked boxes of iced fish in front of them, blocking the door. If anyone was to stop the truck and open the rear door, all he would see would be fish headed for the seafood markets of Taipei.

"I knew I was going to hate this," Hawkins said, taking a deep breath as the truck pulled back onto the highway.

"At least we won't have to worry about breakfast," James said. "I have my eye on one of those sea perch."

"Raw?"

"What's the matter, man—haven't you ever heard of sushi?"

Hawkins shuddered. "Back where I come from, son, we make a point of gutting 'em and cooking 'em before we eat 'em."

JACK GRIMALDI WAS WAITING for the Stony Man team when the fish truck pulled up to the loading dock of the Triad owned seafood warehouse.

"I sent the mission-closure notification to the Farm," he told Bolan, "and Barbara's waiting for your report. She says that Hal's having a cow worrying about the collateral damage."

Bolan smiled grimly. "There was no collateral damage except to the building. Everyone we saw, even the ones in saffron-colored robes, had weapons in their hands, and that made them fair game."

"That sounds about right to me." Grimaldi grinned. As the team's pilot, he usually didn't get involved in the ground operations. But when he did, the rule of engagement he followed was that if it was armed, he shot at it.

Grimaldi had brought the van the team had rented, and as soon as all their gear was loaded into it and they had changed into their civilian clothing, they drove back to the command post at the airfield.

While Bolan and McCarter made their afteraction report to Barbara Price, the other commandos cleaned their gear before packing it up and loading the Hercules for the flight home.

"It's too bad we can't hang around here for a few days," Hawkins observed as he packed his MP-5 in the carrying case. "I was beginning to like this place, and I haven't even had a chance to look around for a good seafood restaurant."

"I think we can arrange that," Bolan announced. "I told Barbara that we might take a few days off and do a little sight-seeing."

"Outstanding!"

CHAPTER EIGHTEEN

Now that they had only to track down one more hit man to wrap this up, Carl Lyons was in a hurry to get on with it so he could close the books on this mission. It had been a bad piece of luck that Zhang hadn't been among the dead at the cannery, but you couldn't expect to bat a thousand every time you stepped up to the plate. The cannery fight, however, had left Zhang on his own, and Johnny Lin's soldiers were combing the city looking for him. As soon as they caught up with the man, the ball would be back in play.

Even though Lyons felt certain that Zhang hadn't called it quits and left town, he'd had Stony Man alert the INS at the airports and border crossings to be on the lookout for him. Knowing that the hit team apparently had used Canadian passports to enter the country, most of the attention was being focused in the north, but Lyons didn't expect the dragnet to snag the assassin. He was counting on seeing him again in San Francisco.

He couldn't begin to claim that he knew how

Zhang thought—they'd never met—but he knew that the man was a hardened pro. Communists, particularly those of the Asian variety, usually had a streak of fanaticism in them, and Lyons was counting on that being true of Zhang, as well.

This had been an important assignment for the Chinese gunman, and he had been humiliated big time. Lyons figured on that playing a role in Zhang's thinking as he made his plans. Fanatics usually didn't have much of a sense of humor. More than likely, the hit man wouldn't be able to laugh at fate and do the smart thing, which was to cut his losses and leave town. Instead, the man would burn with a desire for revenge and would stay to hunt his tormentors.

To each his own, Lyons liked to think, particularly when his opponent's "own" played right into his hands.

IT WAS NO SURPRISE to Lyons when a day later one of Lin's men spotted the Red Chinese agent coming out of an apartment in the Haight-Ashbury district next to Chinatown. Apparently he had wanted to change hiding places, but had no desire to go too far away from the ethnic community he thought he could hide in. And now that they had him, it was time to get back to work.

Lin's men were keeping round-the-clock surveillance of the room he had taken, and they were discreetly following him everywhere he went. It would be easy enough to grab him.

"How are you going to handle this, Ironman?" Schwarz asked. "Now that Zhang's the Lone Ranger, he's going to be more than a little shy about walking into another trap."

"That's true," Lyons said. "But I'm counting on his wanting to get a little payback to get in the way of his common sense. I'm going to have Wong arrange a meeting with both his drug supplier and the assassin in a very public place. That should calm Zhang's fears, and I don't think he'll be able to resist a chance to take his frustration out on Wong. Plus we haven't moved against Hu yet, and this will bring him into the hit zone, too. Once they're together, we're going to crash the party and see if we can ice them both."

"That will put Wong in the line of fire, as well," Blancanales argued. "Don't you want to keep him alive?"

"It's not our job to keep him alive." Lyons shrugged. "And I really don't care if he gets caught in the cross fire. He's a drug dealer who's been selling restricted technology to Beijing on the side. If he goes down, it'll save the taxpayers the cost of a trial."

"There is that."

Lyons got up and reached for the phone. It was time to meet with Lin again and get the ball rolling.

WILLIAM HU WAS at his desk in the manager's office of the People's Republic of China's trade mission, but his mind wasn't on his job. Against Hu's strongest advice, Zhang Liu refused to concede defeat and simply go back to China. Even though there was no chance of his continuing his mission alone, the assassin insisted on staying until Hu could locate the men who had attacked the cannery. And he insisted that Hu help him. Since Hu knew that to refuse the request would cost him his life, he had no choice but to agree.

Because he worked at the trade mission, Hu had a lot of connections with both the local authorities and the criminal underground. So far, though, he hadn't been able to turn up anything. The SFPD and the Oakland police were both baffled. They had no idea what had gone down or who was responsible for the massacre of the Red Cobras and Zhang's last two Beijing agents. Hu had even made contact with the FBI and the DEA, and they were in the dark, as well.

Everyone was taking the easy out and blaming the shooting on Asian gangs, but Hu wasn't certain that was the case. Wong had said that he had been captured by Chinese gangsters, so maybe there was some truth to it. But there were the three white men who'd initially confronted Wong; where did they fit in?

Hu's phone rang, startling him out of his thoughts. "Hu," he answered.

"Bill," Kevin Wong said, "it's me."

"Where are you?" Hu's voice was suspicious.

"I'm calling from a phone booth. That gang let me go."

"Why should I believe you now?" Hu asked. "That's what you said before."

"I know," Wong said, "but I had to say that then. They said they'd kill me if I didn't do what they told me to."

"What's changed now?"

"They think it's all over," Wong explained, "and they don't need me anymore. They were laughing about how easy it had been to take out the Vietnamese at the cannery. They also said that you and Zhang must have been idiots for listening to me when you knew that I had been captured."

"Zhang isn't going to like hearing that."

"I didn't mean to set him up, Bill," Wong said quickly, "but I didn't have a choice."

"Why didn't they just kill you instead of letting you go?"

"I made a deal with them," Wong admitted sheepishly. "I told them that I'd give them a cut of my China White business if they'd let me go."

Hu believed that. Wong wasn't the bravest man he had ever met, and he had no ideological reason not to do anything to save his own skin. That did raise another possible problem for Hu, though. "Did you tell them that I was your supplier?"

"They figured that part out already," Wong said.

"But you don't have to worry. They don't want to get into the business themselves. They just want to suck off my profits."

Hu could believe that, too. The Chinese American gangsters were no better than the Hong Kong and Taiwan drug scum. They wouldn't dirty their hands if they could get someone else to do it for them.

"But," Wong said, forcing a laugh, "I'm not going to stick around and work for them. I'm cleaning out my house and leaving town tomorrow."

"Zhang's going to want to talk to you," Hu said. "Call me tonight, and I'll let you know when we can set it up."

"Tell him that I'm not going to wait for him. I'm out of here tomorrow afternoon at the latest, before the gangsters find out that I'm going."

"Just call back tonight, okay?"

"Okay." Wong sounded reluctant.

SAN FRANCISCO'S Golden Gate Park was within easy walking distance from where Zhang had been hiding out since the debacle at the cannery. It was a very public place, and as Lyons had counted on, the assassin had readily agreed to meet Wong there.

Johnny Lin's people provided early warning by having several pushcart vendors and flower sellers cover the park's entrances. On the odd chance that the hit man had decided to come early, other Chinese Americans were strolling through the park, as well, older men and women, plus young couples with children, looking for him. Even with the number of bums, drunks and drug addicts in the park, it should be easy to spot their target. Lyons was in radio contact with Lin, who had given radios to all of his people. When Zhang was spotted, he would know instantly.

Kevin Wong was very much aware of the unfamiliar pressure of the Kevlar vest he wore under his shirt as he waited by the stone monument in the middle of the park. The short guy had insisted that he wear it, and he was glad to have it.

He was scanning the face of every passerby when his eyes caught sight of an older Chinese man wearing a three-piece suit and carrying a briefcase.

Wong was shocked when he realized who the well-dressed Chinese man was—Zhang Liu. The assassin looked like any of a number of the area's businessmen taking his lunch break in the park. Wong felt his heart race, but he stood his ground because the blond guy had said that he'd shoot him if he tried to run.

WILLIAM HU WAITED until he spotted Zhang approaching before he walked up to join Wong. He still didn't know what the assassin planned to do about Wong, but he hoped this could be resolved peacefully.

When he reached the monument, Zhang opened his briefcase and pulled out an Uzi submachine gun.

Wong raised his hands in surrender. "Don't shoot!"

Without saying a word, the assassin triggered a short burst, catching Wong across the chest. He felt a painful blow and had an accusing look on his face as he went down.

Hu also looked shocked when Zhang's Uzi whipped around to zero in on him. "Don't shoot!" he shouted in Cantonese.

Zhang's finger tightened on the trigger again, sending a burst of 9 mm rounds into his chest.

Hu staggered backward, blood pouring from multiple wounds, and fumbled for the small pistol in his coat pocket. He had his hand on the weapon, but didn't have the strength to pull it out.

The park's visitors were all hardened Californians. The minute the first shots rang out, they either scattered or took cover.

As soon as the fields of fire around the monument were clear, Lyons drew the .357 Colt Python from his shoulder holster and stepped into the open.

"Put it down, Zhang," he called out. "It's over. You're surrounded."

Zhang spun toward him, the muzzle of the Uzi seeking a target, but Lyons had dropped back into cover.

Blancanales clicked his throat mike. "I can't get a clean shot at him, Ironman. There are too many people in the way."

"No sweat," Lyons replied as he thumbed back

the hammer of the Python for a smoother single-action pull. "If you can put a round into the top of the monument, I can take him."

Blancanales raised his sights and triggered the scooped, silenced M-16. When the round caroomed off the stone several feet above Zhang's head, he turned to face the new threat, and Lyons stepped out holding the Python in a two-handed Weaver's grip.

"Zhang!" he shouted.

The assassin was turning back when Lyons tripped the hammer. The Python roared and settled back into zero. He fired again.

Zhang fell to the ground, the Uzi slipping from his hands. His lips were drawn back in a frozen snarl. He struggled, bloody bubbles appearing on his lips, the light rapidly fading from his eyes.

Lyons approached the fallen hit man, standing over the body. "Tell Beijing to send a real man next time."

The last thing Zhang saw was the infuriating smile.

THE INSTANT that the Red Chinese agent went down, Lin's people converged on the scene. Able Team's weapons disappeared into shopping bags, backpacks and strollers, and Lyons and Blancanales slipped away into the crowd. Schwarz, though, stopped to check on Wong.

"Wong's still alive," he reported over the comm

link. "But he took one outside the Kevlar, and he's going to need help pretty soon."

"How soon?"

"I slapped a pressure bandage on it, so he should last an hour or so."

"Make him comfortable," Lyons said, "and tell him that an ambulance is on the way. Also tell him that this squares him with us. If he keeps his mouth shut and walks the line from now on, he won't have to look over his shoulder anymore."

"Will do."

"And take the Kevlar vest with you."

"I already have it."

Five minutes later Lyons, Schwarz, Blancanales and Lin were drinking beers in a small Chinese restaurant one block away from the park when the ambulances and cop cars went screaming past.

"Well," Lyons said, turning to Lin with a big smile, "I guess this about wraps it up for us. Tell your grandfather that we thank him for all the help he has given us for these past few days and that we won't forget it."

Lyons paused and fixed his cold blue eyes on the young gangster. "You should mention to him, though, that this might be a real good time for the Lin family to branch out into other ventures. Something that won't come to the attention of the authorities. He has nothing to fear from us—we owe him—but the times are changing and a wise man changes with them, if you catch my drift."

"I'll tell him what you said," Lin answered evenly.

Lyons drained the last of his beer and stood. "Until next time."

Lin watched the three men walk out and disappear into the sidewalk crowd. He wasn't too sure that he wanted a next time with Lyons and his two partners. And he planned to have a long talk with his grandfather so that he never would.

CHAPTER NINETEEN

Hal Brognola was looking happier this time when Barbara Price met him at the chopper pad. Some of the more recent additions to the lines on his face had faded a bit, and he had a fresh cigar clamped between his teeth. As usual, he didn't say anything of substance before he was safe in the War Room.

Once there, though, he got down to business immediately. "The President has asked me to pass on his personal thanks to everyone for a job very well done. It's going to take Congress a little while to get it together enough to reverse the resolution against Taiwan, but he doesn't think that it'll take too long. As far as he's concerned, we're back to business as usual in the Far East."

"Maybe not," Aaron Kurtzman said cryptically.

"What do you mean?" Brognola asked, frowning. "Has there been a reaction from Beijing to the mission?"

Kurtzman shook his head. "Not that we've been able to pick up on. But like I said back when this whole thing got started, they don't work in cyberspace as much as we do. As far as I know, they could be mad as hell. We'll just have to wait and see."

"When's Striker and the team due back?" Brognola asked Price.

"I didn't think there was any particular rush," she replied, "so I told them to take their time. I don't have a timetable yet."

"Tell them to take all the time they want," Brognola said magnanimously. "See the sights and hang out on the beach. They've earned a little vacation time."

"I'll tell them you said that."

"Once again," he said, "the President sends his regards and hopes all of you will be able to take a little time off."

"Not in this lifetime," Kurtzman muttered under his breath.

AS SOON AS Brognola left for Washington, Kurtzman wheeled himself back to his computer console. Now that the crisis of the moment had been taken care of, he could go back to searching cyberspace for the clues that would point out where the next one was coming from. The battle never ended, and the only way to keep winning was to look for trouble before it came looking for you.

Since the last three events—as he liked to call them—had been sponsored by the Beijing hardliners, he decided that he was going to keep a close eye on China for the next several months. If, that was, Islamic terrorists would cooperate and give him a little breathing room, the Russians didn't lose any more nuclear warheads and the narco barons didn't try to take over any more Latin American governments. The chances were slim that he would get that kind of respite, but hope sprang eternal, even at Stony Man Farm.

He had told Brognola that there had been no unusual activity by the Chinese that he was aware of, but *some* military activity was taking place, particularly on the coast of Fujian Province across the strait from Taiwan. America's alphabet soup of Intelligence agencies, the CIA, DIA, ONI and NRO would be updating the President on that situation on a daily basis. If something broke out there, they'd be sure to pick up on it.

Nonetheless, Kurtzman wasn't content to sit and wait for the CIA to tell him that there was a problem somewhere in the world. On top of that, he didn't have a great deal of confidence in the Company's ability to be able to find its own ass with both hands and a radar set. All too often, the CIA had been eyeball-to-eyeball with the facts and had still been blindsided because they hadn't been able to put the pieces together.

For instance, regardless of what he had told Brognola, he wasn't at all ready to believe that Beijing was going to give up on Taiwan. They'd suffered a couple of setbacks, but the hard-liners were used to thinking of results in terms of decades, not weeks. As Mao himself had said, "The journey of a thousand miles begins with the first step."

So far, Mao's journey had given the Communists control of almost all of mainland China. It was wishful thinking to look at Beijing's takeover of Hong Kong as being the end of that epic journey. More than likely, it wouldn't even be a stopover in the middle of what had already been a very long trip by Western standards.

But, as long as there was a part of Asia that wasn't Communist, Mao's children would still keep walking.

"THE COMMUNIST CHINESE can take Taiwan any time they want," Yakov Katzenelenbogen stated, answering Kurtzman's first question bluntly. The computer wizard had wanted a down-to-earth opinion on several possible courses of action the Chinese leadership might decide upon. And for down-to-earth, it was hard to beat Katz.

"All it will cost them," the Israeli said, shrugging, "is a million men, more or less. But as we've seen several times over the years, they aren't adverse to using up their people that way."

"Could our Navy keep them from crossing the Strait of Formosa?"

"Theoretically," Katz said. "The Chinese navy is less than third-rate. But for us to do anything effective would mean running the risk of a nuclear confrontation. Remember that Beijing mouthpiece last year who asked if we were serious enough about Taiwan to want to trade the island for L.A.? We could stop them on the high seas, no sweat. But if we get involved that way, it would be brinkmanship all the way. One false move, and it would go nuclear in a heartbeat.''

''What about the offshore islands?''

The Taiwanese Republic of China consisted of Taiwan itself and two small islands, Quemoy and Matsu. While the big island was some seventy miles offshore, the two small islands were within artillery range of the mainland. Several minor skirmishes had been fought over them in the fifties and sixties and they were still extremely vulnerable.

''They can take the islands without too much trouble at all. And probably without Washington doing more than screaming and threatening them with a fleet. I don't think the President would risk going to war for Quemoy and Matsu.''

''Okay, then,'' Kurtzman said, changing tack. ''What should I be looking for if I want to find clear-cut signs of a pending Beijing invasion of Taiwan?''

Katz laughed. ''Remember D day at Normandy? Go get *The Longest Day* out of the video library and watch it a couple of times. Everything you see in the film, except of course for the gliders, is what you'll need to be looking for. And, of course, the amassing of troops. Considering the strength of the

Taiwanese army, about half a million people. If the Reds want to take the island, they'll need to commit at least a million and a half men and have a couple million more in position to reinforce the initial landings."

The Israeli stopped and thought for a moment. "Take a real good look at their airborne units. See if there's sign of increased stockage of supplies, munitions and troop-transport aircraft. See if their fighter bases along the coast have more planes parked on the tarmac than usual. An airborne operation has to have fighter cover. Lastly look to see if the ports in Fujian Province are getting crowded with cargo ships."

He shrugged. "The list is endless. If it goes bang, if someone can eat it or if it can be used to move those things, they'll need to be stockpiling it. That's why it took us two years to get ready for Normandy."

Kurtzman shook his head. It was going to be like counting the grains of sand on the beach from ten miles away, but he had wanted something to keep him busy.

"That's enough to keep you busy for a couple of days, Aaron." Katz smiled. "And I've got to get back to the after-action reports. But let me know what you find."

As soon as Katz left, Kurtzman called his staff together and gave them their assignments.

THE CHINA AIRLINES Boeing 777 was at fifteen thousand feet over the South China Sea, forty miles out on final approach to Taiwan's Chiang Kai-shek International Airport outside of the capital city of Taipei. In the cockpit, the pilot was preparing to land his new-generation jumbo jet. The tension between the island nation and its mainland neighbor had reduced Taiwanese tourism to almost zero. His passengers were either American businessmen with interests on Taiwan who hoped that their presence would calm investors' fears, or native Taiwanese returning to their families.

Though the jetliner was owned by Taiwan's national airline, the command pilot on this flight was an American. The 777 was new to the trans-Pacific routes, and China Airlines was making sure that their own pilots were well checked out before turning the expensive planes over to them. The copilot, a Taiwanese air-force reserve officer, was transitioning well to the state-of-the-art machine and was looking forward to the day that he would fly the left-hand seat.

Thirty miles out from the airport, the pilot put the plane into a gentle turn on his final heading and was talking to his air-traffic controller when the copilot caught a flash of red light from the north. He turned to see what it could be and was horrified to witness the starboard engine explode as if an air-to-air missile had struck it.

Jagged chunks of red-hot steel from the turbine

blades slashed into the wing's fuel tanks. Even after the long flight from Tokyo, the fuel tanks were still half-full, and the JP-4 jet fuel was warm so it was well vaporized and the flash point was low.

When the red-hot metal shards came in contact with the vaporized jet fuel, the tanks exploded. The blast cut through the main wing spar like a knife through soft cheese. With the main spar destroyed and most of the wing's box structure with it, the wing couldn't hold its shape against the forces acting upon it. It folded back inboard of the shattered engine pylon mount, ripped off and fluttered away.

With half of the starboard wing gone, the jumbo jet rolled over onto her back and pitched her nose up. At the speed the plane was flying, the effect was like hitting a concrete wall. In an instant, the 777 went from being a graceful flying machine to breaking apart in midair.

The passengers barely had time to scream before they were falling from the sky.

THE AIR-TRAFFIC controllers at the international airport were stunned to see the inbound China Airlines 777 suddenly drop off their radar screens in what looked like a shower of green sparks. One minute the jetliner had been on a textbook final approach, and the next it had been multiple returns plunging into the South China Sea.

A Taiwanese air-force search-and-rescue chopper was immediately scrambled from the airbase at

Sungshan to look for survivors. As soon as the Sikorsky S-70C had been vectored into the area where the 777 had been last seen, it started to circle. It made only half an orbit before the pilot noticed a bright red spot of light appear in the sky to the north. His finger was clicking the switch to his radio mike to report this strange phenomenon when the helicopter exploded around him.

The chopper's demise was also seen on radar, and an urgent warning was radioed to the second machine that had been dispatched. It, too, barely reached the crash zone before it suddenly disappeared from the screen.

After the second chopper was destroyed, the red light from the north winked out.

The Taiwanese navy had also been alerted when the jetliner went down, and they immediately dispatched a pair of fast patrol boats to the area. By the time they reached the crash site, there was little in the water except for debris and floating bodies. No one had survived the crash of the three aircraft.

AARON KURTZMAN WAS cruising through the raw-data feed from the American reconnaissance satellites over China when he came erect in his wheelchair as if he had been shot. One of the U.S. Air Force's Sky Watch nuclear-alert satellites had just sounded an incident alarm.

Running the tape back, he saw that the satellite had just detected a high-intensity energy flash in Fujian Province. He frowned when he watched the replay and checked the readouts. It was the kind of flash that usually accompanied a nuclear detonation. But this one hadn't been the result of a nuclear explosion.

He knew what one of those looked like. The last time he had seen one had been a few years back when the Israelis had secretly tested one of their warheads in the empty-wasteland test area of South Africa. He had also seen the recordings of the last of the Red Chinese aboveground tests. Regardless of the fact that the satellite had automatically sent a nuclear-incident notification to the National Command Center, this wasn't what had transpired.

For one, this energy flash was in the red spectrum, not the blue white of dying atoms giving up their electrons. Plus, by running the tape at a slower speed, he saw that the flash almost appeared to be linear. In other words, this wasn't a flash; it was a beam of light. And a beam of light bright enough to set off the nuclear-detonation detectors in one of the Sky Watch satellites could only mean one thing—a high-energy laser.

The problem was that he didn't know of any laser in the world that had produced enough energy to create that kind of reading.

He was puzzling through this when Huntington Wethers called out from his workstation on the other side of the computer room. "Aaron, the Taiwanese just lost three aircraft. The first one was a China

Airlines commercial jetliner, and the second two were rescue helicopters that had been sent to investigate the first crash.''

A sudden sinking feeling came over Kurtzman. ''Where did this happen?''

''Off the northern end of the island, on the approach to Taipei.''

Clicking onto a map of the region, Kurtzman marked the position of the energy flash the satellite had picked up. It was some fifty miles inside the coast of Fujian Province, slightly north of due west from the island of Taiwan.

He swiveled his chair to face Wethers. ''I just got a nuclear-detonation alert from one of the Sky Watch nuclear-detection birds. The flash was in a direct line with that crash site.''

When Wethers didn't respond immediately, he added, ''I think we have a serious problem.''

CHAPTER TWENTY

Cheyenne Mountain, Colorado

Immediately upon receiving the nuclear-event notification from the Sky Watch satellite, the Air Force's National Command Center in Cheyenne Mountain, Colorado, got ready to go to war. The first thing they did was to flash a Def Con Three message to America's nuclear-response forces. All across the nation, Air Force crews scrambled to prepare their bombers and missile-launch stations. At sea, the Boomers gliding along at five hundred feet below the surface came up to launch depth and checked their positions with the GPS satellites as they readied their Trident III missiles to fire.

The message that accompanied the Def Con Three alert was simple—"Confidence is high"—but those three words sent chills through anyone who was cleared to know what they really meant. They meant that World War III could be starting at any moment.

As they scrambled to respond to the threat, Air Force and Navy officers and NCOs cursed the end of the cold war. The lessening of tensions between the United States and the once powerful Soviet Union had dulled the razor's edge of America's nuclear retaliatory forces. In the congressional defense-budget cuts of the past half decade, training had been cut back, as had the men and equipment needed to keep the first-strike forces at the top of their dangerous game. And this was a game where anything less than the very best spelled a national disaster.

The so-called peace dividend had gutted the armed forces to pay for social programs, and now they were paying the price. If this was the Big One, they couldn't afford to be behind the power curve. The nation's survival depended on it.

As part of the stand-down of America's nuclear forces, the bombers were no longer on airborne alert and the missiles in the silos were no longer preprogrammed to hit their targets. It was true that it didn't take very long for the bombers on ramp alert to be scrambled or for the missiles to be reprogrammed. But what wasn't "very long" in a peaceful world could be fatal in the opening moments of a nuclear war.

If the balloon had actually gone up this time, the first nuclear-tipped missiles would be falling on West Coast American cities in thirty short minutes, and half of that time had already passed.

By the time that the bombers were in the air and the missiles had been retargeted, the National Command Center reevaluated the threat and lowered the alert status to Def Con Two. After the initial flash, the Sky Watch birds hadn't recorded any launch plumes from known Chinese missile-launch sites, and there had been no bombers seen taking off from their airbases. There had only been that one flash.

Nonetheless, the nuclear-strike forces remained at Def Con Two for another six hours before being recalled to their bases.

AARON KURTZMAN WASN'T the only one to look more closely at the Sky Watch tapes and come to the conclusion that he was looking at the energy flare of a gigantic laser. It took a little longer for the NRO and the Air Force to come to that intuitive conclusion, however. Disbelief played a big part in that lag.

Ever since their invention, lasers had been touted as the ultimate weapon of the future. It never happened. While laser beams worked well in the clean, dry air of the laboratory, they didn't fare as well in the real world of the clouds, dust, smoke and rain of a battlefield. As early as the seventies, lasers had been designed that could punch through any known armor plate at any range that it could be seen—just as long as it wasn't raining or the air wasn't full of the dust and smoke of battle. Since no one could guarantee clean, dry air on a battlefield, the plans for ground-based lasers were quickly scrapped.

Development continued, however, for laser space

weapons. The Star Wars antimissile defense program had included the use of space-based lasers. But once again, problems appeared. This time the hang-ups had to do with powering them. It took gigawatts of energy to create the powerful beams of light that were lasers. Short of using nuclear reactors, no other power source that could fit into the small shell of an orbiting satellite would work. Again the peace dividend killed the Star Wars proposal, and laser weapons went back into the science-fiction category.

Until now.

If the Chinese had fielded a laser weapon powerful enough to shoot down a plane from more than a hundred miles away, they knew something about building lasers that the American weapon researchers didn't. And playing catch-up when you were that far behind would prove difficult.

WHILE THE DEFENSE Department's scientists scrambled to recover the ball they had dropped, Congress got into the act, as well. As quickly as they had acted to impose sanctions on the Taiwanese after the death of the CNN reporter, they were just as quick to lift them.

The congressman who had been so outraged about the death of Ken Cunningham in Taipei didn't speak on the floor in opposition to the new resolution to lift the sanctions on Taiwan and to censure China instead. He was still one of the China-can-do-no-wrong crowd, but he voted with the majority this time. He had seen the handwriting on the wall and didn't want to have to go back to fixing parking tickets and defending drug scum in his hometown.

As soon as Congress restored its support for Taiwan, they went back to business as usual. The first item on the agenda was to find a place to fix the blame for the Beijing government having designed a successful laser weapon before America had. Three different House and Senate committees announced plans to hold extensive hearings on what the news media was calling the "laser gap."

WHEN THE RESOLUTION to bring Taiwan back into the fold passed unanimously the President's hands were untied, but now he really had them full, as well. He was free to help Taiwan, but he could do that only by going up against the full might of the Beijing government. That wasn't a prospect any President could take lightly, but it was something that had to be done. To do anything less would be to surrender the entire Pacific Ocean to Red Chinese control and domination.

With the blessings of Congress, the first thing the President did was to release the military hardware that had been promised to the Taiwanese. No matter what happened next, at least he could ensure that they would be able to defend themselves. As a first step, the F-16C jet fighters the Taiwanese had paid for, but had been impounded under the sanctions, were released and immediately ferried to the island.

Next the Patriot antimissile batteries that had been approved after the infamous 1996 Chinese missile tests were finally shipped.

As could have been predicted, the Beijing government protested the American arms deliveries to Taiwan. They claimed that they were provocative and counterproductive to the peaceful resolution of the Taiwan question. The Chinese ambassador was recalled to Beijing for consultations, and an ongoing balance-of-trade negotiation was abruptly halted.

On the island nation of Taiwan, the armed forces went on red alert, and martial law was declared.

EVEN BEFORE Aaron Kurtzman's announcement that the Taiwanese planes had been shot down by a Chinese laser weapon was confirmed by the NRO, Hal Brognola was back at the Farm.

On his way to the War Room, he stopped by Kurtzman's computer room. Choosing the least-stained cup lying around the thirty-two-cup coffee maker, the big Fed poured himself a long shot of the industrial-strength brew. If they ever shut down the Stony Man operation, the EPA would have to declare Kurtzman's coffee station a toxic-waste site and send in a cleanup team to decontaminate the area. Until then, though, it would serve to deliver the high-test caffeine he was running on now.

"What do we know about this Chinese laser?" Brognola asked Kurtzman as he took a seat at the head of the conference table.

"Damned little. In fact, we didn't even know that the Chinese were seriously working on laser weapons until now."

"Why not?"

"There's both a short and a long answer to that question," he said. "The short version is that it's a big world out there, and we only have so much time to devote to trying to keep track of it all."

"And the long answer?"

"As you are more than aware, most of the information we work with here comes from our eavesdropping on other intelligence agencies. And even in the age of cyberspace, they get most of their information from field agents on the ground. China, while being the very large nation that it is, has the fewest foreign agents in place of any potential enemy nation except maybe for North Korea. And with so few agents on the ground, no one gets much information out of there."

"In short, no one has been minding the store."

"However—" he raised a hand to stop Brognola's retort "—now that we know what they are up to, we will start trying to use cyberspace to give us what the field agents in China haven't been able to gather."

"How are you going to do that?"

"I'll start by looking through a backlog of information on China's technology imports to try to find anything that can be tied in to this weapon."

Brognola frowned. ''Shouldn't you have been doing that on a routine basis?''

''In the best of all possible worlds,'' Kurtzman replied, ''yes. Realistically, though, when you're dealing with an economy that is expanding as rapidly as China's, it's simply not possible with everything else we have to do. And,'' he couldn't resist adding, ''that's supposed to be the job of the CIA.''

''I'll mention that to the current director,'' Brognola said dryly.

Kurtzman didn't fall for the bait but continued outlining his plan of attack. ''But we'll only be going over just the legal technology imports. When you consider what they've brought in on the sly, there's simply no way that we can know about all of it.

''At the same time, we're running a worldwide search for the whereabouts of high-energy-laser experts. We're looking for someone who's disappeared under suspicious circumstances, died in a house fire or a flaming car crash and whose body couldn't be identified. That sort of thing.''

Kurtzman shrugged. ''All of this, though, is going to take time. How much, I can't tell at this point.''

Even though he knew how Kurtzman and his team worked, Brognola wasn't liking what he was hearing. The clock was running, and his butt was on the line again.

''I've got to tell the President something immediately,'' he said. ''Do we at least know where the laser is so we can start planning to take it out?''

''We don't have it pinpointed,'' Kurtzman replied as he flashed a map of the Chinese coastline on the big-screen monitor and highlighted a range of mountains opposite the island of Taiwan.

''But you can tell him that it is situated in a mountain range in Fujian Province known as the Dragon's Spine. It's about fifty miles inland from the Strait of Formosa and is in a position where it can fire on almost anything on the western side of Taiwan. And, of course, it's also in position to sink any ship that tries to sail through the Formosa Strait.''

Brognola hesitated before taking another drink of his coffee and popped two of his endless supply of antacid tablets. Using chemicals to defuse the coffee before it ate through the lining of his stomach was playing a fool's game, but he had to get the caffeine somehow.

''When will you know exactly where the damned thing is?''

''The NRO is positioning a couple of satellites for a run over this area right now. As soon as the data is in, I should have something for him.''

Glancing at his watch, Brognola closed his briefcase and pushed his chair back. ''I'm going to have to go back to the office now. There's a top-priority meeting of the National Security Council tonight, but I'll be back as soon as you get something from the recon runs."

"I'll let you know as soon as we have it."

MORE THAN 750 miles in space, a Keyhole 11–series spy satellite passed over the Dragon's Spine Mountains in Fujian Province, along China's southern coast. As per its instructions from the National Reconnaissance Office, it turned its digital-photo-imagery cameras on well before it crossed the coastline of the South China Sea. Its six-inch resolution camera was able to detect objects below that were six inches or larger without needing computer enhancement. After running the digital feed through an enhancement program, it could read the headlines of a newspaper from that altitude.

After the few minutes that it took for the Keyhole bird to make its programmed run, the data was encoded, compressed and readied for the transmission back to Earth as soon as an American satellite-relay station came over the horizon.

An hour behind the Keyhole bird, a satellite code-named Indigo followed on the same flight path. This spy satellite, however, used electrooptical sensors that read the reflected energy from Earth's surface in six electromagnetic bands from visible light all the way to infrared. At the same time, it used a terrain-reading radar to plot the earth below so it could index the electromagnetic readings with the terrain features. When Indigo passed the target area, it also encoded its data and prepared for transmission.

In turn, the two satellites came within radio range of the NRO retransmission facility outside of Anchorage, Alaska, and downloaded their stored data. This information was then forwarded to the NRO's National Photo Interpretation Center for processing.

En route to the NRO, the satellite data was intercepted by Stony Man Farm.

Aaron Kurtzman, Hunt Wethers and Akira Tokaido immediately decoded the input from the NRO feed and got to work deciphering what the satellites had given them. The answers were both informative and troubling.

CHAPTER TWENTY-ONE

"We've confirmed that it's in the western end of the Dragon's Spine Mountains," Kurtzman told Brognola the following morning as he flashed a map of Fujian Province on the big-screen monitor. "There's no doubt about that. It's just that we still can't pinpoint its location."

Brognola had flown to Stony Man Farm in hopes of getting some good news, but apparently that wasn't on the agenda.

"It didn't show up on the optical shots," Kurtzman explained, "and we couldn't even find it with the soft imagery scan. I put Akira to finessing the input from the Indigo run, but he couldn't get the pixels to work out to much more than what we were getting from the digital run, and that's pretty much zip."

"If none of you have any objection," the big Fed growled around the cigar stub in his mouth, "I'd like to have these briefings conducted in plain English."

Before Kurtzman could answer, Hunt Wethers

stepped in. The fact that he had spent much of his life explaining things to college students made him a good briefing officer when the information got a little too technical for the nonexpert.

"What Aaron means," he said smoothly, "is that we couldn't find the laser's location with the normal recon satellite runs, so we tried to find it with infrared and radar-imaging data scans. However, though we got a good run, it wasn't much help, either, even after putting the raw data through a computer-enhancement program."

"Why not?" Brognola frowned. "I thought that those NRO birds could spot a quarter from a zillion miles out and tell you if it's heads or tails."

"That's true," Wethers agreed. "They can if the conditions are perfect. But in this instance, we aren't looking for quarters, and the Keyhole birds can't see through the clouds. The area of the Dragon's Spine we've been looking at is one of those few areas on earth that is almost always shrouded in fog. The conjunction of the warm water of the Jian River meeting cold air trapped by the cliffs of the Dragon's Spine creates a—"

Brognola held up his hand to stop the meteorology lecture. "Why can't the radar cut through it, then? Radar can see through fog."

"Yes, it can," Wethers said, "but the soft imagery radar produces doesn't have the resolution of the Keyhole digital photography. In short, even under the best of circumstances, it can't spot that mythical quarter at that distance, nor can it tell which side is facing up.''

''But,'' Brognola protested, ''I've seen the satellite-radar maps they used to target cruise missiles in the Gulf War, and they're were pretty well detailed.''

''Yes, they were,'' Wethers agreed, ''but they're usually maps of flat areas and the targets stand out well because they're buildings or installations standing high above the ground. We're trying to find a camouflaged installation hidden in a very jagged mountain range. Some of the cliffs and valleys there drop five hundred feet or more.

''If we'd been looking at this area for a number of years,'' Wethers continued, ''we might have been able to spot the construction of this installation and mapped any changes it made to the mountain's topography before it was camouflaged. As it is—'' he shrugged ''—we're looking at this area in depth for the first time now and we don't have any baseline data. We can't compare what we're seeing now with how it looked years before.''

''In other words,'' Brognola said, trying to sum up, ''you're telling me that even though you know where this damned thing is, you can't see it.''

''That's about the size of it,'' Wethers admitted. ''From the targets it has hit, though, we think that it's somewhere around the four- or five-thousand-foot range on that mountain, but we don't know exactly where yet.''

Brognola abruptly shut his briefcase and stood. "You'll call me the instant you do find that thing, won't you?"

Wether's expression didn't change. "Of course, sir."

FIFTY MILES INLAND from the coast of the South China Sea, an ancient upheaval of the earth had created a ridge of towering mountains rising to over five thousand feet. Through the centuries, wind and rain had sculpted this mountain range into a series of peaks that ran parallel to the coastline. To someone with a vivid imagination, the peaks could be taken for the backbone of an impossibly huge animal rising from the earth. Some ancient Chinese with just such an imagination had named this series of peaks the Dragon's Spine.

To the Chinese, the dragon was the symbol of creation. In their mythology, dragons had created their country before returning back to the earth that had spawned them. According to the myth, this mountain range was where the last dragon had tried to go back to his beginnings, but had been a little too late and the earth had closed around him. Here for all the world to see was his skeleton rising from the earth toward heaven.

Even though the Communist government that had ruled China since 1949 paid little attention to classical Chinese mythology, the mountains still bore the ancient name on the official maps. And it was here that the People's Liberation Army had sent several thousand political prisoners to a labor camp in the early 1980s.

For ten years, half of the prisoners toiled halfway up the side of the tallest of the Dragon's Spine peaks. The other half toiled at the bottom of the mountain where the Jian River flowed past the mountains on its way to the South China Sea. The men hammered their way through solid granite to create two huge caverns deep inside of the mountain, and when they were done, those who had survived the brutal ordeal were simply executed and their bodies dumped in the river.

Knowledge of what they had built in the mountain couldn't be allowed to get out. Not even the Communist leaders of China could be allowed to know about it. This project was the brainchild of the hardline faction of the People's Liberation Army and was their most closely guarded secret.

The Beijing leadership was committed to the completion of Mao's journey, but there were those in the PLA who didn't think that they were marching quite fast enough. The secret buried in the Dragon's Spine would get things moving at a swifter pace.

DR. LAM WING SAT at a state-of-the-art control console in a brightly lit room deep inside the Dragon's Spine. Under his fingers were the controls for the greatest laser weapon that had ever been constructed. Its first live-firing tests against remote-controlled targets had been successful, exactly as he had expected, and it was now time to change the history of the world.

Lam was Chinese, but he had been born a Chinese American and had received his Ph.D. in high energy physics at MIT. A man of his academic skill could have worked at any high-energy physics lab in the world, but for a number of reasons he had chosen to return to the land of his ancestors to create the greatest land-based weapon the world had ever seen.

Growing up in a prosperous Chinese community in southern California, Lam had enjoyed a happy childhood with his fully Americanized family. His father ran a large landscaping and gardening service, and the family lived the life of the prosperous American middle class. Lam had excelled in high school and dreamed of becoming a famous scientist, but when he applied for college in his senior year, he ran into one of the academic realities of the 1990s.

Though his grades were in the top one percent of the entire state of California, Lam had been denied entrance to the honors college at UCLA because the "quota" for Asian students had been filled. In the name of cultural diversity, the slot that should have been his by merit had been given to a Hispanic applicant. Not being hampered by California's cultural-diversity rules, MIT's honor school had been glad to take him, but that meant that he would have to be thousands of miles away from his close-knit family.

It had been during Lam's first year of graduate school that a marauding gang had cut off his father's car on the freeway and sent it crashing into a bridge abutment. The gang pulled in behind the wreck and looted the bodies as they lay bleeding. When they were finished stripping the car, one of the thugs threw a lit cigarette into the gasoline flowing from the car's ruptured fuel tank.

Though severely burned, Lam's younger brother had been blown clear of the wreck and lived long enough to tell the police what had happened to him and his family. He died the day Lam arrived home.

The destruction of his entire family at one blow staggered the young man. He had been raised to think of the United States as the great melting pot, a land of opportunity for hardworking immigrants. That might have been true at one time, but it wasn't that way anymore. The death of his family had shown him that America was a land of barbarism, and it was getting worse every day.

Over his family's graves, Lam vowed that he would continue his studies and complete his Ph.D. to honor them. But he also vowed that he would never use his mind to benefit the country that had killed his family. China was a nation that didn't allow a murderous rabble to prey on its citizens. He would return to the land of his ancestors to work so that the family he would someday have wouldn't die at the hands of marauding barbarians.

The summer after Lam graduated as one of the most honored high-energy physicists in MIT's history, he vacationed in Hong Kong. He never returned to the United States. A body wearing his clothing and carrying his identification was fished out of Kowloon Harbour a few weeks later and, when not claimed, was cremated.

Six months later, the People's Liberation Army sent the first labor convicts to the militarized zone in Fujian Province that surrounded the Dragon's Spine Mountains.

HIGH-ENERGY LASER WEAPONS were nothing new; test models had been in operation as early as the seventies. But as had been quickly discovered, one of the things that most limited a laser's effectiveness was the size of its power source, and a laser's destructive power was directly related to the amount of power that went into it. The nuclear generator built into the lower level of the mountain provided unlimited ultrahigh-voltage power for Lam's weapon.

The other limiting factor of a laser's effectiveness was the size of the crystal that focused the photons that turned harmless light into a coherent destructive beam. In the usual high-energy laser, the crystals were cut from synthetic rubies and the synthetic gemstones could be grown only so large. Lam's creation also used a ruby as the crystal, but it wasn't man-made.

The crystal that was the heart of this weapon was a gemstone from the mists of Chinese antiquity. No one knew when and where it had first been discovered. It was first known, however, from a surviving court-jewel inventory dating back to the Chou dynasty of the third century B.C. Over the centuries, dynasties had risen and fallen, but the Dragon's Heart, as it had been named, had somehow survived.

When the Western world brought turmoil to China in the early decades of the twentieth century, the giant ruby dropped out of sight for a while. Some said that it had been in the safekeeping of a Triad leader in a hidden shrine to the old gods of China. It resurfaced during the Cultural Revolution of the 1960s and fell into the hands of the hard-core Maoist faction of the PLA.

Not burdened with the mythologies of old China, the Communists valued the gem for its scientific value, not as the crystallized heart of one of the legendary dragons of creation. When Lam defected to Communist China and set up his high-energy-laser program for the People's Liberation Army, he proved to his PLA superiors what could be done with a laser powered by such a ruby. It had been given to him to experiment with.

Over the twenty-three centuries that the ruby had been in existence, many men had tried to polish the Dragon's Heart to make it even more magnificent.

The results of their efforts had resulted in a stone that was a perfect, unblemished ovoid resembling a large bloodred football. The shape was so perfect for Lam's purposes that he had only to polish a few thousandths of a millimeter off one side to make it completely symmetrical.

Better than its perfect shape, though, was the fact that the ruby was completely unblemished. There wasn't a stress crack or even a single fleck of free carbon in the matrix, as was commonly found as flaws in most natural rubies. This stone was a clear bloodred from one end to the other. Light could pass through it completely unimpeded and come out the other end pure, coherent high energy.

When Lam's initial tests of the ruby brought results even better than he had expected, the Ruby Dragon Project was planned. While the mountain was being excavated, he had finalized the design of the greatest laser weapon the world had ever seen.

From its camouflaged position close to the four-thousand-foot mark of the mountain, the Ruby Dragon had a direct line of fire to any target on the western side of Taiwan. Unfortunately the island was cut by a north-south mountain range that shielded the eastern side. But both of Taiwan's largest cities, Taipei and Kaohsiung, were easily within range. So was anything that approached the island through the air or over the sea.

As soon as he was given the order, Lam was prepared to completely isolate Taiwan from the outside world, then utterly destroy it. He expected, however, that it wouldn't have to come to that. He didn't think that he would have to destroy more than a few square miles of Taipei before the so-called Republic of China surrendered and was incorporated back into greater China.

Lam didn't fear that anything would get in his way of carrying out his plans. The laser was buried deep in the mountain, as was its nuclear power plant. Except for nuclear weapons, nothing known to mankind could disturb his well-camouflaged creation. The rugged topography made it doubly difficult to spot the small, camouflaged firing apertures, so it couldn't be targeted with guided smart bombs or cruise missiles.

The only way the Ruby Dragon could be destroyed would be if the United States started a nuclear war with China and used their largest thermonuclear weapons against the mountain. But as Lam knew full well, not even a nuclear war could prevent China from fulfilling the destiny Mao had planned for her.

CHAPTER TWENTY-TWO

Even with the frantic attempt to locate the laser taking up all of her time, Barbara Price hadn't forgotten that Bolan and Phoenix Force were still in Taiwan. They had been ready to come home, but with the skies over the island closed to commercial air traffic, they had been stranded. When Bolan's scrambled radio call came in, she went to the communications room to take it.

"We're ready to try to get out of here," Bolan told her. "Jack's worked up a wave-top evasion route that he thinks will keep us out of the line of sight of that weapon."

"There's no need to risk that yet," she answered. "Hal wants you to stay there in case he needs you."

"For what?"

"He'll let you know after we locate that weapon."

"If we're going to sit around here waiting on Hal," Bolan said, "I'm going to activate my Triad contacts again and see if they can help us with some information. I know that they run smugglers into the mainland on a routine basis, and they might know something about the region around those mountains.''

''That's a good idea,'' Price replied. ''I know Aaron's been complaining about the lack of Intel coming out of China. Apparently, over the past few months a dozen or so deep-cover agents have failed to report in, and he thinks that Beijing's on a massive rat hunt.''

''I'd be, too, if I were them,'' Bolan said. ''And speaking of Intel and agents, is anything coming together about who's behind this thing?''

''All we're getting out of Beijing is that they don't know anything about any laser weapon. The President even gave them tapes of that initial Sky Watch notification that sent the National Command Center into a panic. They claim that there's nothing in those mountains but solid rock.''

''But they're not about to let an inspection team in to take a look.''

''Right. They say that it's in the middle of a restricted military region since it's so close to Taiwan.''

''What better place to have a secret weapon than in a restricted area?''

''If there's nothing else,'' she said, ''I have to run. Hal's riding us pretty hard.''

''Give him our regards and tell him that we're ready if there's anything we can do to help.''

''Will do.''

"WHAT KIND OF CONTACTS do you have with the mainland," Bolan asked Tung Wu when he visited his office, "particularly with Fujian Province?"

"I do have contacts," the Triad leader admitted. "Certain goods move between the island and the mainland."

Bolan smiled at Tung's comment. Smuggling was a time-honored Triad activity, and tons of material crossed the Strait of Formosa every month. Manufactured goods went to China in exchange for raw materials, spices and foodstuffs. It was a profitable trade and well worth the risks.

"I need to talk to anyone who knows anything about the region around the Dragon's Spine Mountains."

Tung's dark eyes fixed him for a moment. "That is a serious undertaking, Mr. Belasko. The mountains are in the middle of a military zone."

"I know," Bolan replied. "That's why I need firsthand information about it."

"I will see what I can do."

TO THE TAIWANESE government, not only had the renewed American arms deliveries bolstered their defenses, but they had bolstered their confidence, as well. They were prepared to fight to the last man on their own in a last-ditch effort to keep their island from Communist domination. But knowing that their old cold-war partner was still on their side was just as helpful.

Now that they believed they weren't facing immediate invasion, the Taiwanese military also wanted to know the location of the laser that the media was calling the Ruby Dragon. They didn't have any deep-space spy satellites to do their looking for them. But they did have two high-flying Lockheed U-2R spy planes on hand that could pass over Fujian Province and take a quick look with their sophisticated sensors and cameras.

While the U.S. Air Force had operated the famous Lockheed spy planes out of Taiwan for years, these were the first top-secret U-2s that had ever been turned over to a foreign government. The recent U.S.-Chinese treaties had restricted American aerial spying on Beijing's territory. But, as part of the unprecedented deal with Washington, Taipei had agreed to share any information it picked up with their new spy planes.

THE HANGAR AND RAMP lights at the Tainan air base at the southern end of the island had been turned out so the dull black U-2 could be towed onto the runway without prying eyes spotting it. After a final check with the pilot in the cockpit, the special J-75 P-13 turbine was fired up. In seconds, the jet's afterburner sent a twenty-foot tongue of flame shooting out as it quickly accelerated the plane down the runway. With its huge wings, the U-2 was airborne after traveling a mere hundred yards.

Immediately after taking off, the U-2 turned to the

southeast, away from China, but kept at wave-top level to stay off the powerful Chinese radars. After flying two hundred miles, the pilot started an upward spiral, climbing until the U-2 reached its usual operational height of sixty-five thousand feet. Then it turned west, heading for the huge land mass of mainland China, the lair of the Ruby Dragon.

The Taiwanese U-2 spy plane was at sixty-five thousand feet when it crossed the Chinese coastline some two hundred miles south of the Dragon's Spine Mountains and turned east.

Major Ye Chee triggered his U-2's onboard cameras and sensors as he started his run over the target. At his sixty-five-thousand-foot altitude, he knew he was safe from interception by any of the Red Chinese jet fighters. Though the Reds had built up a sizable modern air force, they didn't have anything in service that could operate as high as he was flying.

His only concern was that a radar-guided, air-launched missile from one of the J-8 Fantail interceptors could reach him. The R variant of the U-2 that he was flying had a small ECM suite, but it wasn't as effective at blocking radar lock-ons as the electronic countermeasures equipment on aircraft like the Stealth bomber.

It was possible for the Reds to get a radar lock on him, and if that happened, he would just have to suck it up and die. At its operational altitude, the U-2 flew a unique profile. Because of the thinness of the air and the limited power of the plane's jet engine, the U-2 flew on the edge of a stall. Evasive maneuvering to escape a missile wasn't an option. He also didn't have IR decoy flares or other defensive systems to protect him.

In fact, the U-2's sole defense was the altitude it flew at, and Ye had no doubt that it would protect him from the laser, as well. The China Airlines 777 jetliner that had been shot down had been flying at only fifteen thousand feet. He was over three times that high.

"WE HAVE A TARGET approaching, Dr. Lam," Colonel Ng Lo announced. "The long-range radar has picked up a high-flying spy plane that took off from Tainan airfield on Taiwan and is approaching our location."

Though the Ruby Dragon was Lam's creation, the People's Liberation Army claimed it for their own, and the site was operated completely under military authority. Ng was in command of the site and took his orders from the hard-line faction in the army high command headed by General Pei. Lam was a genius, which was probably why he wasn't interested in politics and didn't involve himself in the factionalism that was so much a part of life in China's Communist elite. He didn't care which faction he worked for as long as they left him alone to pursue his work.

"Do we have a radar lock-on?" Lam asked the

PLA officer seated at the console next to his. As powerful as the Ruby Dragon was, it was only effective if the laser beam hit the target. To direct the laser's fire, equally powerful radars had been installed on the mountain and fed their targeting information into a state-of-the-art fire-direction center built from smuggled American computers.

"Yes, Comrade," the officer replied. "The tracking radar has acquired the intruder and is tracking it. It is coming into range now."

Lam's fingers flew over his Hong Kong–made keyboard as he readied his weapon to fire. First he brought the nuclear reactor from standby to full power. A faint hum could be felt as the turbines came up to speed, sending megawatts of power through conduits the thickness of a man's body. Next he opened one of the firing apertures that had been camouflaged to look like a jagged rock face when it was closed.

When the camouflaged door was rolled out of the way, the laser's gun carriage moved forward into its firing position like any conventional cannon. The gun carriage had been converted from a Russian 230 mm antiaircraft gun mount, but the traversing and elevating mechanisms were now computer controlled, using servos that had been developed for the space-shuttle program.

The weapon on the old antiaircraft gun mount looked nothing like any artillery piece anyone had ever seen except in a science-fiction movie. Where the breech of a conventional cannon would have been was the housing that held the ruby. Instead of ammunition feed trays, power cables the size of a man's thigh were connected to it to send millions of volts into the exciter to create the blue white light. More power cables fed the coolant system that kept the ruby from melting down under the heat. The barrel itself was rather short and was made from an ultrahigh-temperature refractory material polished to mirror brightness on the inside and ringed with coolant tubes on the outside.

Once the gun carriage was locked into firing position, a few taps on Lam's keyboard linked it to the targeting radar. Since a laser was a pure line-of-sight weapon and fired at the speed of light, there was no need for a ballistics program. The radar simply pointed the laser at the target, and it would be hit.

When the diamond-shaped pip came up on Lam's firing control, he hit the firing-sequence button.

The whine of the laser was too high-pitched for the human ear to hear, but it could be felt even through solid rock. No humans were allowed in the Dragon's lair because the heat and radiation would instantly fry them. But had eyes been able to see, it would have looked as if a bloodred sun had burst into existence and then sent a finger of red light lancing into the moonless sly.

The light winked out a second later, but that was all it took.

EVEN AT SIXTY-FIVE thousand feet, Major Ye Chee saw the bloodred flash reach up for him at the speed of light. For a brief moment, he thought that he felt the heat of an impossible sun burn through his helmet visor.

An instant later, the high-flying U-2 spy plane ceased to exist as a unified structure. The plane's matt black fuselage skin glowed, then blew out as the oxygenated jet fuel in its internal tanks flashed into vapor. At the altitude it was flying, the U-2 didn't so much explode as simply turn into a fireball.

LAM'S FACE WORE a satisfied smile when Colonel Ng reported that the radar indicated that the laser had scored another direct hit. He had expected nothing less, but it brought a rush of pleasure anyway.

"Now that the Taiwanese are challenging us," Ng said, "General Pei wants you to move into the second phase of the operation immediately. Are you ready?"

Lam took a deep breath. When this night's work was over, his name would go down in history as one of the giants of Chinese history. His descendants would be honored for all time for simply sharing the blood of the man who had given China domination over all of Asia.

"I am ready," he said simply.

"Good. I will send the message to the fire-control radar to start locating your targets and downlinking the information. As we planned, we will start with the shipping in the strait."

Not only was the Ruby Dragon's laser breath death to aircraft, but the powerful beam was also capable of punching through steel plate as well as thin aluminum. It took longer for the laser beam to penetrate, true, but not that much longer. In the blink of an eye, the Ruby Dragon could cut through a ship, and the Strait of Formosa was full of ships.

The seventy-mile-wide channel between Taiwan and the Chinese mainland was a major shipping lane. On any one day, millions of tons of commercial shipping sailing between Japan, Hong Kong and other South China Sea ports made the passage. This night was the same as any other, and the Ruby Dragon's targeting center marked more than a dozen targets before Lam locked on to the first one and fired.

The first target was a VHC crude-oil carrier, a supertanker, loaded with millions of barrels of Middle Eastern crude oil bound for the ever hungry refineries of Japan. With the altitude of the Ruby Dragon's lair overcoming the curvature of the earth, it was a direct line-of-sight shot to the huge ship.

Although it was night, not even the bridge watch noticed the red beam that slashed out of the darkness of mainland China until it was too late. Even had they noticed it, there was nothing they could have done. The laser's beam hit above the waterline, and the resulting explosion tore off the bow of the supertanker as if someone had taken a chain saw to it.

Flaming oil lit the night sky, and other ships in the area responded to the tanker's frantic SOS calls. Most of them didn't make it more than a few miles before they, too, were destroyed. Leaving half a dozen hulks burning, the Ruby Dragon looked for more prey.

Not all of the ships that were targeted exploded like the tanker had. Only those that were carrying petroleum products or were so unfortunate as to have had the laser hit their fuel bunkers burned. Others simply sunk when gaping holes had been blown into their hulls. Dozens of men scrambled into lifeboats and abandoned their dying ships for the shark-infested sea.

By the time dawn broke, seventeen merchant ships had been sent to the bottom of the Strait of Formosa. Not since the height of the submarine-warfare days of World War II had so many ships been sunk in such a short period of time. Almost a hundred crewmen from a dozen nations were clinging to lifeboats and debris, still not sure what had happened to their ships. Many of the lifeboats were equipped with rescue beacons or radios, though, and the men were confident that come morning they would be rescued.

IN THEIR HIDDEN LAIR deep inside the mountain, Colonel Ng and Lam Wing waited patiently. The radars served as their eyes and let them know what was going on in the Strait of Formosa. With the break of day, the first of the search-and-rescue choppers and planes appeared to look for survivors among the floating wreckage,

As soon as the skies were crowded with aircraft, the Ruby Dragon came out of her mountaintop lair and breathed fire once again. A dozen planes and helicopters were quickly added to the carnage in the strait.

CHAPTER TWENTY-THREE

A weary Hal Brognola took a packet out of his briefcase and laid it on the table in the War Room. "The President has tried to handle the China crisis through diplomatic channels, but it isn't working this time."

That wasn't news to anyone seated around the table. The attack on the shipping in the Strait of Formosa had sent the world into deep shock. Beijing's response to this storm of criticism was typical. First they denied having anything to do with the attacks, then the leadership prepared to go to war.

The President of the United States had no choice but to respond in kind. The military was put on a permanent Def Con Two alert for the first time since the fall of the Soviet Union.

Everyone knew that if a political solution was in the works, Brognola wouldn't be talking to them now. Stony Man Farm was a monument to past diplomatic failures, and they only went into action when the diplomats failed again.

"Even after he gave them the evidence from the NRO satellites," Brognola explained, "the Chinese flatly denied having any kind of laser weapon. They have also denied having anything to do with the destruction of aircraft or shipping in the Formosa Strait. They say that all of this is an American plot to increase tension over Taiwan."

Brognola shook his head. "That's a completely asinine explanation for what is happening, but it's typical of Beijing's thinking lately. British Intelligence has developed information that there is a hard-line faction within the central government that wants to go all out this time. Apparently they feel that now Hong Kong is coming back under their control, they want to go for it all, win or lose, and are determined to take Taiwan.

"Obviously the President cannot allow this to happen. He has ordered a nuclear-armed-carrier task force into the South China Sea to show the Chinese that we aren't going to let them take the island."

"Does he think that a fleet is going to make them back off?" Katz asked. "If they get within range of that laser, they'll get blown out of the water."

"He's hoping that it won't come to that," Brognola replied. "He's hoping the weapon can be taken out with ship-mounted cruise missiles like we used on the Scud launchers during the Gulf War."

"They would work, of course," Katzenelenbogen said, "but you'd have to mount nuclear warheads on them to do it. And even then, for them to be effective, we're back to having to know exactly where the laser is. And by exactly I mean within a dozen yards or so."

"Why wouldn't a ton of high explosives work like it did on the Baghdad command bunkers?" Brognola asked.

"To start, this mountain range isn't concrete like the bunkers of Iraq. It's solid granite just like Cheyenne Mountain, and the laser is buried somewhere in it. Plus, the way the rock is folded and fractured, even using ten- to twenty-kiloton warheads, you'd have to hit within a couple hundred yards of it to guarantee knocking it out."

"You're telling me that the only way to destroy this thing is to start a nuclear war with China?"

"That's about it," Kurtzman stated. "And I think that the Pentagon planners are going to tell him the same thing."

"That isn't going to be acceptable."

Kurtzman shrugged. "It is, however, a fact."

"What about Mack and Phoenix?" Brognola asked. "Is there any way we can send them in to deal with it?"

"Not if we want them to come back alive," Katzenelenbogen stated flatly. "To start with, the target is fifty miles inside China in an area that's crawling with troops. The military buildup in Fujian Province makes the D Day preparations look like a Boy Scout outing. Even if we could get them on the beach and through the fifty-odd miles, they'd still have to climb a mountain, get through whatever security they have at the site, blow it up somehow and then walk back to the South China Sea.''

He shrugged. ''As David would say, it's not too bloody likely.''

''Plan for it, though,'' Brognola ordered. ''The President is going to want options to an all-out nuclear war with China. He's prepared to go to war with them if he's forced to, but no President wants to go down in history for that.''

''That is completely understandable,'' Katz said dryly, ''since the chances are that he'd lose.''

Of all the nations on Earth, China was the only one that could go through a nuclear war and come out of it still able to function. They could lose five hundred million people, almost twice the population of the United States, and still have five hundred million people left over to clean up the mess left behind.

There were those who even wondered if the Chinese leadership was pushing for an all-out war exactly for that reason. They could devastate the United States and still be left the most powerful nation in the world. From that point on, it would be easy enough for them to ensure that no nation ever became powerful enough to challenge them again.

''Since the final decision to go to war hasn't been made yet,'' Brognola said as he closed his briefcase, ''I would like to bring an alternative to the table for discussion, and I'm counting on you people to come up with one I can present. If you can think of anything that might defuse this crisis, I want to know about it immediately.

"Until then, I'll be in Washington trying to keep this from going nuclear. So think hard, people, and come up with a way out for the Man. It's never been needed as much as it is right now."

WHEN TUNG, the Triad businessman, called him the next morning, Bolan didn't know who he would be meeting. But from the Triad leader's tone of voice when he asked Bolan to come with him, it had to be someone important.

Once again Shan picked him up and drove him to a small village on the west coast of Taiwan, an hour's drive from the capital city. Tung was waiting when the car pulled up in front of a large Chinese-style house, and Bolan stepped out.

"What's going on?" the big American asked.

"There is someone here who wants to talk to you," Tung stated.

"Who?"

"He wants to tell you himself. But I swear that there's no danger to you. Please follow me now."

Sensing that Tung was sincere, Bolan followed him through a wooden gate that led into a walled garden.

"At the end of the path," Tung said. "I have to wait for you here."

Bolan followed the twisting path and, around the first corner, saw a man in black Mandarin robes waiting for him. The man was old, but it showed more in his manner than it did in his face. This man could have been seventy or 120; he couldn't tell just by looking at him. There was something about him, though, that told him that his true age was closer to the latter than to the former.

When Bolan got closer, he saw that the man's eyes were clear and youthful, but there was a depth to their darkness. There wasn't an ounce of fat on his body, but he wasn't frail. Power emanated from him like the glow from white-hot steel.

"I am Cam," the man said simply when Bolan stopped in front of him.

"I know who you are," the Executioner stated. He didn't need to see an ID card to know that he was talking to a legend. Cam was the leader of the Golden Dragon Triad, the man who so long ago had brought the petty criminals of China under his control and formed the first modern Triad. He was the grandfather of all the godfathers.

"And I you," Cam replied, smiling thinly.

Bolan didn't doubt that. The Executioner had operated against drug-smuggling Triads from the very beginning, and their sources were almost as good as Kurtzman's. The difference was that Cam used humans instead of electrons to compile his information.

"Why did you ask to meet me?" Bolan said, coming straight to the point.

"I am here to help you with your quest to still the breath of the Ruby Dragon."

"Why do you want to help me?"

"What is happening is bad for China," Cam said simply. "She must come into the new millennium and take her proper place among the nations of the world. But to do that, there can be no war. China's Communist leaders do not want to give up their power, and they see war as a way to keep it. But power without responsibility is no power at all. They have grown arrogant, and their eyes are closed to the future."

Bolan could only agree with that sentiment. If more Chinese thought the way this old man did, it would be a much more secure world. Now that the Soviet Union was gone, China was quickly becoming the new Evil Empire.

"Your people are youthful barbarians," Cam stated. "But you have the strength of youth. You also have the welfare of the people in mind. But you will strike hard at China if the Communist leaders go ahead with their foolish plans. The destruction would be terrible, and it would take many years to recover, years where many would die and many more suffer.

"In addition," Cam added, "they should not have used the Heart of the Dragon for this evil purpose."

"What is the Heart of the Dragon?" Bolan asked politely.

"When the last dragon died and went back to the

earth," Cam explained, "his heart wanted to remain behind so it could guard the Han people and guide them to greatness. When the first emperors rose, the Dragon's Heart revealed itself to them and it became an honored part of the Imperial household. For all these years, a man of wisdom has been appointed to be its guardian."

Cam sketched a brief bow. "When the palace fell, it was my honor to become the guardian of the Dragon's Heart for many years, and I kept it safe from the eastern barbarians when they attacked our land. I also guarded it when Mao Tse-tung's army's marched and drove the eastern barbarians back to their island."

Bolan didn't point out that the United States had had something to do with the defeat of imperial Japan. This was Cam's story.

"After Mao's death, when the children who had been raised with no knowledge of who they were took power in the name of the Cultural Revolution, the Dragon's Heart was taken from its sanctuary. I was away when this happened, and when I returned, the Dragon's Heart had been captured by the Communists. They have had it since then, but they have not learned wisdom from it. Instead, they are using it to power their weapon."

"The Dragon's Heart is a ruby?" Bolan's mind made the leap to identification.

Cam's ancient face cracked in a smile. "It is a ruby like a whale is a fish."

His hands sketched a shape a little larger than a football. "It weighs ten of your kilos. It was flawless as only a dragon's heart could be, a single crystal of bloodred hue, pure and with great power from the heart of the earth."

"And they are using it in the laser," Bolan finished for him.

"Yes," Cam barked. "They have taken the guardian of the people and have turned it into a weapon of destruction that is being used against other Chinese. This is not what the dragon intended to be done with his mighty heart. His heart is for all Chinese to benefit from no matter where they live. Even those who have gone to the Golden Mountain, as we call your country."

Cam studied him for a moment. "I know who you are, Mack Bolan, and the wind tells me that you will be sent to destroy the Ruby Dragon before it is allowed to start a war."

"More than likely, yes," Bolan answered honestly.

"If that is so, you must promise me this one thing."

"What is that?"

"When you destroy this weapon, you must return the Dragon's Heart to the earth. Some day, when the people are wiser, it will return again and will be used for good instead of evil."

Bolan wasn't into mythology, Chinese or otherwise, but he had to agree that the old man had a good idea. A ruby that large would always be a source of trouble of one kind or another. "If it is at all possible, I promise that I will see that it is done."

"In exchange," Cam said, "I will see that your quest is successful."

The old man reached into a hidden pocket in his black robes and pulled out a plain red-lacquered box. Inside was an old ivory chop, the carved stamps that were used to serve as a man's signature in Chinese culture. No Chinese document was considered legal if it didn't have the chop of the official issuing it. This chop was cracked with age, but had a fine dark ivory patina.

"Do you know what this is?"

"It's a chop."

"It is my chop," Cam said, "and it carries my authority throughout the Middle Kingdom. Even those in the People's Army know my mark. When your quest is finished, you will return it to me."

"Of course." Bolan nodded.

Cam then produced a large oilskin packet. "In here is a map showing the location of all of the military units in Fujian Province. I have indicated several routes that will take you to the mountains that hide the Ruby Dragon. I apologize that I do not have information about the mountain itself. Every man I sent has failed to return.

"After you have studied this, tell Tung what you need and when you will need it, and it will be done for you."

"Thank you."

The old man's eyes flashed. "Remember that you must send the Dragon's Heart back to the earth."

"I will do my best."

THE MEN OF PHOENIX FORCE crowded around Bolan when he showed them the box containing Cam's personal chop and explained what the old man had promised.

"That thing sounds like the ultimate 'get out of jail free' card," James said with a grin. "At least for this part of the world."

"You know," he added, "I'll bet that you could go into any bank in Hong Kong and clean out the vault simply by flashing that chop."

"What happens if we lose it?" Manning asked.

"We had better be dead by then," Bolan said dryly. "Otherwise, we would be shortly thereafter. This isn't a government-issue item to be dropped alongside the trail or stuffed into our rucks when this gig is over."

"Bummer," James said. "I was looking forward to taking it to Hong Kong with me."

"In your dreams."

After going over Cam's map in detail, Bolan headed for the fax machine. "I'm going to send this to Katz and tell him that we've found a way for us to get in at that thing if we have to."

CHAPTER TWENTY-FOUR

Mack Bolan's call to tell Yakov Katzenelenbogen that he had been guaranteed a safe passage to the Dragon's Spine Mountains put the Stony Man team back into the game. Now that there was a feasible way to get the Stony Man team in place, the Israeli warrior could start thinking of something useful for them to do when they got there. And when it came to planning strategy, there wasn't a better man than Aaron Kurtzman to bounce ideas off of.

"I think that I've figured out a way to pinpoint the weapon," Kurtzman said when Katz walked into the computer room.

"How's that?" Katz asked as he poured himself a cup of coffee. The fact that the spy satellites hadn't been able to spot the laser rankled him as much as it did Kurtzman. Until they could pinpoint the laser, all talk of taking it out was meaningless.

"I'm going to need a little cooperation from the NRO and the Air Force again, but I think I know how to do it right this time."

"Okay, I'll bite. How?"

"I'm going to send over a couple of satellites, particularly ones with SAR sensors, while I set up an aerial target for the bastards to shoot at. When they shoot it down, the SAR birds should be able to triangulate its location."

"That's not a bad idea." Katz made an intuitive jump. "But I've got a better one. How about having our guys in place as a back-up when you try it. That way if the spy birds fail to pick it up like they did before, our team can spot it from the ground and mark it with a ground-target designator."

"That would work," Kurtzman admitted. "But you know what it's like in that region. Like we told Hal, the place is crawling with thousands of troops. They'd never make it in close enough to get a visual on it."

Katz quickly explained what Bolan had told him about Cam's offer to get him to the site if he would destroy the laser.

"Do you think that we can trust this ancient mystery man?" Kurtzman asked. "Walking through half of the People's Liberation army armed only with a piece of carved ivory sounds a little off-the-wall to me."

"Striker trusts him," Katz stated. "And he's the one who's got his ass on the line. If we can get a pinpoint target grid, the Navy might be able to put a Tomahawk right down the barrel of the weapon."

"It would sure as hell be safer than having them try to go in there and blow it up."

"Do you want to run this one past Barbara?"

Kurtzman's fingers were already moving over his keyboard. "I'm on it."

BARBARA PRICE FOUND Aaron Kurtzman sitting on the front porch of the main farmhouse as he waited to hear from Brognola about the new plan.

"Would you like to take a stroll through the orchards?" she asked as she walked up behind him.

"Sure," he said, knowing that she was using that as an excuse to talk to him away from the farmhouse. The Farm's grounds were completely saturated with sensors and pickups, and everything they said outside would be recorded; she knew that as well as he did. But, it would feel more like a private conversation than if they spoke inside the farmhouse.

She took the push bar of his wheelchair and started down the ramp. Kurtzman was more than able to wheel himself anywhere he wanted to go—his arms had the strength of an old-time blacksmith's—but he knew that she liked to do it for him. They had worked together for a long time, and they knew each other's mind well. He also knew what she wanted to talk to him about.

As she headed for the edge of the orchard, she looked off at Stony Man Mountain looming in the distance over the fertile valley. "This sure is a nice place," she said wistfully. "Sometimes I think how nice it would be to retire here and grow tomatoes or raise chickens. I'd hate to see it blighted by a nuclear winter."

"We're right in the fallout zone if Washington ever gets hit," he stated matter-of-factly. Considering that the capital was a certain target in any all-out-war scenario, he had always wondered why the Farm had been placed where it was. Probably it had been done for ease of travel from the seat of power, Washington. For security, they should be somewhere in the wastelands of Montana or New Mexico.

"Thanks Aaron." She leaned down and hugged him.

"What did I do?" He was surprised but pleased by her gesture.

"You're my reality check around here," she said. "I can come to you, and you'll gently remind me of how things really are in the world. And you'll tell me even if I really don't want to hear it. I need that sometimes so I don't drift off into the same fuzzy fantasy world that the rest of the country seems to live in. Even in this line of work, it's tempting to think that things are the way you want them to be instead of how they really are, warts and all."

She took a deep breath. "I strongly recommended to Hal that the President approve your plan to give Mack and Phoenix Force a chance before he sends in the Navy. As long as there's any option to a nuclear war, no matter how risky it might be, I think we owe it to the world to at least give it a try."

"The good of the many outweighs the good of the few," he said.

"Where's that line from, anyway?" she asked.

"I'd have to look it up," he said. "I don't honestly know."

"It's a good line. It ought to be our motto."

"Better than it being our epitaph."

"I didn't need that much reality, Aaron."

He didn't smile. "Just doing my job, ma'am."

YAKOV KATZENELENBOGEN had a full Pentagon-style dog-and-pony show all ready to go when Hal Brognola showed up for the briefing. Copies of all of the maps and briefing papers were ready for him to take back to the Oval Office when he left, but it would help for him to hear it himself before he explained it to the Man.

After letting Kurtzman explain his plan for the aerial target and the satellites, he got into the role the Stony Man team would play on the ground.

"Considering the havoc the Ruby Dragon has caused to surface travel in the Strait of Formosa, we'll need to borrow a submarine again to send them in. They'll launch from a couple of miles offshore and Scuba in the rest of the way. Their extraction will be a SEAL boat pickup on the coast."

"I can lay on the sub and get the Navy's fullest cooperation," Brognola promised.

There would be no problem this time getting Bolan and Phoenix Force all the military backup they would need. Not when the cards were all face up on the table and the nation was preparing to go to war. Plus, with tensions as high as they were, it probably wouldn't make any difference if it was discovered that the military was involved in a Stony Man operation. If it worked, it could always be written off to something or someone else.

If it didn't work, though, it simply wouldn't matter one way or the other.

"I've talked to Bolan about his mainland contact, and he's confident that he'll be able to get within visual range of the mountains, a couple of klicks or so. Then, with the navsat GPS gear and laser target designator, they should be able to get a fix on that weapon if the satellites screw up again."

"They'll stay in the area until the cruise-missile attack is made, then conduct a damage assessment. At that point, we'll decide what, if anything, they'll do after that."

He took a deep breath. "If need be, we'll then send them in to try to cripple the weapon. But, the go or no-go call will be made then."

There was no comment to that. Everyone at the table knew what it meant if they got the go call. It would be a suicide run, a last sacrifice to try to prevent the unthinkable from happening.

"Lastly," Katz said intently as he laid his laser pointer on the table, "I want to go to Taipei and brief the team in person this time. I want to go over every last detail with them and make sure that every possible contingency has been thought of before they're sent out.''

Usually the Stony Man staff didn't go into the mission area. There were several reasons for this prohibition, most of them having to do with security. For Stony Man to operate the way it did, its very existence had to remain unknown to all but a very small, select handful of people. Were Bolan and Phoenix Force to be discovered in the field during one of their operations, they could always be discounted as a mercenary force, Company contract men or even black-ops personnel. To have one of the Stony Man principals caught, however, would be difficult to explain away.

''I know that's outside of the Stony Man doctrine,'' Katz said when Brognola didn't immediately answer him, ''but this isn't a normal situation even for us. China isn't one of our usual operational areas, and it presents unusual dangers for the team.''

''You can go, Katz,'' Brognola said. ''I'll clear it with the Oval Office. But, I'm going to Taiwan with you.''

''Why?''

''Like you said, this isn't our usual mission. We're facing the end of the world as we know it, and I, too, want to make sure that we've done everything we can do to prevent it. This may be the last Stony Man mission, and I want to be on hand for it.''

''You're the boss.'' Katz shrugged. ''You can

come if you want. I'll be leaving from McCord AFB the day after tomorrow on a C-141 for a nonstop."

"I'll get the President to sign off on this and try to catch up with you before you leave. If I don't make it, though, don't wait for me. I'll catch the next flight."

"Just make sure that your pilot is well versed in nap-of-the earth flying. To keep out of the line of sight of that laser, he's got to stay under the horizon all the way in."

"I'll remind him."

David McCarter and Mack Bolan met Hal Brognola and Yakov Katzenelenbogen when their C-141 Starlifter landed at Sungshan airbase. Now that the two countries were on speaking terms again, military flights were coming in every day.

"How was the flight?" McCarter asked.

"Very interesting," Katzenelenbogen said. "I didn't know one of these ships could fly from wave top to wave top like a fighter. The guy behind the wheel must be an out-of-work fighter jock."

"Actually," Brognola said, pleased to see the unflappable Israeli war horse caught off guard for once, "he was the flight leader of the Thunderbirds not too long ago."

"That figures."

Bolan turned to Brognola. "Do you want to check into your rooms first?"

The big Fed shook his head. "That can wait. We need to get this show on the road ASAP."

"I've got a secure briefing room set up in our survey company's office," Bolan said.

"That'll do."

BROGNOLA LOOKED GRAVE when he stood to address the men of Stony Man. "Gentlemen," he said, "in two days, a U.S. Navy task force will attempt to make passage through the Strait of Formosa. As you know, Beijing has declared that area a contested zone under international law, and they say that any vessel attempting to enter the zone will be fired upon. Our position is that the Strait of Formosa is international waters and that any attempt to restrict our passage will be viewed as an act of war."

McCarter slowly shook his head. "Bloody hell."

The other warriors were silent. War was their business, but their wars had been fought to avoid the ultimate war, the nuclear nightmare. Usually, even though the stakes were high, they worked behind the scenes. Going to war with the shadow of a nuclear holocaust looming over their heads put things in a new perspective.

"Isn't there some way to just knock the bloody thing out and let it go at that?" McCarter asked. "Send in a Stealth bomber, or something like that, and do what you Yanks like to call a surgical strike?"

"Actually," Katz said, "that would be our first choice if it weren't for the fact that we simply don't know exactly where the thing is. The satellites haven't been able to pinpoint it."

"Stony Man has come up with a way to pinpoint it, however," Brognola said, "and the President wants me to ask if you gentlemen will try to carry it out."

Katz quickly went over the plan to send in the decoy target to draw the Ruby Dragon out of its lair and to have the Stony team in place to mark the target if the satellites couldn't find it again. "There is a cutout built into this," he said. "Once you're on the ground, if it looks like there is no chance of your getting into the target, you can abort. This is not to be a suicide mission."

"But," McCarter asked, "if we can mark it, you'll hit it with a cruise missile, right?"

"One way or the other," Brognola answered evenly, "that weapon has to be taken out of action."

"But using nuke-armed cruise missiles means starting World War III with China, doesn't it?"

Brognola met his gaze squarely. "Yes, it probably does, doesn't it? It hasn't been this serious in a long time, gentlemen, but the President can't afford to let them get away with this. If Beijing is able to pull this one off, the world's going to be a pretty sorry place."

All of the men around the table understood that well.

"How are we going in this time?" Bolan asked.

"By submarine," Katz answered. "With the Ruby Dragon controlling the skies, there's no way we can get you in by a paradrop or even a surface ship, for that matter."

"That means swimming, doesn't it?" Hawkins asked.

"We can't bloody well ask the Navy to drive us up onto the beach," McCarter quipped.

"I was afraid of that."

"What's the matter, man?" James asked. "Don't you like swimming?"

"I don't mind a dip at the swimming hole, old buddy, but I'm not much for Scuba gear."

"Piece of cake, as our glorious leader says. I'll show you everything you need to know."

"Wonderful!"

"When's our launch time?" McCarter asked.

"You've got twenty-four hours," Katz said, "and that includes the sub ride to the beach."

"So when do we board?"

"The USS *Seawolf,* a nuclear attack boat, will be entering the harbor in another hour or two. You can board any time after that."

Katz's gaze went from one man to the next. "If there are no further questions, gentlemen, it's time to get ready."

He looked at Jack Grimaldi, who was sitting in on the briefing. "And I need to talk to you, Jack. I have something useful for you to do, as well."

"Outstanding. I was starting to feel like the Lone Ranger around here."

CHAPTER TWENTY-FIVE

The Formosa Strait between China and Taiwan wasn't a good place to play underwater hide-and-seek with a deep-diving nuclear attack sub like the USS *Seawolf.* The bottom of the strait was dotted with seamounts, the greatest of which was the island of Taiwan itself. In other places, the bottom was far too shallow for normal submerged operations.

Captain Bud Burton swore under his breath as he plotted a course through the deepest channel leading to the coast of Fujian Province. Burton was an old-fashioned submariner who had started his career back when there had been no Boomers, the ballistic-missile-firing behemoths that got all the press nowadays. He had first served in one of the early nuclear attack boats, the USS *Sturgeon,* and had devoted his entire service career practicing what submarines were so good at—killing other submarines.

Now he was a four-striper, the Navy's foremost authority on attack-submarine tactics and the commander of the first Seawolf-class attack boat. This was the world's most advanced antisubmarine weapon, and he had been ordered to take his boat into harm's way on a mission that had nothing to do with killing enemy submarines.

Task Force Shield was less than forty-eight hours away from its run through the Formosa Strait and the beginning of World War III. The task-force commander had orders to enter the strait with a MiG Cap in the air and the strike aircraft positioned on the catapults fully armed with war loads. A war load, in this case, meant nuclear weapons. The USS *Seattle* would also make the run with the Tomahawk cruise missiles on her launch racks fitted with war loads.

If the Chinese laser fired on them or any of their aircraft, the task force commander had orders to return fire, and World War III would immediately commence.

Burton didn't know the details of the mission he had been tasked to support, and he had no idea who the six men were that he was transporting. But he didn't have to be a rocket scientist to know that it was somehow aimed at trying to prevent the holocaust. That didn't mean, however, that he liked anything about what he was doing.

"Is that as close as you're going to be able to get us to the shore?" Mack Bolan asked when he looked at the end point of the plot the sub man had marked on the nav computer.

"This isn't some air-sucking, coast-hugging, diesel pig boat, Mr. Belasko. The *Seawolf* draws a lot of water under her hull, and I'm hazarding her by coming that close in. And, yes, that is the best I can do for you."

"I didn't write your orders, Captain," Bolan retorted bluntly. "And just for the record, I would rather have had a diesel pig boat take me and my men in. But your boat is what they gave me, so I guess we both have to live with it, don't we?"

Burton looked away as he sucked back an angry retort. He didn't know who this Belasko guy was, but his orders had been specific about his authority, and they had come directly from the chief of naval operations. Until Belasko and his men departed, the mystery man was in complete command of everything that didn't have to do with the routine operation of his submarine. Belasko had complete mission control and could order the *Seawolf* piloted up onto the beach if he had a mind to.

The captain didn't understand why a Navy SEAL team wasn't being sent to China to do whatever these men were going to do. At least that way, there would be an established chain of command to follow, and he wouldn't have to put up with this crap. This smelled like a CIA operation to him, and if there was anything he hated it was spook games. But if he wanted to keep the stripes on his sleeve, to say nothing of his command, he would do exactly as he had been ordered, which was to follow Belasko's lead.

If the mission went sour, though, he was ready to

testify at the board of inquiry that would want to know why he had hazarded the most expensive submarine in the world. He would explain that a nuke attack boat wasn't a landing craft and that not even orders from the President could turn it into one.

After checking the plot again, Bolan glanced at the clock in the plot room. "If you can get us there, Captain, we'll be able to make it ashore just fine."

"That I can do."

"I'll be up forward with the team."

"WE'RE COMING UP on the launch point, Captain," the navigation officer said half an hour later.

"All engines stop. Maintain navigating speed only."

"Aye, sir."

"Mr. Belasko," Burton said into the intercom to the forward torpedo room, "we're at the launch point. Are your men ready to disembark?"

"Yes, sir."

"I'm going to come up to periscope depth to take a look around first."

"Just give us the word."

Bringing the boat up to periscope depth, Burton raised the scope to take a look at the coastline five miles away. It was raining heavily, and the wind was running at least twenty-five knots. It was nasty, and he didn't like being dead in the water. An attack boat lived by her speed, and the *Seawolf* was barely making headway. Balancing the six-thousand-ton displacement of the submarine against the currents and the weather in the strait required a delicate touch. Nuclear boats weren't designed to spend much time close to the surface, and their round hulls made them wallow like the proverbial round-bottomed boat.

When he didn't see anything threatening on the sea or shore, he ordered "Down scope" and marked their position.

"HERE'S YOUR FINAL PLOT," the chief petty officer in the torpedo room told Calvin James.

James fed the numbers into the inertial guidance unit that he would use for the swim to the beach. "It's locked in," he said, looking at Bolan, "so we're ready to go."

The Stony Man warriors were outfitted with Navy SEAL-issue black wet suits, fins, masks and re-breathing gear. Their weapons, ammunition and equipment were strapped to their bodies. With all the weight they were carrying, they hardly needed any extra weights on their diving belts.

"Let's do it," Bolan said.

After making a final check of everyone's equipment, James was the first to go into the escape hatch. Once he was in the water, the ex-SEAL stayed by the opening in the sub's hull to help the others get out and orient themselves in the darkness. To keep from losing anyone on the long swim to the beach, James had all of the swimmers tied to him and one another with nylon cord. It made swimming much more difficult, but it ensured that no one would get lost. Anyone who got lost this night would be lost forever.

As soon as they were all hooked up, he signaled and they started to swim away from the *Seawolf*. They had to be at least a hundred yards away from it before its screw started to turn to make sure that they were not sucked up in the prop wash.

"TORPEDO ROOM ALL CLEAR, sir," the chief petty officer called up to the bridge.

"Get us under way immediately, Mr. Williams," Burton growled at the engineering officer. "I want deep water under my hull."

"Aye, aye, sir."

Burton headed for deep water and took the *Seawolf* down until he could no longer feel the effects of the waves above. His boat was safe now, and he had time to think of Belasko and the five men he had left in the water. He had no use for spooks, but he wished them Godspeed anyway. No matter what they were, they were Americans and they were sure as hell going in harm's way.

HAD IT NOT BEEN for the inertial guidance unit Calvin James was using to navigate, the Stony Man warriors would have surely been lost at sea. Even at a depth of twenty feet, the wind and currents turned the water into a giant whirlpool. But as bad as it was on the way in, it became almost impossible when they reached the shallow water of the surf.

The wind was rising, and the surf pounding the beach made it almost impossible for the men to get out of the water without being smashed by the surging waves. Leaving the others hugging the bottom sand beyond the surf line, James tried his luck first. Before he went, he took a roll of nylon mountain climbing rope from his pack and handed one end to McCarter.

After fighting his way through to the beach, he finned his way well above the surf line before turning around and digging his feet into the sand. Taking a firm grip, he tugged on the line, signaling for the others to follow it to shore.

"Leave on your gear," James said when he pulled McCarter out of the water first. "I haven't seen our guy yet, and if we don't find him, we may have to abort."

McCarter nodded as he caught his breath and tugged on the nylon line to indicate that he was safely ashore.

As soon as everyone was out of the water, they broke out their weapons, loaded up and set a perimeter around their beachhead. The instructions were that Hang, their Triad guide, was to show a light every fifteen minutes for a two-hour period. It was a long quarter hour before Hawkins spotted a faint light a hundred yards farther in.

"I've got him," he said over the comm link. "He's on our right front, about a hundred yards."

"I've got him, too," McCarter stated. "Go out and bring him back. We'll cover you."

"I am so sorry," the man said in English when Hawkins escorted him to the beach. "The waves made me have to wait back here and not on the beach."

"That's okay," Bolan told him. "Where's your truck?"

"Not too far away."

THE TRUCK WAS ONE of the Red Chinese copies of the Korean War–vintage U.S. two-and-a-half ton GMC. They were rugged vehicles and well suited for China's primitive road networks, so they were still in production. Hang's vehicle looked as if it dated back to the war itself, but there was no way to tell how old it was, only how much use it had seen. It did have the canvas cover over the bed, however, so they could ride out of sight.

The six commandos climbed into the back of the truck, and Hang started out. After a slow half hour on the badly rutted road, he pulled the truck over and walked around to the back.

"The first People's Army checkpoint is just up the road," the driver said. "Just stay quiet and there will be no problem."

"They won't search the truck?" McCarter asked.

"Oh, no." Hang smiled. "They know that I am a smuggler, and I always bring them things."

The PLA troops at the checkpoints were used to seeing Hang's truck. He was a frequent traveler, and he always had a 'gift' for them each time he came through—cigarettes, audio tapes, batteries. In another country, these would have been called bribes, but since good Communists didn't accept bribes, they were gifts. By any name, though, they ensured that none of the guards bothered themselves with looking into the back of his truck.

Nonetheless, the Stony Man team readied their silenced weapons just in case. It was nerve-racking to have to sit and listen to a conversation that they couldn't follow. They could tell, however, that it was a good conversation. Hang was laughing at what could only be jokes, and everyone was having a good time.

"Damn!" Hawkins said quietly as Hang finally got back in the cab and drove off. "I thought that guy was never going to stop talking."

"As long as he was talking, we were okay," Encizo commented. "If he'd have stopped, we'd have been in trouble."

The next two checkpoints posed no problem. Hang stopped and swapped jokes with the guards, handed out his gifts, and then drove on. At the last checkpoint, however, there were complications.

None of the Stony Man warriors spoke enough Chinese to understand what was going wrong, but they could hear Hang arguing with the soldiers. Hearing at least three voices other than their driver's, McCarter pulled his Beretta 93-R and getting James's and Encizo's attention, mimed screwing on a sound suppressor. The three men prepared their pistols and were ready to take out the guards when they heard the footsteps of two men walking back to the truck.

Hang was talking pleasantly, and they heard the other man's gruff answers as he opened the passenger-side door and got into the cab. When James mimed shooting the soldier, McCarter shook his head. He didn't want to get blood in the cab. He looked over to Encizo and mimed choking himself. The Cuban nodded and took the nylon-cord garrote from the side pocket of his combat suit.

Hang knew that the Americans would have to do something about the unwanted passenger in the cab and purposefully drove slowly. Like the old GMC it had been copied from, the truck had a canvas top with a button-in plastic window in the rear. The window was missing, and all that separated the Stony Man commandos from the two Chinese in the cab was the canvas flap of the cover over the bed.

Motioning for James to lift the flap, Encizo readied his garrote. The roar of the unmuffled engine masked any sounds as James lifted the flap, exposing the back of the passenger's head. The soldier felt the draft, though, and was turning when the Cuban slipped the nylon cord over his head. With a twist of his hands, the knot in the middle of the cord bit into the soldier's neck. Another, harsher twist broke his neck.

The minute he slumped dead, Hang slammed on the brakes. "He was a sergeant," he explained, "and he wanted me to take him to his girlfriend's house in the next village."

"Is anyone going to miss him?" McCarter asked.

"I don't think so," the driver replied. "I could tell that the other soldiers didn't like him, and they will think that he is staying with his woman."

"We'll take him with us and dump him later."

AN HOUR LATER, as the sun was coming up, Hang stopped the truck. "This is as close as I can get to the mountain," he explained. "The road turns away from it here."

"How far away is it?" McCarter asked.

"Only about fifteen kilometers."

That was only a three-hour walk if they didn't have to dodge too many patrols.

"I will wait with you here," the driver said, "until the man comes who will guide you the rest of the way."

It was light enough to see the distant mountains when a young Chinese man wearing peasant's clothing walked up to the truck. Hang got out to meet him and they exchanged passwords.

"These are the honorable long noses that Cam spoke of," Hang told the man in the Fujian dialect when he took him around to the back of the truck to meet the Stony Man team. "You are to do anything that they ask of you. Anything."

The man bowed at hearing Cam's name and turned to Bolan. "I am Chin," he said, "and I am honored to serve you. I must ask, though, to see the chop of Ancient Cam."

Bolan took a square of rice paper from his breast pocket and, unfolding it, handed it to Chin. The Chinese glanced at the red-ink imprint and stiffened in respect.

"It is true," he said in English, his astonishment evident. "And you, a foreigner, have actually talked to him."

"Yes, I have," Bolan confirmed. "And he told me that you would guide us to the Dragon's Spine Mountains."

Chin sucked in his breath past his teeth, the Chinese sign of expressing respect. "Yes, I can," he said proudly. "The soldiers will never see us."

"Let's go, then."

CHAPTER TWENTY-SIX

For a facility as critical to the plans of the Beijing hard-liners as the Dragon's Spine laser site was, it wasn't very well protected. After having passed through massive troop concentrations on the road in, Bolan had expected the area directly around the mountain to be crawling with guards and weapons emplacements. But the closer they had gotten to the mountain, the fewer troops there had been. It was as if the hard-liners didn't trust even the men of the People's Liberation Army to keep their great secret.

Whatever the reason that it was left unprotected, the Stony Man team's job became a lot easier. By early afternoon, they had reached a small hill overlooking the Jian River, which separated them from the mountain, and McCarter called a rest halt.

"What I don't understand," Manning muttered as he scanned the base of the mountain with his field glasses, "is how in the hell they're powering that thing."

"What do you mean?" Hawkins asked.

"There are no power lines running up to the

mountain. Lasers eat up a lot of power, and one that big should use a hell of a lot of it, gigawatts in fact. I would've expected at least a couple of sets of high-tension power lines feeding the thing."

"You're right," James said. "I wonder how the Bear's people missed that little point."

"They were probably too busy trying to figure out a spectacular way for us to get ourselves killed this time."

Bolan had overheard the interchange and turned to Manning. "How would you power the laser if you were doing it?"

"Well, since money is apparently not a limiting factor around here, I'd probably build a small nuclear plant on-site and hide it in the mountain. Or with the river running close by it like that, they might have diverted some of the water to run a turbine. Why?"

"I was thinking," Bolan mused, "that if it comes down to it, we might be able to take out the power plant and save everyone a lot of trouble."

"You've got a point," Manning agreed, "particularly if they're using a nuclear plant. The Chinese build most of theirs to the same specs as the old Chernobyl plant. I think the Russians called it an R-43. And if they built one of those things here, we could easily slag the core and that would be the end of it."

"How long would it take them to repair it and go back on-line?"

Manning shrugged. "Ten thousand years, give or take a few hundred, if we can slag the core. That's how long it's going to take for Chernobyl Number Four to cool off enough to be rebuilt."

"That should do it."

"If they're using a nuclear plant," Manning reminded Bolan.

"I guess we'll have to get closer to see for ourselves, won't we?"

"Actually," Hawkins said as he looked at the towering, jagged peaks of the Dragon's Spine, "I was kind of hoping that we wouldn't have to get that close to it. I'm content to admire that thing from a distance. A good distance."

"Get real, T.J." James said with a grin. "You've been working with us long enough by now that you know we always get up close and personal when we do our thing."

"A man can dream, can't he?"

AN HOUR LATER, the team had reached a point half a mile from the river that provided them a good view of the eastern face of the mountain range, the side of the towering peak that hid the Ruby Dragon's mouth.

McCarter looked over at the mountain. "T.J., can you light that place up from here?"

Hawkins nodded. "We're close enough to get an accurate reading now."

"Get ready to do it, then. I'll let them know that we're in place."

Hawkins readied his Army-issue laser target designator while Manning took a GPS reading to get the exact location of where they were within a nine-foot radius.

Normally a laser target designator was used to "paint" or "illuminate" a target with its low-powered laser beam so that it could be seen by the guidance system of a smart bomb or a cruise missile. The weapon's guidance system would then lock on to the laser's reflection and follow it to the target. That meant, however, that the laser had to be trained on the target continuously until the weapon struck. Even so, the system worked well and had been used extensively in the Gulf War, where it had been responsible for many of the mobile Scud launcher kills and all of the bunker hits.

This time, though, the Stony Man warriors wouldn't stay in place to light up the target, not when it was scheduled to be hit by a nuclear warhead. The target designator was being used in conjunction with the GPS to get a dead accurate fix on the target. That fix would then be sent by sat-link to the Task Force Shield's missile cruiser and would be used to program the cruise missiles that would deliver the opening salvo.

And when that took place, the teammates would need to be miles away.

McCarter looked around their hiding place with a

professional eye. They hadn't seen any troops since the last checkpoint, and there were no signs that patrols were working the area. But it was always the guy you didn't see who kicked your ass. "Rafe, how about you two setting up a little flank security while we wait?"

"Got it covered."

WHILE HE WAITED for Stony Man to give them the word that the decoy was coming into range, Manning examined the vista in front of him with his field glasses. He was particularly interested in the veil of mist that seemed to hang over the river. Rather than just hanging over the water at random, it seemed to have a point of origin as if it were being artificially created.

Suddenly it hit him what could create a fog like that, and he called McCarter over to his position. "Do you remember the Bear saying that this place was fogged up all the time, and he was having trouble seeing through it with the optical satellites?" he asked.

McCarter nodded.

"I think I know why it's always foggy here, and it's a dead giveaway to how they're powering the laser. They have a nuclear plant in the mountain, and they're using the river as a heat sink for the cooling water. Dumping the hot water in the river creates the mist."

The Chinese weren't unaware of the capabilities

of the American spy satellites that kept a close, unblinking eye on their vast nation. They knew that the deep-space spy birds could read a change in temperature on Earth's surface as small as ten degrees. If they had simply dumped the hot water from the reactor's heat exchanger into the river from one large opening, it would have shown up on the infrared scans like a searchlight. Diffusing the heat by using several openings would keep the heat signature to a minimum and create a fog.

"This also answers the question of how the laser is able to shoot through the fog without the beam being diffused. If they just shut off the hot water and wait a few minutes, the constant wind should clear the fog pretty quickly. The rest of the time, the fog can hide the details around the base of the mountain from our aerial observation."

One of the main reasons that lasers hadn't been more widely used as weapons was that clouds, rain or fog tended to scatter the beam, breaking up the coherent light. In the simplest sense, a laser was nothing more than a powerful light beam, and moisture in the air blocked light very effectively. A light rain or even thin morning mist could render the weapon almost useless.

The Chinese hadn't been able to revise the laws of physics when they designed their Ruby Dragon, but even the laws of physics could be bent. They simply built the biggest laser that had ever been conceived and had hooked it up to a nuclear power plant so it would have unlimited power to drive the beam through any kind of weather.

It was an Oriental use-a-bigger-hammer approach, rather than being a Western-style technical breakthrough, but it was still effective.

"Good work," McCarter said. "I'll pass that on to the Farm."

AARON KURTZMAN HAD ALMOST the entire resident Stony Man team crowded into his computer room to watch the results of the decoy flight. The flight wouldn't be a success unless the information that had been leaked about it had been received by Beijing and would be acted upon. But that was something that they wouldn't know until they saw if their bait was taken and the Ruby Dragon roared.

If it didn't work, they wouldn't be able to try it again. With Task Force Shield on its way into the South China Sea, they would have to fall back on Plan B. The problem with Plan B was that it was nuclear war.

"Are you in contact with Mack and Phoenix?" he asked, turning to Hunt Wethers.

"They're on the sat-comm radio."

"Tell them that it's coming within range."

"Roger."

IN THE CORNER of the geological-survey-company office leased by Bolan in Taipei, Jack Grimaldi was sweating bullets as he flew an empty Boeing 727 jet through a TV-camera hookup. He had jumped at the chance to do it since he had been left behind and didn't like being left out of the action. Nonetheless, this was one of the most difficult flying jobs he had ever tried to pull off.

The screen in front of him showed a split view of the 727's instrument panel on one side and a view out of the cockpit on the other. He had everything at his command that an actual pilot in the airliner would have had to work with. The only problem was that the satellite link to the plane's flight controls had a split-second delay in it. The delay wasn't much now because the plane was so close to his transmitter, but he still had to anticipate his control inputs so the flight would appear as smooth as if he were actually on board.

Now that the 727 had come over the curvature of the earth, he dived the plane to almost wavetop level as if he were trying to get under the enemy's radar. Under the circumstances, that's what any pilot who knew about the laser would be doing and he didn't want to make it too easy for them. That would be a dead giveaway that the flight was not what it had been advertised to be—a planeload of American scientists en route to talk to the Taiwanese authorities about the Ruby Dragon.

A target that important would be difficult for the Red Chinese to pass up.

KURTZMAN FOLLOWED Grimaldi's masterful piloting on his own monitor screen. The time lag was greater in his case because the signal from the on-board TV cameras had to be sent up to a satellite, then bounced back down to Virginia several thousand miles away. But since he wasn't trying to fly the plane, the delay wasn't as critical for him as it was for Grimaldi.

"The spy satellites are coming into position," Wethers announced as he watched the data flash across his own screen. "We're ready to record whenever they decide to kill that plane."

The NRO had brought a pair of Vega-series birds into position to monitor the 727's flight. These satellites had SAR capability along with radar-image mapping that should be able to do the job. As a backup, they also had wide-angle infrared sensors on board that were usually used to track missile launches. Even though the laser beam wasn't as hot as a missile exhaust, it should be hot enough to register on the sensors.

Backing up the satellite's detectors, the 727 had been fitted with several additional sensors that were designed to lock on to the laser beam in a split second. Once they had it, they would transmit a bearing in the microsecond before they were destroyed along with the rest of the plane. These devices had never been tested in this role before, but John Kissinger and Gadgets Schwarz had both guaranteed that they would work in this application.

Between the satellites and the on-board detectors,

they should be able to get an azimuth to the laser and a detailed map of the terrain. And that was all they needed to pinpoint its exact location for a cruise-missile strike.

"That should do the job," Wethers said. "They'll have to be able to hit it when this is done."

"If they decide to shoot at it," Akira Tokaido reminded him, "rather than sending in our guys."

"Bite your tongue," Kurtzman snapped. He didn't need to be reminded of what was riding on this.

"GET READY," Manning said as he focused his field glasses on the mountain. "Something's happening up there."

"Where?" Hawkins asked.

"Azimuth 309, almost halfway up, a little over four-thousand-foot elevation." He read the numbers off the digital readout he could see through the lens of the field glasses.

Hawkins looked through the optics of the laser designator and fed in the azimuth and elevation. "I think I have it. An opening some ten yards across and about five high right under that overhang?"

"That's it."

For several minutes, nothing happened at the opening in the mountain. And had Hawkins not seen the opening appear as the camouflage was rolled back, he would have thought that he was looking at a shadow cast by the huge cliff above it. It was no wonder that the spy satellites hadn't been able to spot it from deep space. Looking down, all they would have seen was the overhang and not what was under it.

Suddenly, an impossibly bright finger of bloodred light lanced out from the opening in the mountain. Almost before the image could be registered it was gone, leaving just a retinal imprint behind.

"Jesus!" Hawkins said as he rubbed his eyes. "That was quick."

"It doesn't take long when you've got a nuclear reactor powering your giant laser," Manning replied. "All it takes is a single poof and you've blown the target out of the sky."

"One way or the other," Hawkins stated, "we've got to stop that thing. Our Navy flyboys won't have a chance against it when the task force rolls in."

"You've got that right."

CHAPTER TWENTY-SEVEN

Jack Grimaldi didn't have a screen at his remote-piloting console that showed him the decoy plane's on-board laser detectors. It was believed that he would have enough to do just trying to fly the plane without having to worry about that, as well. Therefore, when the Ruby Dragon locked on to the low-flying Boeing 727 and fired, it caught him completely by surprise. One second he was concentrating on flying right at the tops of the waves, and the next, the screen in front of him went blank.

"Jesus!" the pilot gasped as he wiped the sweat from his forehead.

"Congratulations, ace," Yakov Katzenelenbogen said with a grin when he saw the screens blank out. "You just got your ass shot down again."

"Man, that's quite a feeling. Usually when I get shot down, at least I know that it's coming. This just came out of nowhere and zapped me."

"How do you think those poor bastards in that airliner felt?"

"Do you think it worked?" Grimaldi asked.

"We ought to know in a few minutes," Katz replied. "It'll take that long for them to transmit the data to the Farm."

IN THE RUBY DRAGON'S control room, Lam smiled to himself as he powered down his weapon. Once more he had struck a blow against the Yankee imperialists for his ancestral land. He felt nothing for the twenty-three scientists he had been told were on board that jetliner. Some of them might have even been men that he had known at his old university, but that had been in a life he no longer recognized.

He was all Chinese now, not some bastardized half American, half Chinese. Anyone who threatened his country in any way was his enemy, and he would destroy them if he could.

"I do not think the Yankees will try anything like that again," Colonel Ng stated, allowing the trace of a smile to cross his face. "The island is completely cut off now, and when the fleet comes, we will destroy it, too."

Lam was well aware that the Americans had assembled a fleet and intended to run the strait between Taiwan and the mainland to test China's resolve. That the arrival of the fleet would coincide with the first of the planned attacks on Taiwan itself was fortuitous and fit well into the hard-liners' plans he would carry out. Not only would he destroy half of the city of Taipei, he would deal the Americans a heavy blow at the same time.

The fleet's presence was proof of American arrogance, and had been the typical response to China since the gunboat days before World War II. This time, however, it wouldn't work. This time China wouldn't have to cower from the threat of an American fleet. This time the naval threat would simply be blasted to the bottom of the South China Sea. The Ruby Dragon would see to that.

And while Lam was blasting the American Navy out of the water, he would remember the land of his birth and would remember the insults and injuries he and his family had suffered at the hands of Yankee barbarians.

"WE GOT IT to within ten yards," Hawkins announced. "If they can hit that mark with a Tomahawk or a smart bomb, they can't miss taking it out."

"Send it," David McCarter said.

Using the uplink on the sat-comm radio, Hawkins sent the target-designation data to Stony Man Farm.

"They sent us a confirmation," Hawkins said a few minutes later. "They have it."

"Smash that thing and bury it," McCarter said, nodding at the laser target designator. "There's no point in carrying the extra weight."

"Are you sure we won't need it later?"

McCarter looked across the river at the forbidding

mountain looming over them. "Not where we're going if it didn't work the first time."

Hawkins followed his leader's gaze to the jagged cliff and peaks across the river. He'd done his share of mountain climbing with the Rangers, but he'd never had to tackle anything as formidable as this. Hopefully the missile would take care of it, and he wouldn't have to try. No matter which way it went, though, if he survived this gig in one piece, he'd definitely have something to tell his grandchildren.

Now that the first part of their job was done, the Stony Man warriors settled in to wait for the decision to be made about the missile strike. If the attack was made, the Farm would want them to do a post-strike assessment, a BDA as it was known. Only then would they know if they were finished with the Ruby Dragon.

It had been raining on and off ever since they had hit the beach, and it started to pour steadily now. They hadn't brought wet weather gear, but rain was a minor issue in a warrior's life and they were hardened to it. For now, nobody was shooting at them, and for now, they still had a future.

AARON KURTZMAN SAT BACK in his wheelchair and smiled as he saw the graphics form on his computer monitor. "Got ya!" he said, grinning broadly.

The feed from the first NRO birds was turning into a low-angle view of the topography of the peak on the west end of the Dragon's Spine. The graphic was so detailed that each peak and valley stood out as clearly as if it had been mapped by a team of surveyors. By the time that the graphics program reached the base of the mountain, though, Kurtzman's triumphant expression changed.

"Damn it!" he exploded. "They built the thing under an overhang. That's why we haven't been able to see it before."

"What do you mean?" Barbara Price asked, frowning. She had been in the computer room for several hours monitoring the mission's progress and wasn't happy to hear this.

Kurtzman rolled his mouse to bring a blinking arrow onto the screen to use as a pointer. "You see that blank spot right there—" he ran the arrow up to the center on an area of closely spaced lines that looked exactly like a line drawing of a massive rock face "—the place that would be in shadow if this was an aerial photograph? Well, that's a radar shadow instead. A place that the satellite couldn't see because of this rock."

"A rock?"

"Yes, but it's a damned big rock, and it sticks out several yards over this cliff. Exactly how many I don't know, but the team's data puts the firing aperture somewhere under the rock."

"Does that mean that the cruise missile won't be able to see it, either?"

"I don't know," he admitted wearily. "I'll have to talk to the targeting officers on the missile cruiser.

I don't know what kind of profiles the Tomahawks can fly. If it can't fly there directly at exactly the same altitude, rather than having to fly above it until the last moment and then diving down on it, we're screwed."

"How about the backup GPS fix from the guys?" Price asked. "Maybe they got a better look at it."

"They spotted it, all right, but their reading puts it in the middle of the radar shadow of that big rock, as well."

"Can we combine the two to make a composite targeting graphic?" Hunt Wethers offered.

Kurtzman shook his head. "I don't know if that will be good enough for the missile to follow. And again it will depend on the flight profile."

Kurtzman was annoyed more than he could express. Once more he had been foiled by something as simple as the Chinese having hidden the laser under a rock. Granted, it was a big rock, but it was just a rock nonetheless.

"Send it in anyway," Price said, her voice revealing her disappointment. "We still have to try it and let them make the decision."

"Right."

"HAL JUST CALLED," Price announced, "and he said that there's not going to be a missile strike. He said that the President doesn't want to go with that option because of the problems with the targeting data. He's afraid that the missile won't hit the laser dead-on and he'll have started a nuclear war anyway."

Kurtzman took a deep breath. "Okay, so what's the plan now?"

She looked up at the big-screen monitor displaying the map of Taiwan and the south coast of China. "The task force has been ordered to enter the Formosa Strait as soon as the weather clears."

"In other words," he said, "we have a few hours before the end of the world."

"At least the end of the world as we've known it," she said, and her eyes had a faraway look in them. "The Chinese missiles can't reach us here on the East Coast, but I'm afraid that the West Coast isn't going to be in too good shape when this is all over."

"Did he order us to pull the team out?"

"He left the details of that up to them. But at the very least, they'll need to get as far from that mountain as they can before the laser starts firing and the Navy starts shooting back. No matter what else happens, that mountain is going to become a radioactive hole in the ground. They don't want to be within twenty miles of that when it happens."

"You want me to talk to them?"

"No," she said, shaking her head, "that's my job."

WHEN THEY WERE TOLD that the preemptive strike had been called off, Bolan and McCarter called a council of war. They knew that Brognola had given them a way to save their lives and bail out. But they also knew that it would be at the cost of millions of others losing theirs if the task force was fired upon.

The vote was unanimous to stay and see if they could do anything to prevent Armageddon.

"Exactly what are we going to do to destroy the Ruby Dragon so they can't rebuild it in a couple of months?" James asked.

All eyes turned to Manning.

"I'm not really sure," the Canadian admitted. "I have no idea what the thing looks like and know only a little about how it works. All we know is that it's built into the side of a mountain and apparently is well camouflaged. It's machinery, though, and machinery is always vulnerable.

"I did pack plenty of my favorite demo charges," Manning added, "but like I told David earlier, the best way to destroy that laser is to take out the nuclear reactor that's powering it."

"How's that?" Encizo asked.

"For one thing," Manning replied, "its not so far up the side of that mountain, so we wouldn't have to climb. For another, if we lay some demo charges on that laser gun, we can blow it up, true. But like Cal said, they'd probably be able to rebuild it, and we'll just have to go through this exercise again.

"But, if we slag the reactor's core, and do a Chernobyl number on it, no one's going to do anything up there for the next ten thousand years."

"Okay, so how do we destroy the nuke?"

"Real easy," Manning said. "First you dump the coolant, then you dump the control rods to turn the reactor on full blast. The nuclear fuel will melt in the heat and burn through the bottom of the containment shell, and the whole thing will be contaminated."

"No nuclear detonation?" Hawkins asked. It was a big deal because nobody had to tell him that being at ground zero while a nuke went off wasn't something he'd ever be able to tell anyone about, much less his grandchildren.

"Maybe," Manning conceded. "It depends on a lot of things. If they're using U-238 or plutonium for the fuel rods and they melt down, you could get a critical mass going. That could cause a chain reaction and boom, yeah, it would go up. You probably wouldn't get a complete mass-to-energy conversion like you would with a warhead, but it would be enough for our purposes."

"To do this," Bolan broke in, "you'll need to get into that control room, right?"

Manning nodded.

"After you got in, how long do you think it would take you to figure out how to work the controls?"

"That's the problem," Manning said. "I don't read Chinese, and I doubt that they've got everything labeled in English, French or anything else I can read."

"You want to give it a try anyway?"

"Sure. I haven't blown up anything in the past couple of weeks, and I don't want to get rusty."

"This won't be your usual firecracker, Gary."

"No sweat, boss," the demo man said with a grin. "They all go boom one way or the other."

McCarter turned to the others on the team. "Are you guys willing to go for it, too?"

Encizo shrugged. "Sure."

"Fine with me," James answered.

Hawkins swallowed hard. "Why not? I kind of like the scenery around here. And since it's stopped raining, we might as well go sight-seeing."

Bolan's face was set. "Let's do it."

"You want to call Barb?" McCarter asked.

The Executioner nodded. "It might as well come from me."

The two men exchanged glances. Bolan and the Stony Man mission controller had a history, and this might be the last time they had a chance to talk.

"MACK JUST CALLED," Barbara Price announced, "and they're going to go in. Gary thinks that he can slag their nuclear reactor core and destroy the laser that way."

Kurtzman was shocked. "He's going to try for a Chernobyl event?"

"That's what he said. And he wants to know if you have any good ideas on how to go about doing it."

"It's really not that difficult," Kurtzman said

thoughtfully. "Not if it's a Russian-designed reactor. They aren't too big on using the automatic safety devices we use to prevent meltdowns."

"Can you find out anything about that particular reactor in the next couple of hours?"

"It won't be easy," he said grimly, "but I'll try."

"Do it."

THE JIANG RIVER WAS DEEP where it passed within a half mile of the base of the mountains, but it wasn't very wide. That made the current too fast to try to swim, but since Cam's men had been prepared for every contingency so far, McCarter explained to their Triad guide what they wanted to do.

"There is a fishing village a few miles away," Chin said. "I can go there and get a boat."

McCarter opened his map. "We will wait here." He pointed to a spot on their side of the river.

"I will be back soon," the guide promised.

CHAPTER TWENTY-EIGHT

Task Force Shield was waiting out the end of the tropical storm on the open waters of the South China Sea well out of range of the Ruby Dragon. As soon as the skies over the Formosa Strait cleared, the fleet would challenge the power of the laser weapon, with the fate of the world hanging in the balance of the encounter.

Inside the task force's flagship, the guided-missile cruiser USS *Antietam*, the gunnery officers were pre-loading the target coordinates they had received from Bolan and Phoenix Force into the guidance systems of the Hughes TLAM-N Tomahawk III cruise missiles. These missiles were different than the Block II TLAM-C Tomahawks that had been used so successfully in the Gulf War. For one thing, they had nuclear warheads, but they were also more accurate, had a longer range and flew a little faster.

Even though they still flew at subsonic speeds, the Tomahawks' small size, low radar cross section and reduced heat signature made them almost impossible to spot with either radar or IR targeting systems. Plus, for this mission, they wouldn't have very far to fly, and the Chinese wouldn't have much time to react. Unless they had almost solid fighter cover on all of the approaches to the target, there would be no way to stop the Tomahawks. And even then, most of them would still get through.

Captain Richard Jackson, the task force's operations officer, had no doubts that the missiles would hit their targets. The only question was whether the *Antietam* would still be afloat when they struck. If the Ruby Dragon got the cruiser in its sights, the flagship might not last long enough to see her Tomahawks strike home. The cruiser's hull plates were thicker than the hulls of the tankers and merchant vessels the laser had sent to the bottom before. But no matter how thick the steel was, lasers went through steel like butter.

He knew that if the task force was fired upon, the United States would extract a terrible vengeance from the Chinese Communists. But knowing that he and his shipmates would be avenged was cold comfort. Jackson's family lived in Seattle, and they would be within range of the Chinese nuclear missiles that would surely be launched in a counterstrike.

Nonetheless, this was what being a sailor was all about. And he had done everything he could to ensure that if the *Antietam* was called upon to pay the price, she would go out in a blaze of glory. That was also what being a sailor was all about.

AS SOON AS Chin left to get them a boat, the Stony Man warriors broke camp and headed for the rendezvous point on the west riverbank. Again McCarter put James and Encizo on as security detail. While they waited for Chin to return, Manning talked with Aaron Kurtzman and the Farm's staff about Russian-designed reactor controls. They didn't know much about them, but this was one of those times when a little information was better than nothing at all.

It was midafternoon before Chin returned. "The boatman will come soon," he told McCarter.

"How long?" the Briton asked.

"Not long. You stay here. I will wait by the river.

Chin was back in fifteen minutes. "The boatman is here, and we cross the river now."

The boat Chin led them to was a typical Chinese river craft, an oversize canoe, with a shaft-drive outboard motor attached to the stern. In this case, though, the motor's exhaust had been muffled to the point that it was almost silent. Their crossing point wasn't visible from the side of the mountain that hid the Ruby Dragon, but it wasn't wise to attract attention to themselves.

Even though Chin had assured them that the riverbank wasn't patrolled, the Stony Man team kept its weapons at the ready during the short ride. As they approached the other side, the boatman steered them toward a clump of trees overhanging the water.

When the vessel slipped under its branches, he cut the motor and grabbed onto a limb to stop the boat.

"Thanks for your help," McCarter told Chin. "It's better if you leave now."

"How you get back?"

"We'll head straight for the coast when we're done here."

"Show me on the map."

Chin studied it for a moment. "When you go," he said, pointing to a small village some twelve miles away to the south, "you go here. I will meet you, and I will take you to the coast."

"It's a deal," McCarter said. The Briton wasn't all that sure that they'd make it out of the mountain alive. But stranger things had happened, and it never hurt to be prepared for things to go right for a change.

NOW THAT THE COMMANDOS were closer to the forbidding mountain, they could see the trafficked areas where supplies were offloaded along the riverbank and taken to the subterranean reactor and laser site. From space, they could have looked like natural terrain features, but from ground level, they were obviously trails.

Knowing better than to travel along trails, even ones like this, the six men moved off to the side and cautiously made their way toward the mountain. This time Manning walked point to keep an eye out for unpleasant surprises the Chinese might have scattered around to guard their most secret weapon.

"WE HAVE INTRUDERS in the area," Colonel Ng announced as he turned away from his security console in the control room.

"How is that possible?" Lam asked, puzzled. "You said that no one could get here except by passing through the army checkpoints."

"They are here regardless," the colonel stated flatly. As a military man, he was used to dealing with whatever transpired, and he knew that no security plan was ever foolproof. Men willing to take the risk could infiltrate, and that was why he had placed sensing devices around the base of the mountain. "They were detected by the security sensors down by the reactor's cooling vents."

"You have to do something about them immediately," Lam insisted. "We are only a few hours away from the end of the storm, and I cannot have anything distracting me from carrying out the strike on Taipei."

"Nothing will be allowed to distract you from your mission," Ng said soothingly. "I will personally see to that. I am going down to the security-force barracks. You stay here and finish programming the laser. No matter what happens, you will be safe here."

The hardest part of Ng's job was to keep Lam happy. But until Taiwan was back under Beijing's control, the half-breed and the weapon he had designed were necessary. What would happen to him after that was accomplished was yet to be seen. If Ng had his way, the American, as he still thought of Lam, would spend enough time in a political reeducation camp to knock the Yankee arrogance out of him.

As soon as Ng left, Lam went back to his preparations. Since a laser didn't need ammunition, only electricity to fire, Lam didn't have a gun crew to attend to it. He also didn't have assistants in the control room: the computerized controls he had designed for the weapon were state-of-the art, thanks in large part to the sophisticated equipment that had been smuggled into China from the United States, Japan and Taiwan. All he needed was the tracking information from the radars and power from the reactor to command the most powerful weapon of all time.

Nonetheless, he ran the complicated systems through a second self-diagnostic check just to make sure. When everything came up green again, he switched over to the weather radar and checked on the progress of the storm. As expected, it was rapidly dissipating and the skies would soon be clear between Taiwan and the mainland.

It wouldn't be long now. In an hour or so, a new age would begin in Asia, an age when China would once more take her rightful place in the world.

UP ON POINT, Gary Manning spotted the motion detectors too late, but he did spot them. "I think we've been made," he called back to McCarter. "They've got motion detectors and heat sensors planted in the rocks."

"Can you fix them?"

"I can try," Manning answered, "but I think it would be better if we just got a move on it before they call the cops on us."

"We're on the way."

The entrance leading into the side of the mountain was well camouflaged, but the beaten path leading to what looked like a gigantic boulder gave it away.

"That's got to be it," Manning said. "It's the only big rock around here that has a packed trail leading right up to it."

There were other boulders spaced around the base of the mountain that concealed hidden ventilator shafts, but nothing else was big enough to serve as an entrance to a subterranean cavern.

"Let's give it a try," McCarter agreed. "If that's it, there's got to be a way to open it from the outside."

THEY WERE STILL a hundred yards from the camouflaged door when they saw it start to roll away to one side. There was no shortage of cover in the area, and breaking up into two-man fire teams, the Stony Man commandos dived for cover behind the massive rocks.

When the rock was completely out of the way, troops started to pour out of the tunnel the rock had closed off. They were all dressed in the olive fatigue uniforms, soft caps and canvas chest-pack magazine carriers of the Chinese People's Liberation Army.

"I don't see any heavy weapons," Hawkins reported from his position behind the boulder closest to the door. "They're all just packing AKs."

"Let's hit them with grenades," McCarter ordered, "and give them a warm welcome."

The troops were bunched up as they hurried out of the tunnel, presenting a good target for Encizo's over-and-under M-16/M-203. Sighting in at a hundred yards, he triggered the launcher. The 40 mm grenade arced out and fell into the middle of a clump of some dozen PLA troops. Half of them fell victim to the deadly sharpnel, and many more were wounded.

From behind his boulder a dozen yards to the right of Encizo, James cut loose with a grenade from his launcher, as well, the 40 mm round causing havoc when it landed.

Staggered by the grenade blasts, the troops hesitated. Hawkins snapped burst after burst from his MP-5 into their ranks as James loaded another grenade.

The ferocity of the attack threw the Chinese into a panic. The area immediately in front of the boulder door had been cleared of other stones, and there were few places to find cover. Most of them went to ground where they were and tried to return fire, but the grenades continued to fall on them. Those men the grenades didn't kill faced a withering barrage of well-aimed automatic-weapons fire.

THE CAPTAIN OF THE PLA guard force watched his troops getting chopped to bits and cursed his superiors in Beijing. Their need to keep the Ruby Dragon the ultimate secret had made them paranoid to the point of stupidity. He had asked for a thousand troops to guard the facility, but they had only allowed him to have a hundred men at the site. And not all of those hundred were fighters. The technical and support personnel were counted against that number, leaving him less than fifty fighters.

After watching a dozen of them get gunned down in seconds, he had to pull the rest back or risk leaving the site defenseless.

"I am being forced to pull back," he radioed to Ng, who had remained safely inside the cavern. "There are too many of them, and they have the opening of the tunnel under intense fire. I've lost at least a dozen men already."

"Break off the combat," Ng replied, "and pull back, but leave the door open."

"But what about the intruders getting inside?" He couldn't believe what he was hearing.

"Let them come on into the cavern," Ng told the captain. "Then, once they are inside, we will have them trapped and can destroy them."

The captain thought that was one of the stupidest ideas he had ever heard, but he also knew better than to express his opinions to Ng. Better men than him had died for less at the colonel's hands.

"As you command, Comrade Colonel."

"I will be up in the laser-control center."

"Of course, Comrade Colonel," the captain answered. Where else would the colonel be in times of danger? Ng wasn't known to be a man who took many chances.

"THEY'RE PULLING BACK," James said as he slapped a fresh magazine into his M-16. Snapping the weapon back up to his shoulder, he triggered the grenade launcher and sent his last 40 mm round downrange after them. The spray of shrapnel from the small but deadly round seemed to hurry the Chinese along.

In their rush to get out of the line of fire, the Chinese hadn't closed the camouflaged door after retreating into the mountain.

"They left us an invitation," Encizo commented.

"They're trying to suck us into a trap, you mean," McCarter observed accurately. "So I guess we'd better accommodate them."

"Say what?" Hawkins muttered. "Doesn't anyone remember the one about the spider and the fly?"

"We were going to go in there anyway," McCarter commented, "and they just opened the door for us a little early."

"Right."

Without bothering to check the enemy dead, the Stony Man warriors dashed the last hundred yards to the opening. Manning paused by the doorway to the three-yard-wide tunnel while the others filed on inside. The concrete "rock" had small steel wheels on the bottom that ran on a rail sunk into the ground. "Let me fix this thing so they can't close it behind us."

"Good lad."

Taking two demo blocks from his pack, he ripped the tape off the adhesive strips and slapped them on each side of the track the boulder rolled on. Setting the timers to sixty seconds, he looked around to make sure that everyone was out of the way.

"Fire in the hole!" He shouted the age-old blaster's warning before dashing into the tunnel after the others and pressing himself against the inside wall.

The twin blasts echoed through the tunnel, sending clouds of dust showering on them.

"Let's go," McCarter said over the comm link.

CHAPTER TWENTY-NINE

Aaron Kurtzman sat in front of his big-screen monitor and watched the real-time satellite shot of the weather patterns superimposed over the computer-generated map of the five-hundred-mile circle around Taiwan. Once more the contested island was in the center of the storm, and in more ways than one. In a very short time, the rain would have passed, and Task Force Shield would sail into the confrontation with the Ruby Dragon.

While he could watch the storm fade in real time, he was out of contact with Bolan and Phoenix Force and that worried him. The mass of the granite mountain they had entered effectively blocked all radio communication with them. He wouldn't know if their plan was a success until they emerged into the sunlight again. If, that was, any of them ever saw the light of day again.

As much as he hated to admit it, Gary Manning's idea of melting down the reactor core made good sense. In fact, it was something that they should have thought of at the Farm. But he wasn't sure that the men would be able to carry it off at this late date. They were woefully unprepared for the task, being armed with little more than their wits and raw courage. But there was so much that the Farm could have done to help them if they had gotten started in time.

For one thing, it would have been helpful if the team could have been given intelligence information on the construction of the reactor. He hadn't been able to give Manning diddly when he had called, aside from the bare fact that it was almost certain to be a Russian-designed facility.

Some specialized demo charges tailored for the job would have been very helpful, too. With them in their packs, the team could have simply sneaked in, cracked the containment dome, then gotten the hell out. As it was, the six of them trying to hold the control room long enough to figure out how to destroy the reactor was tantamount to suicide.

He was aware that they knew their chances of getting out alive were slim, but they had chosen to try it anyway in a last attempt to keep the world they knew intact. It didn't make him feel any better knowing that they had chosen the sacrifice themselves instead of being ordered in to do it. Either way, they would be dead.

"I think they've got a pretty good chance of pulling this off." Price tried to sound lighthearted when she read the expression on Kurtzman's face.

"In fact, if we would have been a little more on

the ball when we first learned about that laser, we'd have suggested this right from the start instead of wasting all this time."

"That's what I was thinking, too."

"Next time we'll look for a simpler solution right from the start," she said, trying to lighten his mood.

"If there is a next time."

"Do you want a cup of coffee while we wait?"

He shook his head.

She poured herself one and silently went back to her seat to stand the death watch with him. She was the Farm's mission controller, and regardless of the outcome, it was her job to oversee every Stony Man mission until she knew the fate of the men.

AS SOON AS the dust from Manning's door-blocking exercise cleared, the commandos moved out. Even though there was a line of light fixtures on the ceiling overhead, the tunnel wasn't lit. With a nuclear reactor providing an unending supply of electricity, a shortage of power shouldn't have been the reason. More than likely, the circuit had a built-in trip switch that shut the lights off when the outer door was open.

The lack of light wasn't an obstacle to the commandos, however. As soon as they lost the light from the door opening, their night-vision goggles turned the dark tunnel into a green-lit hole in the rock.

They stayed spread out, half-expecting to meet

the defeated Red Chinese at any moment. A tunnel was a good place to pull an ambush. Thirty yards inside, they came to another steel door blocking their way and halted.

Manning was reaching for a demo block to blast it open when James reached out and punched a button on the control panel on the wall. With the click of an electric lock, the door swung open.

"You're always in such a big hurry to blow something up," he said to Manning. "You've just got to have the right touch, my man."

"You just lucked out this time."

After putting a wedge in the lock so it wouldn't trip behind them, they closed the door, and the overhead lights in that section of the tunnel came on. Quickly raising their night-vision goggles, the commandos pressed themselves against the walls. When they weren't attacked as they expected, McCarter motioned for James and Hawkins to take the point as they continued down the tunnel.

"Do you think they're going to let us get all the way inside?" Hawkins asked James as they approached an intersection in the tunnel.

"If they do," the ex-SEAL replied, "they're going to drop the hammer on us the minute we break out into the open."

"Let's take this side branch, then," Hawkins suggested, pointing to the smaller tunnel leading to the right. "Maybe it'll come out someplace where they won't be expecting us."

"Good idea," James replied. "But let me check that with David first."

When the Phoenix Force leader gave his okay, the two pointmen turned down the side tunnel. After bearing to the right for twenty yards, the tunnel turned left and continued on into the heart of the mountain. Another ten yards brought them to a doorless opening covered with a ventilator grille.

"Geez!" Hawkins said quietly as he peeked through the grille. "Take a look at this place!"

The chamber inside the mountain looked like a set from a James Bond movie. The cavern was bigger than any two civic stadiums he had ever seen, and had been carved into the solid granite. Walkways circled the cavern at several levels, and tunnels led off of it to drive deeper into the mountain. A bank of elevators on one side were capable of traveling both up and down inside the hollowed mountain.

In the middle of the cavern was the familiar rounded shape of the concrete dome that had to contain their target, the nuclear reactor. On the wall behind it was what looked like a miniature electrical substation, complete with transformers and massive power cables to send the power it generated up to the Ruby Dragon.

On their side of the containment dome was a small structure built onto the middle walkway overlooking the reactor, which had to be the control room. Even though there was no way to see inside the dome, it was human nature for a man to want to look at what he was controlling.

When they all got to the vent grille, McCarter and Bolan surveyed the cavern themselves before making their battle plans. From their vantage point, they couldn't see any of the uniformed troops who had challenged them outside the tunnel, but they knew they had to be waiting for them. The question was, where?

"You want us to take out the transformers?" James asked Manning when he recognized them for what they were.

"No," the Canadian said, shaking his head. "We damage them, and we'll probably lose the power to the control room. I have to have everything powered up so I can work the controls."

"Good point."

"I've got the grille loose," Encizo reported.

"Okay." McCarter turned to Hawkins. "Here's the drill. I want you to go with Manning and cover him while he tries to do his thing. We'll try to hold them from here so we can use the same tunnel to get out of here when you're done."

The two men nodded.

"And I want you to go out first. Your best chance of reaching the control room is to do it before all hell breaks loose in here."

That, too, was understandable.

Manning turned to Hawkins. "You ready?

"Let's do it."

THE TWO COMMANDOS WERE able to walk all the way around to the control room without being challenged. When they reached the control-room door, Manning sent two clicks on the comm link and got two clicks in return. McCarter and the others were ready to cover their move.

"Remember," Manning whispered as he and Hawkins flattened themselves against the wall outside the control-room door, "don't shoot up the control panels. I'm going to need everything intact."

"Roger," Hawkins replied as he took a firm grip on his MP-5.

Planting his boot against the door of the control room, Hawkins shoved while Manning tripped the latch. The door slammed open, and the two men stormed in, their subguns blazing.

The half-dozen men in the control room turned as one when the two commandos opened up on them. Two of the men wore PLA uniforms and had AKs slung over their shoulders. They didn't even get a chance to swing them into action before they were cut down where they stood.

The technician seated at the far end of the control console spun with a pistol in his hand and snapped a shot at Manning.

Hawkins caught the movement out of the corner of his eye and answered by sweeping a burst across the room that stitched a neat line of holes across the man's chest.

The last two technicians dived for cover, but were too slow. The MP-5 in Manning's hands stuttered, and the two Chinese fell sprawling on the concrete floor.

Slinging the subgun over his shoulder, Manning stepped over the bodies of the control-room staff to reach what looked like the central-command chair. At least it was the chair in the middle of the largest control console and the most likely choice.

"I'll be right outside the door if you need me," Hawkins said as he kicked the fallen weapons over toward the far wall.

"Right," Manning said as he slipped into the control chair.

Outside they heard the first bursts of automatic-weapons fire as the battle inside the cavern commenced.

Wiping the blood spatters off a couple of the gauges, Manning studied the panel in front of him. Some of the instruments and gauges were still labeled in their original European languages with Chinese translations added. This was going to be a lot simpler than he had thought.

The first thing he needed to do to sabotage the reactor was to retract the carbon-graphite control rods that modulated the nuclear reaction. When they were in the down position inside the reactor core, they soaked up the neutrons emitted by the fuel rods and kept the reactor cool. To start the reaction running, they were withdrawn from the core, exposing the fuel rods to the full neutron emissions of the other rods. This caused heat, and all any nuclear reactor was, was a source of heat.

His eyes raced over the maze of knobs, switches, sliding-bar controls, gauges and meters. Finally he located a slide-bar control that was marked 100 percent at one end and zero at the other. It was set at twenty percent. Next to it was a big gauge also marked in percentages, with a red zone covering the face from ninety-five to one hundred percent. The chances were good that these were the controls for the graphite rods in the fuel core.

When he found a prominent temperature gauge, he was sure that he had it figured out. If he was reading the meters properly, the reactor was running at twenty percent and the core temperature was a respectably cool 320 degrees. There was only one way to find out, however.

Reaching out, he ran the slide bar up to the fifty percent mark and kept his eye on the reactor-temperature gauge. Within seconds of withdrawing the rods to fifty percent, the temperature shot up dramatically. Now that he knew how they were controlled, he pulled the rods all the way out until the reactor indictor was in the red zone at one hundred percent. Almost immediately, the temperature needle shot up toward the red zone, six hundred degrees.

"You'd better get a move on it in there," McCarter's voice said over the comm link, breaking his concentration. In the background, he could hear a storm of gunfire. "I don't know how much longer we can hold these guys off."

"I'm almost done," Manning answered. "Just give me another five. I've found the moderator-rod controls, but I still need to shut down the coolant."

"No more than that," McCarter warned, "or we're all going to be in deep shit."

"Roger."

WITH HAWKINS AND MANNING at the reactor-control room, the other four commandos had their hands full dealing with the PLA security force. They had found cover behind the concrete buttresses that supported the walkways, but the enemy had taken cover behind them, as well.

The main thing they had going in their favor was that while Ng's guards had been handpicked, they had been chosen for political reliability, not combat effectiveness. Regardless of their loyalty to the hard-liners' cause, their hearts weren't set on facing sudden death inside a mountain.

But even with the casualties they had taken outside, there were still several dozen of them, and as always happened, the sheer numbers were making a difference.

On the plus side, though, the guards weren't using heavy weapons, probably out of fear of damaging something vital to their subterranean existence.

Nonetheless, the AKs they carried were threat enough.

"Manning," McCarter said over the comm link, "move your ass in there."

"I'm working as fast as I can."

"Work faster!" McCarter snapped as he sent another short burst at a guard who was trying to inch his way closer by crawling along the floor.

HAWKINS WAS STILL guarding the door to the reactor-control room while Manning worked inside, but he wasn't sure how much longer he could hold out. He had burned through most of his ammunition and had only a magazine and a half left. His teammates were spaced out along the walkway between the control room and the tunnel that they had followed to enter the cavern.

So far, the PLA troops seemed to be content to simply keep the commandos pinned down where they were and prevent them from moving deeper into the cavern to threaten the reactor. If the Chinese knew just how unprepared they were to tackle the thing, they would end this charade pretty quickly.

When Hawkins noticed that several of the PLA looked to be massing behind a buttress twenty yards away, he took the last hand grenade from his belt, armed it and skittered it down the concrete walkway. When it detonated, several bodies went flying.

That should hold them for a while.

CHAPTER THIRTY

Even after he had positively identified the coolant controls, Manning was having difficulty figuring out how they worked. They were labeled in Russian, which he couldn't read, and the numbers didn't make much sense to him, either. Again, though, the coolant valves appeared to be controlled by electric servos, as were the control rods through a large vernier knob.

Needing to do something quickly, he turned the vernier knob to the right and watched the gauge measuring the coolant temperature. After a few seconds, it appeared to fall a degree or two, which was the wrong way. He wanted the temperature to rise.

Turning the knob all the way to the left, he was rewarded with seeing the temperature spike again. He also noticed that the needle of another gauge that was marked CMM fell to zero. That had to be the coolant-flow meter, graduated in cubic meters per minute, and if it was registering zero, that meant that the coolant was completely cut off.

It also meant that it was time for them to get clear

of the cavern. He had no idea how long it was going to take for the fuel rods in the core to melt down, but he wasn't about to hang around to time them.

Alarm bells and sirens were sounding all through the underground complex when Manning left the control chair. "That's it!" he shouted over the comm link. "We'd better get the hell out of here fast! It's going to blow!"

Picking up his MP-5, he sent a long burst of 9 mm slugs across the control panel. It was too late for anyone to save the reactor core now, but he wanted to make sure that they couldn't even try. As an added measure, he took a quarter-pound demo block and slapped it on top of the coolant controls. After setting the detonator for two minutes, he tripped it and raced for the door.

"Let's get out of here," he told Hawkins.

"After you."

IN THE LASER'S control room halfway up the mountain, Lam looked with horror at the instruments on his master console that gave him information about the nuclear reactor.

"They've dumped the reactor-core coolant," he shouted in English. "It's going to explode!"

"Get hold of yourself!" Colonel Ng roared, "and speak to me in Mandarin."

"The reactor," Lam explained. "The raiders have sabotaged the reactor, and it's going to explode."

"When?"

"I don't know. I'm not a nuclear-power engineer."

Ng flew across the room and punched the button to the intercom connected with the reactor's control room. When there was no answer, he tried the security-force office. Again there was no answer.

Without a word, he turned and ran for the elevator that led to the lower cavern over two thousand feet below. That's where the reactor was, but it was also the only way out of the mountain. He was halfway down when the elevator suddenly jerked to a halt and the lights went out.

Ng's screams echoed inside the elevator shaft as he hammered his fists on the walls of the car, rocking it from side to side. There was an emergency-escape hatch in the top of the car, but he would never find his way down the shaft in the dark.

IN THE CONCRETE containment vessel of the reactor, the uranium fuel rods were glowing red with the heat that wasn't being carried away by the coolant, instead of the usual blue from radioactivity. It took several minutes for the metal to heat to the melting point, but when it did, molten drops started to fall off the rods.

As the drops of molten uranium pooled in the concrete bottom of the containment vessel, the neutrons it emitted were being soaked up by the metal itself, knocking electrons out of the orbits of the atoms and releasing even more energy in the form of heat, which kept the melted metal from solidifying.

When over twenty-two pounds of the molten uranium had gathered in the ever growing puddle, it did what pure uranium always did when it came together in large enough quantities. It achieved critical mass. From there, it was only microseconds until it converted itself to energy.

It detonated.

Manning had been wrong about the fuel rods not completely converting their mass to energy if a critical reaction occurred. The Chinese had a wealth of uranium ore, and they didn't need to stint. The fuel rods they produced were pure U-235 to within a few thousandths of a percent, the same purity of material that had ushered in the atomic age over Hiroshima. In the United States that was called bomb-grade fuel and was rarely used in reactors.

With that kind of purity, the fuel rods didn't need to be in contact with each other to go critical. In the microsecond that it took for the molten uranium to go critical, the neutrons it released were soaked up by the unmelted fuel rods, and they went critical, as well.

Deep within the mountain, a miniature sun burst into being with the force of forty thousand tons of TNT.

T.J. HAWKINS WAS GIVING it his best, but he wasn't sure that he was running fast enough. With the aid of their night-vision goggles, the Stony Man warriors had had no difficulty racing back through the tunnel to reach the outer world. They had covered almost two miles in the past ten minutes, and the ex-Ranger was well out in front of the pack. But trying to get away from a nuclear detonation on foot wasn't one of the brightest things he had ever done. The options, however, were even worse.

Encizo was bringing up the rear of the party when he felt the earth move under his running feet, and he immediately dived for cover as if it were an earthquake. As if following orders, all six men turned to look at the mountain so as not to miss the results of their handiwork.

From where they watched, it looked as if someone were shaking the mountain. Ground shock after ground shock rocked them as they hugged the earth. Smoke and dust shot through with orange flame jetted from the entrance tunnel, the ventilators and from other previously unseen apertures in the mountain.

The biggest gout of flame shot out of where they had seen the Ruby Dragon fire. They had been impressed by the bloodred fire of the laser, but it had been nothing compared to what they witnessed now. A broiling ball of flame the size of the cavern they had been in filled the sky.

Suddenly they felt more than heard a rumbling from deep beneath the earth. A Chinese peasant would have said that it sounded like one of the dragons awakening under the earth. But this was like no dragon that any Chinese peasant had ever seen.

At first it felt like another, but stronger, earthquake to the commandos. But as they watched, the mountain changed shape in front of their eyes. Rocks and cliffs that had stood for millennia tumbled to the ground. Cracks appeared in the cliffs, and steam started venting from the cracks.

With a deafening roar louder than anything they had ever heard, the entire top of the mountain blew off in a gigantic volcanic explosion.

A shock wave rolled over the men, flattening them to the ground. Molten lava shot into the sky and cascaded over the shattered rocks. Huge chunks of rock blasted from the peak fell from the sky like artillery, drilling deep into the rain-soaked ground.

"ARE THEY OKAY, Aaron?" Barbara Price asked, not able to take her eyes off of the drama unfolding on the screens in the Stony Man computer room.

The Keyhole 11 satellite that had just come over the horizon was giving them a full-color view of what hell had to look like. And even from hundreds of miles in space, the effect was stunning.

The mass of solid rock the nuclear reactor had been buried under kept the nuclear detonation from exploding upward as had happened in Chernobyl. Instead, when the Chinese reactor cooked off, the force of the explosion had been directed into the earth.

As with most mountain ranges, the peaks of the Dragon's Spine were the upper portions of fault lines that went down through the crust of the earth to the molten magma below. The nuclear blast had followed one of those faults, drilling deep into the earth, cutting a channel all the way to the magma.

The molten interior of the earth soaked up even the force of the nuclear blast for an instant before the pressure became too much. Then, with a blast hundreds of times stronger than that of the exploding reactor, a volcano was created.

Though it was hundreds of miles above the earth, the satellite view of the volcano was like looking into hell.

"I don't know." Aaron Kurtzman's voice was hard. "The radiation is playing hell with our communications. It's like a big sunspot, only worse."

Suddenly there was a burst of static from the satcom radio. "Stony Man, Stony Man," David McCarter's voice said, "this is Phoenix One, over."

Price snatched up the microphone. "This is Stony Base, go!"

The transmission lag seem to stretch for hours before McCarter's voice came back. "This is Phoenix. Be advised that we have completed the mission. The fleet can sail anywhere they want now."

"We've been watching it," she said, "and it's awesome, completely unbelievable."

"It is rather spectacular, isn't it?" She could almost see the grin she knew McCarter's face wore.

"Are you going to be able to get back out to the coast okay?"

"We still have our Chinese guide, so we should be okay," McCarter answered. "I'll call if we run into a problem, but I think that the opposition is going to be a little too busy for a while to worry too much about us.

"You also might want to alert the Navy," he continued, "to be ready to pick us up. We'll be several miles northeast of where we went in, so we don't have to go back across the river again. I'll call in the coordinates as soon as we're within a couple of miles of the coast."

"I'll have them standing by."

"Phoenix, out."

When Price put down the mike, she turned back to the inferno on the color monitor. This time it could be truly said that the team had gone into hell and had lived to fight again. She shuddered.

TASK FORCE SHIELD came over the horizon and steamed for the northern end of the Strait of Formosa. It wasn't a large task force, but the power of its weaponry was many times more than that of all the fleets that had ever sailed. It was simply the most powerful fleet of all time.

As it sailed within range of the Ruby Dragon, the destroyers were well out in front, offering their thin hull plates as the first target. If the laser was still functional, they would be blown apart like so many paper boats. The crews weren't anxious to face eternity, but they knew that if they did die, they would be avenged.

The USS *Antietam* followed the destroyers into the strait under general alert, her launch racks loaded with preprogrammed, nuclear-tipped Tomahawk missiles. At the first sign of an attack, they would be launched in a first strike designed to take out both the laser and as much of China's nuclear missile and bomber arsenal as they could reach.

To back up the *Antietam* if it came to a fight, two Ohio-class Boomer subs were cruising a hundred miles away at launch depth, their Trident missiles ready to launch, as well. These missiles had multiple independently targeted warheads capable of taking out eight targets each. What the Tomahawks didn't get, they would, along with a number of other strategic targets such as ports and rail centers.

If the balloon went up, China would go back to the Stone Age in less than fifteen minutes.

Lagging behind the rest of the task force, the nuclear carrier, the USS *Nimitz* had already launched her MiG Cap to cover the rest of the fleet. The carrier's E-2C Hawkeye AWACS aircraft were also aloft, watching the Chinese air force, and the F-14D Tomcats were flying north of the fleet along the edge of China's international boundary. Their Maverick air-to-air missiles were hot and their "look down–shoot down" radar was scanning the air looking for incoming hostiles.

Throughout the task force, fingers were poised on the firing controls as the lead destroyer came within range of the Ruby Dragon. As the minutes passed, radio messages snapped through the air between the ships and the aircraft overhead. The messages all asked one question, where was the Ruby Dragon?

In the command center of the *Antietam*, the first of the real-time photos from the Keyhole 11 satellites passing over Fujian province started coming in over the fax.

"I'll be a son of a bitch," Admiral Michael Dover said softly as he scanned the photos. "They really did it. They took out that damned laser."

Captain Richard Jackson, the task force's operations officer, couldn't resist asking, "Who's that, sir?"

"I can't tell you, Jackson," the admiral replied, smiling broadly. "If I did, I'd have to kill you afterward."

Jackson grinned back. The admiral was an old SEAL turned fleet man, and his sense of humor was famous. It was a bit grim at times, but it was famous.

"Send all units are to stand down to Def Con Two," the admiral ordered. "But leave the MiG Cap up and the Tomahawks on the launch rails until we clear the other end of the strait. The bastards still might want to play their stupid games."

"Aye, sir."

"And, Jackson..." the admiral's voice suddenly turned serious.

"Sir?"

"Make sure that you remember this day for the rest of your life."

"Believe me, sir, I will," Jackson said, equally serious. "My family lives in Seattle."

EPILOGUE

Three days later, Mack Bolan was led into the garden of the house outside of Taipei again and found Ancient Cam waiting for him. Taking the box containing Cam's chop out of his pocket, he handed it over with a small bow. "Thank you for the loan of this. It was helpful."

Cam returned the bow. "I am glad that I could be of some small service."

Bolan smiled at the customary self-deprecation. "It was no small service, Mr. Cam, believe me. We couldn't have accomplished our mission without your help."

"But the mission was completed."

Although Bolan was sure that the Triad godfather knew as well as he did what had happened, he reported anyway. "I couldn't personally see that the Dragon's Heart went back into the earth," he said, "but I believe that it is safe now for all time. The volcano has destroyed most of the mountain, and the radioactivity from the power plant will make sure that no one goes there for thousands of years."

"You did well, Mr. Bolan. The dragon is satisfied now."

"I'm just glad that we were able to work together on this. It would have been very difficult if not impossible for us to do without the assistance of your associates."

"I do not think that we will ever speak again," Cam said, "so I will bid you farewell now. Live long, Mr. Bolan, and never give up your fight."

Bolan was surprised to hear Cam wish him well in the future. It wasn't as if they were on the same side of the war. Over the years, he had cut a bloody swath through the Triads several times, and he would do it again in a heartbeat if it was necessary.

Cam caught the look of puzzlement that flashed across Bolan's face and smiled. "In the fight of good against evil," he explained, "too often evil has the strongest hand, and that is not how it should be. Without good to stand against evil, the world is not in balance."

"Yang and yin," Bolan said.

"Exactly." Cam smiled. "I knew you would understand."

"But," Bolan cautioned, "if I'm sent against your people again, I won't spare them just because we worked together this one time."

Cam studied him for a long moment. "I would expect nothing less from the Executioner."

There was nothing Mack Bolan could answer to that.